I0661110

Frank J Sullivan, Charles N. Felton

A Contested Election in California

Testimony of the qualified electors and legal voters of New Almaden

Frank J Sullivan, Charles N. Felton

A Contested Election in California
Testimony of the qualified electors and legal voters of New Almaden

ISBN/EAN: 9783337378110

Printed in Europe, USA, Canada, Australia, Japan

Cover: Foto ©Andreas Hilbeck / pixelio.de

More available books at **www.hansebooks.com**

A CONTESTED ELECTION

IN

CALIFORNIA.

.........*vs.* HON. C. N. FELTON.

Testimony of the Qualified Electors and Legal Voters

OF

NEW ALMADEN.

REPRINTED FROM THE SAN JOSE DAILY MERCURY, SANTA CLARA CO., CALIFORNIA.

1887.

INTRODUCTORY.

At the general election held in California, November 2nd, 1886, Hon. Charles N. Felton and Frank J. Sullivan were rival candidates for election as members of Congress in the Fifth Congressional District. The official returns gave to Hon. Charles N. Felton a plurality of 118 votes, and the certificate of election duly issued to him.

Sullivan afterwards inaugurated a contest for the seat. In this contest the vote of New Almaden precinct became a very conspicuous part. The majority against Sullivan in that precinct was 164, so that if Sullivan could have that precinct thrown out, or the votes cast for Mr. Felton counted for Mr. Sullivan, he might reasonably expect to unseat Mr. Felton and fill the place himself.

The New Almaden precinct is the seat of the great New Almaden Quicksilver Mine, which for many years has been the principal quicksilver producer of the American Continent, and employs about 500 men in all capacities, of whom 156 were voters, and voted at the election in 1886. The total vote of the precinct was 256.

The grounds of the attack upon the vote of New Almaden precinct by Sullivan were, that the voters of the precinct were coerced, intimidated, and held in a state of peonage or slavery and compelled to vote for Mr. Felton against their will.

In support of this he attacked the method of conducting the mine, the system of trade at the mine, and the general condition of the miners; claiming that those who did not vote as pleased the management of the mine would be discharged.

On behalf of Sullivan the testimony relating to Almaden was almost entirely hearsay so far as it could be in any sense pertinent to the issue; being generally a statement by witnesses that they "had heard," or "it was generally understood" that so and so had happened at Almaden.

On behalf of Mr. Felton a large amount of evidence was taken, very much of it at New Almaden. Of the 256 persons who had voted in that precinct in 1886, 243 were personally examined, the other 13 being dead or having removed to a distance, or for other reasons their attendance as witnesses being impracticable. Of the number examined there was not one but what testified in the clearest terms, that for more than fifteen years past the subject of voting, or candidates, or elections had never been mentioned to any employee of the Company by any one in any way connected with the management of the mine; that the Superintendent of the mine was the only person in the precinct who voted the American ticket in 1886.

That the voting employees of the mine consist very largely of natives of Mexico and Cornwall, England, who here, as elsewhere in California, vote the Republican ticket almost exclusively. It was also shown that there were in the employ of the Company, and always had been, several Democrats who were always outspoken in favor of that party and its candidates, and who had never had their relations with the Company affected by that fact.

That the vote for Sullivan had been about the average vote given to his party. But that some candidates of the Democratic party on account of acquaintance or personal popularity had received a larger vote.

As to the system of trade at the mine, it was proven that at the mine were two extensive and well stocked general merchandise stores, the proprietors of which are in no way connected with the mine, or its management, or officers. That the employees of The Quicksilver Mining Co. have facilities for purchasing goods at these stores upon a system of credits or orders, known as boletos, issued by the stores, and based upon wages earned, but not yet due to the employees.

The social and financial condition of the employees of the company, was shown in considerable detail. It appearing that they are better fed, better paid, better clothed and better housed, than any other laboring class in the State. A large collection of photographic views was introduced in evidence for the purpose of showing the homes, surroundings and conveniences supplied for the laboring people. It was also shown that a majority of the miners had money on deposit in savings banks, and owned stocks in dividend paying corporations. That the management, and especially J. B. Randol, the Manager of the properties of The Quicksilver Mining Company, had devoted much time and attention to the elevation of the people living at the mine. They were supplied with handsome churches, schools, clubs, lodges, and societies all well sustained and flourishing. That a very large number of daily and other periodicals representing all political views were taken regularly by the employees at the mine.

That nearly all the work at the mine is let and carried on by the contract system. The work being let in small monthly contracts (employing from two to twelve men each) to the lowest bidders, in a competition open to all, no favors being dependent upon politics or any thing else.

That not a man in the employee of the company, who had voted previous to coming here, had changed his party fealty after coming to Almaden.

In fact the investigation showed that there was no possible ground for the assault upon this precinct, or this mine or its management, unless it be found in the undisputed statement of one of Sullivan's witnesses, who testified that about the time of the initiation of the contest Sullivan told him in his private room at the La Molle House in San Jose, that "he intended by this contest to cast a shadow upon the entire Congressional District," and then rely upon a Democratic majority in the House of Representatives, to give to him Mr. Felton's seat.

The following pages contain a condensed statement of the evidence taken at New Almaden. The collection of photographic views of the mining camp are the work of Dr. S. E. Winn and R. R. Bulmore, amateurs, both residents of New Almaden.

CONTENTS.

———◆———

MANAGER'S RESIDENCE, HACIENDA.

AT NEW ALMADEN.

The Sullivan-Felton Contest in Santa Clara Co.

Superintendent Jennings Enters a Vigorous Protest—"A Lurking Mixture of Gush and Hoodlumism."—A Resume of the Management of the New Almaden Mine. At New Almaden, Santa Clara County, April 19th, 1887, the taking of testimony in the congressional contest of Sullivan against Felton began. Messrs. C. W. Cross and Moore represented Mr. Felton, and N. Bowden appeared for Mr. Sullivan.

TESTIMONY OF HENNEN JENNINGS.

Hennen Jennings, Superintendent of the Mining Company, the first witness called in behalf of the contestee, testified as follows:

By Mr. Cross:

Q.   Please state your name?

A.   My name is Hennen Jennings, but before giving my testimony I desire to enter a protest.

Mr. Bowden — Contestant objects to the witness entering any protest.

Witness resumes: On behalf of The Quicksilver Mining Company, of which I am Superintendent, and also on behalf of the voters of the New Almaden Precinct, whose exercise of the right of franchise has been attacked and villified in this contest, I protest against the method pursued by the contestant and his assistants in this investigation on the ground: First—That much of the matter given in evidence, is entirely irrelevant and immaterial to the issue involved. Second—That villainous and unnecessary attacks have been made upon the management of the mine, the voters of the precinct, and upon the motives and character of the manager. Third—That nearly all the testimony is mere hearsay and a repetition of idle and malignant gossip. Fourth—That most of the direct testimony has been obtained from former employees of the mine discharged for incapacity or inattention to their duties, and from disappointed candidates for office who desire to obtain, and made every effort to obtain the vote of the employees of the company. Whilst recognizing the fact that most of the testimony regarding us is irrelevant in the contest and is adduced principally from thoroughly unreliable sources, actuated by occult malevolence on the part of the contestant, he having no considerable personal acquaintance or even business relations with the parties attacked, and by some of his witnesses for the mere gratification of personal spleen. Still, from the fact that by the course pursued, much publicity has been given through some of the press to these statements, I deem it proper to lay before the public a plain

statement of facts regarding the conduct of the affairs of the mine and the condition of the people here. I also protest against the course of such of the press as by means of virulent headlines and distorted statements of the evidence, and unjust editorial comments, have done their best from political motives or personal spite to produce false and unjust impressions upon the public mind with regard to the conduct of the mine and the character and condition of its employees. I submit this protest in writing, in order that it may become a part of the record of the contest, and so that there may be no mistake as to what the protest is.   HENNEN JENNINGS.
April 19th, 1887.

Mr. BOWDEN—Contestant moves to strike out the so-called protest.

By Mr. CROSS:

Q. Mr. Jennings, state your connection with this mine, from your first connection with it up to the present time. It is the New Almaden Quicksilver Mine, is it not?

A. It is called The Quicksilver Mining Company, that is the title of the property, but it is known as the New Almaden Mine. The Quicksilver Mining Company is the correct title. The first connection I had with this mine was in November, 1877. I was then introduced to Mr. Randol by Hamilton Smith, and received the position of Assistant Surveyor, under Ross F. Browne. Ross F. Browne was then Surveyor of the mine. I remained as Assistant Surveyor until December, 1878, when Mr. Browne severed his connection with the mine, and took the position of Instructor at the University of California; after which I was made Surveyor of the mine, and remained in that capacity until August, 1880, when I left to take the position of Assistant Superintendent of the North Bloomfield Gold Gravel Mining Company in Nevada County. After holding that position for over a year, I took charge, as Superintendent, of the Ruby Gold Gravel Mine in Sierra County, in August, 1881; I remained there until September, 1883, when I received the appointment of Superintendent of The Quicksilver Mining Company, in which capacity I have acted ever since.

Q. What is your nativity, and when were you born?

A. I was born in Kentucky in 1854.

Q. What business was your father in at that time?

A. My father was the owner of some coal mines there.

Q. State what your education for the business of mining was?

A. I spent four years at school in England before entering Harvard College, and graduated at the Lawrence Scientific School, a branch of that University, with the degree of Civil Engineer, in 1877. I am a member of the Institute of Mining Engineers, a volumn of whose proceedings I will put in testimony as an exhibit; and I will also state that I am a charter member of the Technical Society of the Pacific Coast.

Q. State your acquaintance with the contestant, Mr. Frank J. Sullivan.

A. The only time I ever met the contestant previous to the present was just before the last Presidential election. It was the Cleveland election. He was then making a canvass of this precinct as a candi-

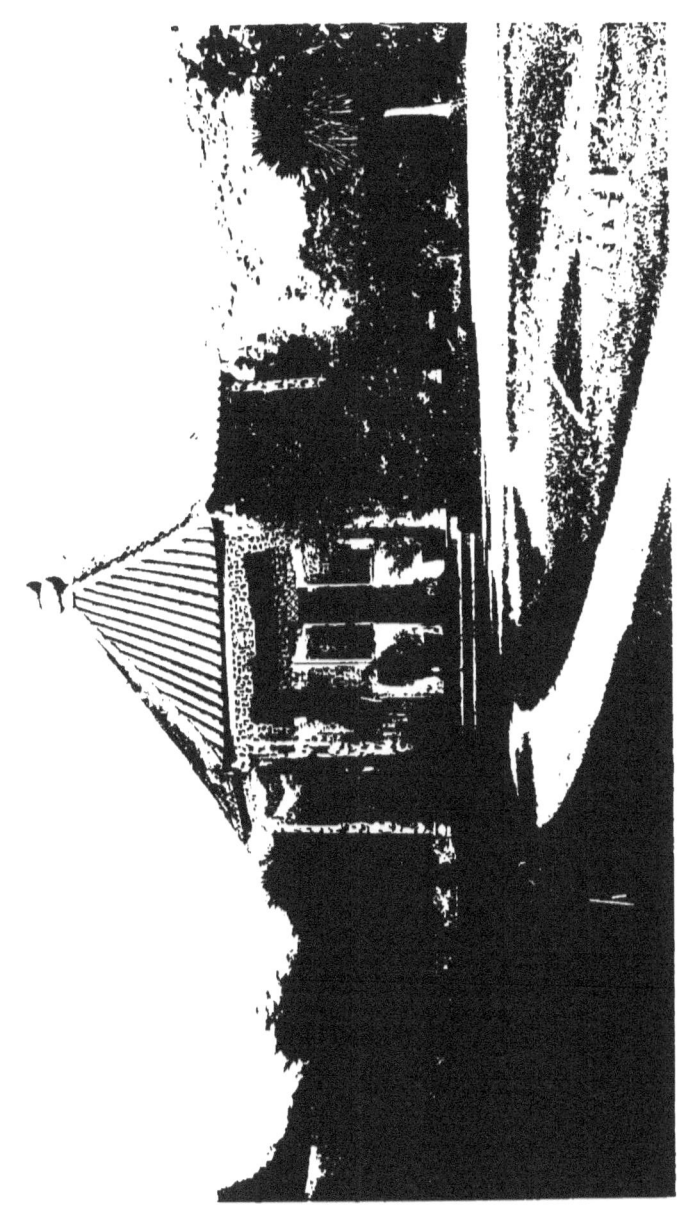

date for Congress. I believe I have already stated that I do not remember the month or date, but the day of the week was *Sunday*; he came out with a letter of introduction from Dr. Thorne to Mr. Randol, and in the course of conversation with Mr. Randol he asked him for his support in the ensuing election. Mr. Randol in reply told him he had no personal objection to Mr. Sullivan, but his political views were those of a Republican, and consequently he could not support him; but he turned towards me and said: "Mr. Jennings is a Democrat, you probably may influence him." After conversing some time at Mr. Randol's house, I took Mr. Sullivan through our furnaces and lower grounds. I was in the main voting the Democratic ticket, but after being thrown in contact with Mr. Sullivan for the length of time that I was, I concluded that I did not wish to vote for him; my reasons for so doing were that he impressed me unfavorably, for in my conversation with him he exhibited a lurking mixture of gush and hoodlumism, which his subsequent exploits have not removed. After Mr. Sullivan's departure I told Mr. Randol that Sullivan was one vote worse off than when he came out here. I would like to say that this is, so far as I know, the only meeting between Mr. Sullivan, Mr. Randol and myself.

Q. Have you had any further acquaintance with Mr. Sullivan?

A. None at all, in any form.

Q. State what acquaintance, if any, you have had with Mr. Felton.

A. I have no recollection of any acquaintance with Mr. Felton at all, though it may be probable that I have met him at the house of Dr. Thorne; that is some years ago.

Q. Mr. Jennings, I would like to have you give some history of the mine management during Mr. Randol's incumbency as Superintendent and Manager, so far as you are acquainted with it. First, you may state if you will the condition of the property when Mr. Randol took charge.

A. The condition of the property. I will try to confine myself to such as is seen from the records of the company, and I would like to state here that in all my testimony I will try to deal with facts as far as possible. The financial condition of the mine when Mr. Randol took charge was a most embarassed one. There was an interest-bearing debt of $1,600,000 against the mine. The production of quicksilver for the year 1870, at which time he took charge, was one of the small ones in the history of the mine. The amount of ore in sight was small, and its extraction very costly, and the stockholders were so pressed to carry on the working of the mine that it was necessary to raise money. The stock being unassessable, the money was raised by subscription, the subscribers becoming preferred stockholders. I believe the amount thus raised was $200,000. Mr. Randol, then secretary of the company at New York, which position he had held for seven years before coming out here, was sent by the company with command of the money raised to suggest remedies and new methods of working, and soon after his coming out and reporting he was appointed manager.

Mr. Cnoss—Now, then, you may state the condition of the mine itself, you have stated the financial condition.

A. As to the technical condition of the mine, it would be well to first speak of the furnace plant, which at that time was very crude in comparison to the present one. The furnaces being only of the intermittent type, an intermittent furnace being a furnace that is capable of roasting only coarse ore, or, when fine ore is used, only in the form of adobes, and it has to be periodically charged and fired, requiring intervals for cooling and discharging, thus causing considerable loss of time, and also the possibility of loss of quicksilver by the shrinkage and expansion of walls; this method of operation was costly, the chief cost being the making of adobes. The condenser system also was crude, and has undergone entire modification since then. The mine was then developed no deeper than what we call the 800-foot level, the datum point for levels being taken at the summit of the mine hill, which is 1,700 feet above the sea-level. The only machinery in operation at the mine was one engine, working underground, in the main tunnel above the main shaft, the steam being generated by boilers outside, and conducted to the engine by pipes, a distance of several hundred feet As to the condition of the underground work; the main Day tunnel of the 800-foot level, though started, was not then connected with the main shaft, and it was necessary to export a large amount of ore from the lower to the higher levels by means of cerrones, which are bags made of hides used by Mexican miners, and carried by means of a strap over the forehead of the packers; these packers would go up notched ladders, and would carry as high as 150 to 200 pounds at a load.

Q. You may state something of the improvements that have been made in the furnaces under Mr. Randol's administration, Mr. Jennings.

A. As to the improvements in the furnaces made during Mr. Randol's administration, I do not think I could give a more complete and comprehensive showing than by introducing exhibit A, an article on "Quicksilver Reduction at New Almaden," by Samuel B. Christy, University of California, Berkeley, Cal.

Q. You may read any portions of that that you wish to, Mr. Jennings.

A. It commences on page 547, and ends at 587. It is a very complete history and minute description of the workings of these furnaces and accompanied by plates of the furnaces themselves, and the furnace yard.

Q. You may read any particular portions of that that you see fit, Mr. Jennings, as briefly as you please.

A. I may say, previous to giving this in evidence, that this work before its publication, was submitted to me for correction or approval of any of the details.

Q. Do you as an engineer and a man familiar with these departments of industrial science, endorse the correctness of the statements of that article?

A. Professor Christy's reputation is well known, and from my own personal examination, and in fact from aid to Mr. Christy, I know, as far as it is possible for me to know, in professional work, that it is correct. I would like to read certain parts concerning the first attempt made for the reduction of quicksilver.

HOISTING WORKS, 1870.

Q. You may read such as you think is pertinent to the matter.

A. Page 551. "The first attempt at quicksilver reduction was made by treating the ore in whalers' trying vats. These were made into retorts by luting on iron covers; but so much salivation of the men resulted from their use that they were soon abandoned, and regular iron retorts were introduced instead. The retort process necessitated crushing all the ores in order to mix them with lime, and was so expensive that only the rich ores would pay for treatment. As a consequence, concentration by washing or a total rejection of the poorer ores was necessary, in either case giving rise to considerable loss. Hence, even before 1850, attempts were made to treat all the ores as was then done at Idria, Austria, and at Almaden in Spain, by roasting them and condensing the quicksilver from the product of combustion. The first furnaces built were badly constructed, with poor materials, and gave rise to the loss of much metal in the foundations. But experience soon led to the type of intermittent furnace afterwards widely used in California. One of these furnaces, known as the No. 6, is still in use at New Almaden, and with the other furnaces now used will be described in detail later on."

This No. 6 is the only one of those primitive furnaces now in use, and it is made use of only when there is an actual demand for quicksilver which we cannot meet by our ordinary continuous furnaces.

(Reading) "The next important improvement was the introduction of the continuous coarse ore furnace. This furnace was first invented and built for burning lime near Berlin, by the celebrated Count Rumford. It was first introduced at Idria, Austria, by Bergrath Adolph Exeli, in 1871, and proved so effective there that its introduction at New Almaden followed in 1874. The first furnace worked so well that a second was built in 1875. These furnaces, locally known as Nos. 7 and 9, are also called monitors in allusion to their shape and to the fact that they are iron-clad. With the introduction of these furnaces, the economical treatment of the coarse ore was satisfactorilly accomplished. But the most serious problem yet remained. Two-thirds of all the ore had still to be worked into adobes, whether it went through the monitors or the intermittent furnaces. The fine ores of Almaden in Spain are even yet made into adobes, while at Idria, Austria, this class of ores is treated in continuous reverberatory furnaces. At New Almaden, the problem has been solved in a much happier manner by the invention of the Huttner & Scott furnace."

At this point I desire to state that I consider without the invention of the Huttner & Scott furnaces the New Almaden Mine could not have been run for this term of years, and would have been a bankrupt concern.

By Mr. BOWDEN:

Q. Who is the inventor or who were the inventors of that furnace?

A. (Reading) "This must be regarded as the most important contribution to the art of quicksilver reduction that has originated at New Almaden. The inventors of this furnace are Mr. H. J. Huttner, the well-known mechanical engineer, who devised nearly all the details of the various furnaces of this type, and Mr. R. Scott, the furnace mason at New Almaden. To the careful and patient experiments of its inventors and of Mr. J. B. Randol, the Manager of The Quicksilver Mining Company, and the introduction of several important improvements of his own, the practical success of this furnace is due."

I said that without this furnace this would have been a bankrupt concern; that may have been too forcible a statement, and, if you please, I will modify it.

Mr. Cross—Very well, you may modify it.

A. I would add, not perhaps bankrupt, but the profits would have been very much less. The whole present plant now consists of eight furnaces, as seen by the exhibit, which with the exception of No. 6 are of the continuous order, of a daily capacity of 145 tons. Formerly salivation of the furnace employees was a very common occurrence, but during my term of office the physician has reported no case of severe salivation among the furnace workmen which of itself is a proof of the efficiency of their work. Salivation is caused by the escaping quicksilver fumes from the furnace. It is very injurious to the nervous system and health of the employees. I have already touched upon the furnaces. I will now introduce an exhibit as to the mining growth.

Q. Please state, Mr. Jennings, the improvements upon the mine and the methods of working the additional plant and other improvements besides the furnace improvements.

A. This I have no notes of at all, but I will take an exhibit which I present as Exhibit B. which has the maps of the mining property of The Quicksilver Mining Company, New Almaden, California.

Q. What is the date?

A. Dated January 1st, 1880. I would desire to explain my exhibit a little. It is entitled "Map of the property of The Quicksilver Mining Company, New Almaden, California, January 1st, 1880." This book of maps first shows the map of the property of The Quicksilver Mining Company, showing the extent of the grant and its boundary lines owned by the Company, and containing 8,580 acres. Also, next is a topographical map of the central part of the property of The Quicksilver Mining Company. This shows the position of the houses; the hachures showing the steepness or hilliness of the country; the relative positions of the three camps, namely the Hacienda, the English Camp and Mexican Camp are given by this map, and the position of the houses and the shafts and the general working. All these exhibits are only for 1880, and there are a great many improvements which have been added since, some of which have, however, been placed on this map, though not on others, as it will figure more hereafter in evidence; next a series of colored mining views, showing the plans and vertical cross-sections of the underground works of the mine, commencing with No. 3, and extending to and including No. 9. The next, No. 10 is a plan of the furnace yard, the data for which, and surveys for which I made myself in 1879. No. 11 is the furnaces and condensers of The Quicksilver Mining Company. Considerable improvements have been made, especially in the form of condensers, since that date. From the mining maps it will be seen that

GARDEN, MANAGER'S RESIDENCE.

in 1880 there were three main shafts in which work was carried on, namely, the Randol, Isabel and Cora Blanca. The work at the latter has been discontinued. Since the date, 1880, the Buena Vista, the St. George, the American and the Washington shafts have been started, and thus we have six shafts at present in operation, and there is a network of underground passageways that have been made since the beginning of this mine, amounting now to nearly fifty miles. The different shafts are equipped with effective and modern machinery, and the mining work has been carried on to a depth of 2,300 feet below the datum point, making a total increase of depth since Mr. Randol's management of 1,500 feet. Further statistics of the mining work will be given later on in the testimony.

Q. I will ask for a statement showing the production of the mine during Mr. Randol's administration.

A. For this purpose I present exhibit C, which shows the production and other statistics. Exhibit C is entitled " The Quicksilver Statistics of New Almaden," in which the detailed statements are given of the years 1884, 1885 and 1886—the years that I have been connected with the management of the Company, and it also gives a statement of the statistics, making a showing of the whole term of Mr. Randol's administration, including 1886.

Q. What has been the total amount of ore reduced by the Company during Mr. Randol's administration?

A. The total amount of ore reduced in the sixteen years Mr. Randol has been in the management amounts to 396,212 tons, producing 317,822 flasks of silver, giving an average percentage of 3.07.

Q. That is 3.07 per cent. of quicksilver?

A. Yes.

Q. How much quicksilver in a flask : how many pounds?

A. There were 76½ pounds of quicksilver in a flask. The percentage of yield has fallen from 1871; commencing with the percentage of 6.44, the yield has fallen from 6.44 through various fluctuations until it has reached a minimum in 1886, of only 1.69 per cent., and that is the percentage of the quicksilver to the ore reduced, the lowest percentage making it much more necessary and vital to have the best and most economical methods of extraction and reduction. The total operating expenses for the sixteen years has amounted in round figures to $7,500,000.

Q. How much of that amount has been distributed for labor?

A. Over $5,000,000 has been distributed for labor on the mine and Hacienda pay rolls.

Q. What are the taxes and miscellaneous expenses?

A. Over $700,000.

Q. What has been the cost of materials consumed in that time?

A. Over $1,600,000.

Q. What have been the receipts of the Company during that time?

A. The receipts have been $11,800,000.

Q. How much of that has been realized from the sale of quicksilver produced?

A. Over $11,000,000.

Q. What has been the total profit?

A. A total profit of over $4,000,000. This is the gross profit, part of which has been put back into improvements, $4,300,000 in round numbers.

Q. What amount of that profit has been expended in permanent improvements upon the mine?

A. Over $850,000.

Q. What amount of profits have been remitted to the New York office during that time?

A. Over $3,000,000.

Q. How has that $3,000,000 been disposed of?

A. The funded debt of $1,500,000, with interest, has been paid, and over $1,000,000 declared in dividends. Before we leave this exhibit I will call attention to another portion of it. I want to state here from these statistics: What I want to bring out is the drifting, sinking, prospecting, page 49, called *dead work*, from which it is seen to amount, for the past ten years—previous to that time accurate statistics not having been kept—to a total of 77,400 feet of tunnels and shafts and passageways, drifting for prospecting purposes and for developing ore chambers, which bring no ordinary return; but this policy of the mine in keeping this dead work ahead, while it has yet good ore chambers, has been to a great extent its salvation, as the ore chambers are of a capricious character and liable to give out at very short notice.

Q. Does the ore lie in continuous veins or deposits which may be traced from one to the other, or do they have to be found, each by exploration?

A. There are generally connecting links between ore chambers, especially noted in the main branch extending from the mine hill down to the 2,000-foot level; but in places it is very unproductive, and again in other portions of the mine, such as the American and the Washington shafts, the ore bodies are disconnected as far as yet known.

Q. Will you make some statement or offer some exhibit showing the relative results of the methods pursued at this mine and other quicksilver mines in California?

A. For this purpose I desire to put in Exhibit D. This shows the production of quicksilver in the entire State of California from the year 1877 to 1886, both inclusive, from which we see, starting from the maximum produced in the year 1877 of in round numbers, 79,400 flasks, the production has gradually crept down year by year until it has reached its minimum in 1886 of not more than 30,000 flasks of which amount the New Almaden Mine produced 18,000 flasks in 1886, and the next highest producer at present being the Ætna Mine of only (for the year 1886), 3,500 flasks. The quicksilver mines of the country have to contend not only with the difficulties of nature but also with a fluctuating market, and most of the quicksilver mines of the coast have gone under or have got behind in their production by the excessive low price of quicksilver, and under these difficulties it has been necessary to have a very close industrial as well as financial management to keep this mine working.

Q. Make a statement of the classes of labor employed at this mine, with reference to the term and kind of employment.

BIRD'S-EYE VIEW OF HACIENDA.

A. There are three classes of labor employed at this mine, namely, men working by the month, by the day and on contract.

Q. State what kinds of labor are performed by the employees working by the month.

A. The employees by the month consist of officers of the company, mechanics, engine drivers and other skilled branches of work.

Q. The specially skilled branches of the work?

A. Yes, including bookkeepers and the accountants.

Q. What classes of labor are performed by the day?

A. The work about the furnace, landings and shafts,. workers on the road and sorters of the ore.

Q. What class of work is done by contract?

A. The main body of the work of the underground department is done by the contract system. Exhibit E shows the names of all employees of The Quicksilver Mining Company residing on the Hill, alphabetically arranged regarding their names, and giving their occupation, wages, how long they have been in the Company's employ, nativity, whether voters or not, age, married or single and the number of family.

Q. What does Exhibit F show, Mr. Jennings?

A. Exhibit F shows a similar chronicling of the men at the reduction works.

Q. Have you any exhibits the summary of those books, Exhibits E and F?

A. Yes, for this purpose I present Exhibit G, inserted in book Exhibit E and also Exhibit H.

Q. What does Exhibit G show?

A. Analysis of men employed by The Quicksilver Mining Company; the numbers and nationalities of the men employed by the Company November 1st, 1886, are: Mexicans, Chileans, etc., 115; English, from different parts of England, 172; Americans, including descendents of Mexicans and English, but born in the United States, 90; Spaniards, 6; Swiss, Swedes, Norwegians, Russians and Italians, 12; Irish, 2; nationality unknown, 19. Sixty-one are employed at the Hacienda, whose nationalities are: Mexicans, Chileans, etc., 5; English, 9; Americans, 19; Swedes, Norwegians, 16; Dutch, Germans, Austrians, Canadians, 6; Irish, 1; unknown, 5.

Q. What is Exhibit H?

A. Exhibit H shows the earnings of the yardage contractors for the year 1886, and the first three months of 1887; their wages not being given in the table of the wages on account of the fluctuation of their earnings from month to month.

Q. Can you show by any exhibit or otherwise about the number of men employed in each of these different classes, that is day laborers and laborers by the month and contractors?

A. This information is obtainable from the book and will be inserted later.

Q. Now from Exhibit H you may state the work done on the so called yardage contracts, the total during the whole of 1886, and the first three months of 1887.

A. The general average wages per man per day of extraction and reduction has been $2.48; that is the general average earnings per man per day.

Q. What was the total number of days work on yardage contract for that particular period of time ?

A. By this particular class of contractors 25,800 days in round numbers.

By Mr. Cross:

Q. What has been the total amount paid for that work ?

A. About $64,000.

Q. Mr. Jennings, explain what has been the highest daily earnings per man under these contracts during that period of time ?

A. The highest average of any particular company was in May, 1886, when one set of contractors made $5.96 a day per man.

Superintendent Jennings resumed his testimony at New Almaden yesterday in the Sullivan-Felton contest. Contract Work Let Publicly to the Lowest Bidder—What the Sullivan-Felton Contest is bringing forth — The Company Building Schools, Churches, Etc.

By Mr. Cross:

Q. Explain the method of advertising and letting and performing work under what you term the "contract system ?" First, as to the advertising for contracts ?

A. I will explain the classes of contract work; the contracts are offered at public bid once every month; a notice is given as to the last taker, last price, number of men required, location and size of drift and the character of the work done.

Q. When and where is this notice posted ?

A. In front of the company's office, several days before the day on which the contracts are let, usually three or four days.

Q. Where are the notices usually posted ?

A. On the company's bulletin-board at their Hill office, on the outside.

Q. Are any advertisements of this kind inserted in the papers ?

A. Frequently general advertisements stating that miners are needed for these contracts, are published in the San Francisco daily papers a week or ten days before contracts are let.

Q. To whom are the contracts, so advertised, let ?

A. To the lowest bidder.

Q State the method of bidding for and awarding the contracts.

A. The method of bidding for is shown by the exhibit of the contract bid which is printed in the company's office and freely distributed several hours before the closing of bids, then the bids are made in writing and signed by captain of the contracting company and also the men that go in with him; these bids are then tabulated in a book for the purpose, so that the lowest or most advantageous bid can easily be picked out.

Q. By what different methods of estimating the work are these contracts let ? a few moments ago you spoke of yardage.

A. There are five classes of contracts. The first is the yardage contract, requiring the greatest skill from the miners. The contrac-

FRAME... FT. LEVEL, RAW O- SHAFT.

tors are paid on yardage contract by the number of lineal yards
driven in a tunnel or a drift or a winze or a shaft, the size of these
various workings being given on the posted notices. The next class
is the drillers by the foot.

Q. Explain what that means.

A. Drilling by the foot, the men are paid by the length of the
drill hole which they drive into an ore chamber under the direction
of the shift boss, who measures and reports the length of the drill
holes. The next class is the tribute system; in the tribute system
the contractor is paid for the amount of ore after it is cleaned upon
the planilla or dressing floor, which he sends out from the ore chamber to which he is appointed. He blasts and does the whole exca-
vation of this ore and gives it to the trammers. Tramming is the
next system of contracts of which I treat and consists of taking the
material from the ore chamber to the shafts in cars, it being generally impracticable to use mules for propelling the ore. It is estimated by the ton, which is arrived at by the number of skip loads
sent from a particular level to the shaft to the outlet tunnel of the
cars. The next is the skip-filling, and the men being paid for the
number of tons they fill in the skip. The trammers deposit their
ore in various plats on different levels connected with shafts, and
the skip takes the ore from the different plats through the shaft to its
outlet, in other words is a hoisting elevator for the ore. After the
ore is taken from the mine it is deposited upon the cleaning floor,
known locally as the planilla. The ore is here subject to assortment, and it is divided into two classes of ore which are shipped to
the Hacienda, known as coarse ore and tierras; tierras being the fine
ore, or the ore that goes through the bars of the screens over which
the ore is dumped. The ore, after it has been cleaned, is hauled in
wagons over the road of the company to chutes, where it is loaded
into cars, and for a short distance is conducted by rail to the incline,
down which the cars are sent on the gravity plan, the full car pulling
up the empty car from the lower end of the incline. That work is
also done on contract, the teamster getting so much a ton for taking
from the planilla to the ore chutes of the railroad, and the men who
run the incline also being, as a rule, paid by contract. Under the
contract system there is natural selection and weeding out going on
among the employees, the less competent miners and dissolute miners not being able to compete with the more skilled and better class
of miners.

Q. I will now ask you, Mr. Jennings, as to anything like nepo-
tism being exercised on the part of the manager ?

A. I think Mr. Randol is singularly free from any cause for such
complaint, and, although he has a large family and social connec-
tions, I have never known or heard of the employment here of but
two in the whole course of his management. These were, for a time,
the resident physician, who had supervision of the Miners' Fund,
and also one of the accountants in the office for a time. The physician was his brother. The accountant was the husband of his
wife's sister.

Q. Now, Mr. Jennings, I desire to take up the social condition
of the miners, and what has been done here on the grant for their

improvement; and you may state, first, with reference to the churches on the grant.

A. The material wants of this community have received very careful attention in the shape of dwellings and gardens and water supplied, etc., which will be treated later on. There are now two churches—Methodist and Roman Catholic.

Q. What nationalities principally attend the Roman Catholic Church here?

A. The Mexican element.

Q. State whether or not those churches have regular clergymen.

A. The Methodist Church has a regular clergymen resident here.

Q. Does he have any other church under his charge except this?

A. He preaches at both camps—the Hill and the Hacienda; at the Hacienda camp, in the school-house.

Q. You may describe the Methodist Church upon the Hill, and give what you know of the history of the church structure—the Methodist Church structure.

A. The Methodist denomination have been unfortunate in their church building. It has been damaged twice by severe windstorms, requiring almost reconstruction, and once destroyed by fire. In all cases the Manager has been appealed to, in his capacity as Manager, and as an individual, for aid in the reconstruction of this building, and has always responded. The last time it was re-built, which is the present church, the total cost of construction was about $3,400, and the amount donated by the company was about $500, and by the Manager, individually, $300.

Q. From what source were the other contributions derived?

A. They were derived from the miners themselves, and by entertainments given on the grant, in which the Superintendent assisted at one, when there was a collection of $200 made. One remarkable feature of the reconstruction of the church was that on its opening the entire debt for the reconstruction was paid off.

Q. State in regard to the Catholic Church.

A. The last building of the Catholic Church was erected about two or three years ago, and it also received aid from the management in the form of money and material. The amounts I could not state, and it is now a creditable and pretty structure.

Q. Now you may take up the subject of schools. First, how many school buildings are there on the grant?

A. There are three—all public schools; all managed on the public school system in vogue in the State, at present employing six teachers—one male and five female. There are two teachers at the Hacienda school district and four on the Hill district.

Mr. Cross—Counsel for contestee states that the reason for taking testimony of the particular character now under consideration, is that it is claimed by contestant that the people living upon this ground are in the condition of slaves and peons. Counsel for contestee claims that this evidence tends to show first, that there is a condition of intelligence and means of intelligence which will render such conditions impossible, and that these facts in themselves tend to show that the people are not in the condition of either serfs or

CLEANING ORE, RANDOL PLANILLA, HILL.

peons, but are pursuing a course of intelligence and prosperity in advance of the laboring classes generally in this country.

The WITNESS—After the tilt between counsel, I am more than ever convinced of the value of my photographic exhibit for I do not believe that it is possible for the contestant or his attorneys, with the art of photography, to make any claims that it has been intimidated, coerced or gives misrepresentations of facts.

Witness here introduced in evidence a book of 53 photographic views, showing the schools, churches, stores, club building, works and homes of operatives upon the mine, including exterior and interior views of the same.

Q. Do you know about how many months per year schools are maintained in these respective buildings?

A. Ten months per year.

Q. What social organization is there, if any, maintained upon this grant, and state what you know about its organization and maintainance?

A. A social organization known as the "Helping Hand" was organized about one year and a half ago, with the idea of supplying the wants of the single men in the matter of a place of amusement and also an evening resort, independent of the drinking saloon, a club. The company supplied the building and the stage and greatly aided in fitting up the hall. For a more comprehensive description of this club and its advantages I desire to read an extract from the San Jose *Daily Mercury* of June 15, 1886, and I know it to be written by one of the members of this club. "The manager of the mine conceived the idea that by fitting up a nice, cozy, and in every respect comfortable hall where all kinds of popular games could be indulged in, and have attached to it a reading room and kitchen, that by so doing a great public want would be met; that the social sphere here would be enlarged in usefulness and our community become better natured and consequently more happy and contented. Our rules and regulations are very simple. Everybody and their families, if they have any, who pays $1 per month to the Miner's Fund are members, and entitled to all privileges and can come to the hall when open, play games, read or take a cup of tea, coffee or chocolate with cake at less than cost. No gambling or drinking of spirituous liquors is allowed, smoking is allowed in the main hall but no games; no talking or smoking is allowed in the reading-room. We have a library of about 450 volumes, consisting of stories, biography, history, etc. Our list of magazines, weekly and daily newspapers comprises the best in the State and nation." That is all that I propose to read of that article.

Q. In speaking of this club, the Miners' Fund has been mentioned; will you explain the Miners' Fund, how it is collected, cared for and applied, and you may also state what was the occasion of the Miners' Fund, if you recollect.

A. Various efforts were attempted by the miners to organize a system of contribution to secure to themselves economical, skillful medical attendance. The result of the experiments did much to convince the miners that compulsory contributions were necessary to make such a scheme a success; so that in the latter part

2

of 1870, soon after the direction of the mine was assumed by the present manager, Mr. J. B. Randol, the miners were ready to petition that he assume control of the Fund, and that contributions be made compulsory. After convincing himself that this was the wish of a large majority of the employees and residents, Mr. Randol established what is known as the Miners' Fund, and assumed entire control as Trustee. He has occupied this position for over thirteen years, without salary; and to his skillful management is due the high state of practical usefulness which the Fund has reached, in spite of previous failures.

Q. What amount is contributed per month to this fund by each employee of the mine?

A. One dollar per month by each employee of the mine is contributed. This is compulsory. A printed statement of the rules and regulations of this Miners' Fund is posted in conspicuous places in front of the main offices, shaft houses and the prominent buildings in connection with the general rules and regulations of the company, and is referred to in slips which new men sign. "Contributors are entitled without further payment to the attendance of the resident physician for themselves and their immediate families (except that cases of confinement will be charged $5 each), and will be furnished with medicines prescribed by him, on payment of cost; also for the relief of contributors whom circumstances may entitle to the same, and for other contingent expenses."

Q. I will ask you first as to the medical attendance. What means has the Trustee provided for supplying the medical attendance paid for out of this fund?

A. He has provided a resident physician.

Q. How is he paid?

A. He is paid a regular salary by the month.

Q. Of how much?

A. I would say here, it is an embarrassing position to be placed in, my present one, as regards what right I have to lay bare before the public the private business of its employees. I have aimed to present such facts as have already appeared in print in various forms.

Q. State whether or not the physician employed by the Trustee of the Miners' Fund devotes himself exclusively to that service?

A. Most exclusively; he is here and ready at every call, night or day.

Q. State whether or not he has office hours at which he receives calls in his office of those who are able to attend the office for treatment?

A. Yes, he has an office hour on the Hill. Let it be here stated in that connection, that when I make the statement "the Hill," it includes the English and Mexican camps; it is a general term for that portion of the mining industry away from the reduction works. Those two camps lie near together.

Q. Are those office hours daily?

A. Daily.

Q. State whether or not those who are contributors to this fund are treated by the physician without any further charge to them or their families.

A. Yes, every one as long as he is an employee or a voluntary contributor to the fund, is entitled to any and all services of the physician except the one mentioned in the rules (that is cases of confinements will be charged five dollars) free of charge.

Q. Does that go into the fund?

A. That goes back into the fund.

Q. State whether or not the members of his immediate family are also entitled to that treatment without further charge?

A. Yes, that treatment; all members of the family are treated for that consideration, and in that connection let me state that one of the contestant's most malignant witnesses against the management of this company was a Mr. Kennett; he testified against the improprieties of this fund, but had, before his leaving this mine, great cause for the use of this fund, inasmuch as he had one, two or three children, I am not certain which, taken down with scarlet fever, and the doctor was required greatly, and the only amount he paid was the amount of one dollar a month.

Its Management—The New Almaden Mine and its Employees. A Searching Inquiry by the Contestee's Attorney. Political Complexion and Personal Character of the Mine Workers. The third days's testimony at New Almaden in the Sullivan-Felton contest was as follows, Superintendent Jennings being on the stand:

By Mr. Cross:

Q. I desire to examine you now as to the industrial management of The Quicksilver Company and its property. First, who is the present manager of the property and the company's affairs?

A. The present General Manager of this mine is J. B. Randol. He became manager in 1870 or 1871. He resided in New Almaden till 1880, though often visiting San Francisco for business purposes, when the sales of the quicksilver were entrusted to his hands, in addition to his control of the mine. Mr. Randol during his residence at New Almaden practically filled the position of both General Manager and Superintendent, but since that date it has been necessary to have a resident Superintendent with absolute authority during his absence.

Q. What are the duties and responsibilities of the Superintendent?

A. The Superintendent is under control of the General Manager, who has absolute control of the property in California, the company being a New York corporation, with its President and its Board of Directors in New York City, and he is thus an agent on this coast, with absolute authority to act for this company in all matters.

Q. That is, in all matters relating to the management of the mine?

A. The management of the mine, and under the general control is the position of the Superintendent, who has the entire power of employing and discharging men, and has direct supervision of the industrial work, and has a corps of assistants under him to aid him in the general overseeing of the property.

Q. Give the grades and names of these different assistants who come next to the Superintendent in authority.

A. The general mine foreman, the present incumbent being Captain Harry; the Hacienda foreman and accountant combined, which position is filled by Mr. Bulmore; the foreman on the Hill, Mr. O'Brion; the clerks, of which there are two, one on the Hill and one at the Hacienda, who, in addition to their clerical duties act in the capacity of telegraph operator and apothecary; they are Mr. Carson and Mr. Hall; the surveyor who has the surveying and mapping of the different underground excavations and passageways accomplished during various months of the year, and also assists the general mine foreman in some of his duties. Other positions would be the shift bosses who have the directions of the details of the underground work, though under the supervision of the main mine foreman. A very important position is the furnace foreman at the Hacienda, who has charge of the details of the furnaces and men. This position is occupied by Mr. William Stiles, and under him are the watchmen and weighers. The position of chief engineer is also a very important position on the Hill, and is filled by Mr. James Harrower, who has charge of all the machinery on the company's property and the mechanics working under his direction.

Q. What is about the average number of men employed at the mine during the year 1886.

A. Between 450 and 460.

Q. Mr. Jennings what can you say of the length of time that the men in the employ of the company have continued in its employment?

A. To answer that question I desire to turn to the exhibits already presented, E and F, from which it will be seen there have been men in the employ of this company from thirty-four to thirty-five years.

Q. Can you make any statement as to the average length of time of those employed in the company?

A. That would be a pretty hard statement to make, but if you would designate any letter of the alphabet, I will turn to the exhibit and read from it.

Q. Well, take from letter C. The employees' names commencing with C. You need not read the names.

A. The length of employment by this company is given as follows in regular rotation in years: 21, 23, 20, 24, 22, 11, 9½, 9, 22, 14, 25, 24, 2, 4, 5, 30, 6, 2, 5, 9, 5, 1½, 25, 12, 25, 6, 6, ½, 2. Frequently men who have left the service of the company afterwards return to get work.

Q. Seeking re-employment from the company?

A. Seeking re-employment from the company and in giving out some of the positions on day pay we make it a point to try and take care of and tide over the miners that have been a long time here by giving them the preference on day work to strangers and though they may be working for one month or two in this manner in day pay they return again to their contract system.

Q. Mr. Jennings, what can you say with regard to strikes or threats of strikes during Mr. Randol's time?

A. The great satisfaction of the men with the administration is very well illustrated by the fact that during Mr. Randol's entire administration of sixteen and one-half years there has not been a single strike or even threat of a strike.

Q. What are the principal nationalities employed at the mine?

A. The chief nationalities are English-Americans—that is descendants of both English and other nationalities who were born in America, in the United States rather, and the Mexicans and Swedes.

Q. How do you account for these being the nationalities chiefly employed?

A. The proportion in which these elements have remained here is greatly due to the natural competition going on in the contract system. These nationalities also harmonize well together, for although the Cornish and Mexicans do not associate very much with each other, they agree to let each other alone, and thus have no tendency to affiliate in combinations against the management.

Q. Mr. Jennings, how do you account, for instance, for there being so many Cornishmen employed in working the mine?

A. They have been the most successful men in making wages under the yardage system, that is to say, in open competition for the running of drifts and tunnels, and the sinking of shafts, winzes, etc.

Q. How do you account for that?

A. It may be accounted for from the fact that their ancestors were miners, and they were brought up in Cornwall on a system of contracts somewhat similar to what is carried on here.

Q. Now what can you say as to the physical characteristics of those men?

A. When spurred by the impetus of large pay made on their contracts, they perform, as far as I am able to judge, the greatest amount of labor of any set of men I know.

Q. What have you to say with regard to the Mexican miners. How do they come to be employed here; and how is it that so many of them are employed here?

A. In the early history of the mine the Mexican element seems to have been the only one used here. The original owners of the mine receiving their grant from Mexico, and introduced the Mexican system of mining; in this manner a great many of them came from Mexico, and their descendants have grown up at the mine, and they have made a specialty of working in ore chambers more than in competition with the Cornishmen on the yardage contracts, though at times they are the lowest bidders on the yardage system.

Q. What department of work are those of the Swedish nationality mostly employed in?

A. They are employed on the furnaces and in tramming and in skip filling, a class of labor not requiring as great mining skill, but often great physical endurance.

Q. Mr. Jennings, I notice from your report of the nationalities the number of Irish birth is very small. What have you to state about that?

A. We have but few Irish. Those few that we have retained are especially efficient and faithful, but this element does not harmonize with the other elements here. As I have noticed, even in other mining localities, the Cornish and the Irish do not assimilate well together, and no great exertion has been made on the part of the management to keep this element here when harmony with the others could not be expected.

Q. In reference to the contract work you speak of, the contract being let to an individual and his assistants, how many men are employed upon one contract?

A. From four to sixteen.

Q. In going over the table of the nationalities employed by this mine I see no statement of the number of Chinese employed in the mine. Owing to the sentiment about the employment of Chinese on this Coast, I will ask you to make a statement with regard to that matter.

A. Previous to August, 1884, some Chinamen, amounting to about forty or fifty, were employed around the furnaces or in working the old dumps, but since that date no Chinaman has been employed. This date of August, 1884, I would desire to say, is previous to the last crusade against the Chinese in this State.

Q. Was the discharge of those men accomplished by any strike or any act upon the part of the men, or was it the voluntary act of the employers?

A. It was the voluntary act of the Manager.

Q. Now, Mr. Jennings, I will request you to give some comparison of the results and cost of production, amount of production and average wages of the miners in the Almaden Mine of Spain and the New Almaden Mine here?

A. For this purpose I will present exhibit M. I desire rather fully to explain exhibit N, entitled "The Quicksilver Mines of Almaden and New Almaden, a comparative view of their extent, production, costs of work, etc., printed for private circulation." The origin of Exhibit M was that some time in the early part of 1886, the Manager, discouraged by the small profit made at the mine in 1885, as shown on page 47 of exhibit C, sent witness the pamphlets, articles, etc., alluded to in the report, and desired him to make a formal examination and comparison for the purposes of seeing if he could gain points of advantage for the working of this mine, and also to show him what a formidable competitor the mine had in the old Almaden Mine in Spain.

Q. Does the product of this mine have to compete with the product of the Almaden Mine in prices.

A. Yes. The product of the Almaden Mine in Spain, is controlled by the Rothchilds of London, who control the quicksilver markets of the world; and after carefully examining the statistics thus sent me, I returned, as Superintendent, my conclusion as follows page twelve of Exhibit M, as to the relative efficiency of the methods and workmen: I again request your careful attention to Table D, for I believe that in no mine on this coast are similar results obtained for less money. Even if it be possible to reduce these rates of labor per day, I believe it could only be at the expense of having a poorer class of workmen who would not accomplish as much per dollar paid out as our present force of skilled and energetic men at wages now paid. The illustration of the accomplishments of cheap labor at Almaden, Spain, is certainly not encouraging. Of course if our production keeps on decreasing, something will have to be done to lessen expenses, and the only way I can see to accomplish this will be to decrease the number of men employed. On the other hand if prospecting is not energetically continued until new discoveries are found the life of the mine must be brief. At the old Almaden there are employed 2,825 men and 301 boys, a total of 3,126 workers.

Q. What is the aggregate production of ore?

A. The extraction of all material from the old Almaden Mine amounted to only 19,475 tons for the entire year under discussion.

Q. Now state the number of men employed, and the amount extracted at the New Almaden Mine.

A. A total, including boys, of but 423, employed for the mining department. The amount of material extracted from this mine, however, was 138,600, or an average per worker of 326 tons a year. It is hardly fair, however, to leave the inference that this vast difference in work is entirely due to our superior methods of work and workmen, as there is one serious disadvantage connected with working the Spanish Mine that I have not before mentioned, viz: the workmen are seriously affected by the mercurial emanations from the mine, and do not work on an average over one day in three, and then only six hours at a time; but even taking this into account, and assume they cannot work more than one-fifth the number of hours our men do, it is seen for equal time working per man there is ten times the material extracted from this mine in equal time. The Almaden Mine, although with this small production of material produced over 40,000 flasks of quicksilver, and at an expense of only $7.10 a flask, and the production of the New Almaden was only 21,-600 flasks at an expense of over $26 per flask. In other words the old Almaden ore chambers are ten times as rich as the New Almaden.

Q. Now, Mr. Jennings, leaving the industrial management of the mine, as such, I wish to inquire something regarding the political complexion of the mine, and first I will ask you whether you have any prepared table of the voters of the precinct at the last election?

A. Yes. A table made up from the poll list of this precinct and Great Register of the county. The voters in the employ of The Quicksilver Mining Company was 156.

Q. How is the nationality of that vote divided?

A. Those in the employ of the company are divided as follows: American, 52; English, 71; Mexicans, 25; Irish, 2; other nationalities, 6. Of this number there are 64 on day pay, and contractors, 92.

Q. Mr. Jennings, have you been acquainted with the residents, miners in other portions of California besides New Almaden?

A. Yes, I have been engaged both in Nevada and Sierra Counties.

Q. From your acquaintance with the miners there and at New Almaden can you state what are the generally political party leanings of the Cornishmen?

A. My observation is that they are Republicans.

Q. What have you to say about the partisanship of the Mexicans?

A. The Mexicans exhibit little partisan feeling, they have stronger race feeling.

Q. State whether or not you have observed that this race feeling has had strong influence at times in affecting their vote ?

A. This race feeling being strong there would be a chance of its influencing them in this last election of November 1886, at the time Mr. Sullivan was a candidate for Congress. At that election a prominent candidate on the Democratic County ticket was a man who, in the exercise of his duty, was forced to kill one of their race. He was a candidate on the same ticket and at the same election as Mr. Sullivan.

Q. What have you to say with regard to the general partisan leanings, so far as you have observed them, of the Irish voters in the mines of California?

A. It is the accepted verdict of the country that their leanings are Democratic.

Q. What have you to say with regard to the native Americans who vote in California, so far as you have occasion to observe them, as to their partisan leanings?

A. They are largely descendents of Cornish and Mexican nationalities, and their opinions are largely in accordance with their ancestry.

Q. State what you know of the history of the social condition and character of the parties who are employed on this mine as employees in early days.

A. The early history has been, as I cull it from old inhabitants and articles in the newspapers, I would conclude that there was a great amount of lawlessness pursued here; the men were making large wages, and not much restraint was exercised over them, they had almost unlimited freedom to gratify any gambling or drinking tendency and it was no uncommon occurrence for a man to be killed after pay day; it was a rendez-vous for Mexican banditti; a curious incident occurs to me in this connection, about a year ago there was a skeleton of a miner found in one of our drifts that had caved together and in running a new drift, this drift was again entered, in which was found the skeleton of a man with a bullet hole through his head.

Q. Do you know of any noted banditti who were reputed to have frequented the place in the early days?

A. Yes, the notorious Vasquez.

Q. What can you state of the condition at the present time in these respects as compared with the condition at that time?

A. The present management outside of the industrial and financial condition of the mine takes also great interest in the condition of the people and have made strenuous efforts to exclude from the mining property notably obnoxious, disorderly and habitually intemperate people and also to make the non-producing class of the community as small as possible. Gambling and intemperance and prostitution may be carried on secretly, but is very vigorously fought when it openly appears.

Q. Now what example can you give and what statement can you make tending to show the present condition of the mine as compared with the former lawless condition?

A. That for some time past the community was unsupplied with a Constable or any peace officer.

Q. Now what can you say as to the industrial management and the management with regard to the improvement of the condition of those who reside upon the mines as to their savings and accumulations? What I desire to call your attention to is what has been the result to the employees in the way of savings and accumulations resulting from this management?

A. I will answer your question generally as it is asked. I would state that the improvident are improvident the world over, and the saving and careful get ahead. It is the same here as elsewhere. Speaking of it in regard to the nationalities, I would say that the Mexicans are a far more improvident and pleasure-loving race than either the Cornish or the Swedes. Their saying is: "Mañana es otro dia," (to-morrow is another day), and they take the sweets as they come. The Cornish believe more in saving. Many of them have their own houses here on the company's property, and also, I understand, other accumulations. In this connection I would state that there are a considerable number of Mexicans who also, by saving, own their houses, and are saving. The number of men employed in November, 1886, was 477; being contractors, 249; day pay men, 155; men employed by the month, 73. I submit in evidence the printed rules and regulations of The Quicksilver Mining Company, which are posted about the furnace works and in front of the offices and the shaft houses and other conspicuous positions about the property, in connection with the rules of the Miners' Fund, as already stated and given in evidence.

Q. What is done to call attention to these rules of the miners seeking employment by the company?

A. They are officially required to read them or have them read to them before being employed.

Q. From what sources are these rules in the main derived?

A. In the main from the Civil Code of California.

Q. Mr. Jennings, what is the reason of that provision of rule 7, which provides that an employee by the month, if he desires to quit the company's service, must give one month's notice?

A. That is to protect us from the sudden leaving of a skilled employee whose position cannot be filled at a moment's notice.

Q. As I understand you, these positions, on account of the special skill required to fill them, if one of them becomes vacant, cannot be filled ordinarily, immediately?

A. Yes; and it requires time to enable us to find a suitable man to fill the vacancy, and so we require a month's notice of quitting.

Q. State whether or not during your incumbency as Superintendent, there has been any rule requiring employees to trade at any particular place, and whether there have been during your term any men discharged from employment on that account?

A. No.

Q. Mr. Jennings, in dispensing with the services of employees or discharging them, does the company or its representatives give any reason to the persons discharged, for discharging them?

A. No; it has been the established rule of the Manager for years that he declines so doing; the reason being almost self-evident, as it is not politic or advisable to enter into personal discussion which will lead to heated, endless and needless controversy with discharged employees of such a large industrial establishment as this, and the management reserves the right, and believes they have it, to employ and discharge whom they please.

Q. What right has the company to the land included in this grant; what title?

A. The company have now the United States patents to the whole tract.

Q. We will now discuss the improvements upon the company's lands. First the roads: What is the extent of the roads owned by the company upon this grant?

A. About six or seven miles of private road constructed by the company.

Q. Who maintains these roads?

A. The company.

Q. Over what kind of a country do these roads run?

A. Over a hilly country, as shown by the map. The roads have serpentine windings and declivities over which they pass.

Q. What difference in elevation is there in the one road that extends from the Hacienda to the American shaft?

A. Over 1,100 feet vertically. The main part of this road was constructed in the early history of the mine.

Q. Speaking of this grade how was it necessary to construct the road for the purpose of overcoming this grade?

A. By excavations in the hillsides. The width of the road is varying. For the most part there is room for two teams to pass each other at a pinch, but there are places where it is dangerous.

Q. Who maintains these roads?

A. The company.

Q. What is the expense?

A. At least $500 for the total system of roads, per year.

Q. What means has the company provided for preventing trespassers upon its lands?

A. Fences and a gate, such as are generally maintained about private lands in this country. The company claims the right to maintain fences about its property and to exclude all trespassers. This company considers itself a private industrial institution, and claims the right of excluding people from its property as any other private individual is allowed to by the laws of the land. We understand that that is what the right of property is, in part.

Q. What means of entrance and egress to the mine is furnished.

A. Through a toll gate in connection with the roads already described.

Q. Are there other parties besides the manager, officers, and employees of the company allowed to use this road?

A. Yes, by obtaining permission and paying reasonable tolls. It acts favorably to the interests of the people themselves on the grant, inasmuch as it gives the company the power of excluding nonproducers, who, in almost all communities of the country are found to subsist on the earnings of the workers.

Q. Is there any other reason for practicing this exclusion of teams from the roads of the company?

GATE LEADING TO WORKS, HACIENDA.

A. Yes. At times when we are getting in our supply of coal and timber and lagging for the mine there is great activity, especially as the ore teams are continually running on these roads, and at times I have noticed as high as twelve or thirteen teams at one time in going up from the Hacienda to the Hill on horseback, and parties not acquainted with the country would embarrass the hauling by getting in positions on the road where it would be impossible to pass each other.

Q. Now to meet that objection, what has been the custom latterly as to who shall handle teams upon the road other than those directly engaged in the business of the company?

A. It is thought proper not to allow strangers and visitors to drive themselves on the Hill, for their own best interests, and also to protect the company against any lawsuit that might arise from accidents, and from interference with the traffic of the company on the road. A livery stable is provided here and kept by a Mr. Bohlman who supplies visitors, if they so desire, with a suitable driver and reliable horses to go on these mountainous roads.

Q. State whether or not these teams hauling on this mountain grade, that you state is narrow in places, wear bells.

A. Yes.

No Coercion or Intimidation of Voters —No Man Discharged for Political Reasons— Conclusion of Superintendent Jennings' Testimony. The taking of testimony in the Sullivan-Felton contest was resumed at New Almaden yesterday morning, Superintendent Jennings being still on the stand:

By Mr. Cross:

Q. What can you say as to the employees of the company as to having families or being single men ?

A. A large proportion of our employees have families here, and the management desire to encourage this class of labor.

Q. What means have they provided for the housing of their employees having families ?

A. The cottages before alluded to, built by the company. The employees can also erect dwellings of their own on the company's ground, by paying a monthly ground rent of fifty cents a month.

Q. You have given some testimony that the ore bodies are scattered and have to be prospected for; what effect would it have upon the best interests of the company as to the right to prospect for and develop ore bodies in the ground if the company was parting with the title to portions of its land for the erection of these cottages ?

A. I think it would be disadvantageous.

Q. Can you state what number of cottages the company owns for occupancy of its employees?

A. More than 100 are rented to employees for the occupancy of their families.

Q. What are the rents the company charges for those cottages ?

A. From $2 to $8 per month; a fair average would be about $5 a month.

Q. What number of cottages on the company's land are owned by private parties other than the company?

A. There are 119 such houses owned by 91 different parties.

Q. How many of these are owned by the employees of the company?

A. Ninety-one of them, though there are some held by old residenters, who were formerly in the employ of the company, but are not now. These are leased by such parties to employees of the company.

Q. State whether or not the company encourages or discourages the occupancy of cottages upon its land by other persons than those who are employed by the company or directly administer to the necessities of those so employed?

A. No. They do all in their power to exclude such persons.

Q Is there any exception to that?

A. In the case of families, or those who have formerly been employed by the company; the families are often allowed to remain to suit their own convenience until they can locate elsewhere.

Q. State the material and character of these cottages furnished by the company for these employees.

A. They are built of redwood with a shingle roof and board partition walls as a rule (though some are plastered), and lined in with such linings inside as are usually used in these climates of Calfornia; the repairs are in the main kept up by the company.

Q. What can you say concerning the grounds, and fences, and improvements about these cottages?

A. The management desires to have them neat and orderly as far as possible, and encourage in every way the people to make them so by giving them cuttings of plants from the main garden, and free use of whitewash and such like encouragement free of charge.

Q. State whether or not these cottages are fenced and have flower gardens about them?

A. Yes, and that is shown in the photographic exhibits already presented.

Q. What is done with the rents received from the cottages that belong to the company and the ground rents for such cottages?

A. They are turned into the funds of the company and appear on their books as receipts outside of the sale of quicksilver.

Q. Mr. Jennings, can you state the nationalities of the heads of families which rent houses from the company?

A. Yes. Americans owning houses 2; French, 3; Mexicans, 38; English, 48.

Q. Who owns the largest number of houses outside of the company?

A. One of the oldest residents here, Mr. Francis Meyers. He owns sixteen. He was formerly one of the chief mechanics, and his last hard work was in the capacity of chief carpenter and architect of the Santa Isabel shafthouse building.

Q. Has he any connection whatever with the company or its management?

A. None at the present time.

Q. Make a statement of the water supply for the residents in these cottages.

A. The water supply for the Hill cottages is one of the purest I know of anywhere. The water is taken from an adjacent mountain ravine, some two or three miles away, and is conducted in iron pipes up and down declivities, and is disbursed and distributed to the various shafts for the use of generating steam power, and is also distributed at different prominent and easy accessible points to the cottages from large tanks.

Q. What about protection from fire in connection with this water supply?

A. A hydrant is placed near the central portion of the English camp, with the water under pressure of over 100 feet with large supply tanks in case of necessity.

Q. What price does each cottage pay for water?

A. Fifty cents a month. This water system was established somewhere about 1881 or 1882, at a cost to the company of $15,000. Before this system was in use the company had made efforts to put in tanks at some points, by leading the water from adjacent and local springs to one or two places in the camp, but it was comparatively inconvenient for the people, as they would have to carry the water some distance, and in the Spanish camp it was even necessary for the cottagers to supply themselves with water by purchasing water from a Mexican water-carrier—in the early times the water being transferred in little barrels on burros.

Q. Who owns the buildings in which the business of merchandizing is carried on, on this grant?

A. The Quicksilver Mining Company.

Q. Who owns the business and stock of merchandise handled in those stores, and who conducts the business?

A. The stores are leased to Messrs. Derby and Lowe directly from the New York office, the lease being signed by the President of the company there. Messrs. Derby and Lowe sell provisions and other merchandise to the employees and other persons on the company's grant, and outsiders who desire to trade with them, and they do not furnish the supplies or materials used by The Quicksilver Mining Company, except in small quantities. Messrs. Derby and Lowe have in no way any control over the employees of this company, as the management is alone invested with the power of employ and discharge. Messrs. Derby and Lowe are private individuals, and in my whole term of office I have never in one solitary instance discharged a man at the request of either Messrs. Derby or Lowe, and I have received no formal complaint from the employees against their prices.

Q. Have Messrs. Derby and Lowe any other connection with the company except that they lease stores from the company?

A. No.

Q. How many stores do they lease?

A. Two stores, with store houses and cellars.

Q. Mr. Jennings, you may state anything you may know of the Boleto system, so called, as practiced at those stores?

A. The Boleto system arises in this way: The company pay but once a month, at a regular pay-day. That pay-day is well known to employees; and in the whole history of Mr. Randol's management that pay-day has not been missed in one solitary instance. The company make no provision to advance men pay before the regular pay-day, but if the men desire advances they get them at the store; the store gives no credit on goods, but issues orders payable in goods at their store; these orders are printed on small pieces of card-board and called boletos. These orders when advanced to them are charged against them by the store-keepers on their books, and the amount charged against each man is reported to the company at the company's main office before pay-day, and the money thus advanced by Derby & Lowe for the convenience of the employees themselves is refunded to Messrs. Derby & Lowe by The Quicksilver Mining Company.

Q. How many butcher shops are there on the grant?

A. There are two butcher shops on the grant; one at the lower camp called the Hacienda and the other at the Hill camp in Spanish town; the butcher also supplies the inhabitants by means of a regular butcher cart or delivery wagon. These butcher shops are leased at the present time to Mr. Dulion.

Q. How many stables are there on the company's land?

A. There are quite a number of stables that are made use of by the main contractor Bohlman, who does our hauling of all descriptions by contract. It is found by experience that it is better to concentrate all this work in the hands of one reliable party rather than several, and Mr. Bohlman has numerous teamsters and over 100 head of horses in connection with his work, but the only relationship that this company have with Mr. Bohlman is that of a contractor and lessor.

Q. Are any of these stables so leased to and occupied by Mr. Bohlman's livery stables?

A. One is.

Q. What provision is made for furnishing board and rooms to such employees of the company as have no families of their own with whom to reside, upon the grant?

A. There are several boarding houses on the grant which are managed by different parties. The party that has the boarding-house at the lower camp is a Mrs. Hancock, whose husband was killed in a sad mining accident some years ago; and the main board-house on the Hill is conducted by Mrs. Robins, and there is also a Mexican boarding-house. These boarding-houses are leased to the occupants by the company.

Q. How many employees of the company are accommodated at these boarding houses?

A. It is a very variable matter because the single men class of labor is the most fluctuating. At present about a hundred.

Q. What rates do they pay for board?

A. Seventy-five cents a day I believe for table board. If they room at the boarding-house about ten cents additional per day.

Q. On what condition are vegetable peddlers allowed to go upon the grant?

A. Vegetable peddlers have been allowed the privilege by simply paying ordinary toll for their class of vehicle, and on their showing themselves reliable parties for the employees to deal with.

Q. What privileges have the occupants of the cottage outside of the cottages and land referred to in connection with the cottages?

A. They are allowed the pasturage of their live stock on the company's grant. I think there must be altogether say nearly 200 head of stock thus pastured upon the company's ground.

Q. How are the materials and supplies for the mine obtained?

A. There are various kinds of supplies that we need, and they are purchased here and in San Francisco, as is most favorable for the company. All such supplies as foundry work, and steel, iron, candles, hardware, fuse, powder, etc., are bought by the Manager in San Francisco, who has a reputation there as a very close buyer for the company.

Q. How is the wood and timber used at the mine obtained?

A. That is obtained by contract made by the Superintendent with such parties as have such material to sell in this vicinity. The coal is bought by the Manager in shipload quantities. We are now consuming over 5,000 tons a year at the different engines.

Q. How is it transported to the mine from the ship?

A. Formerly it was sent to San Jose, but now since we have railroad communication it is taken from the ship to the terminus here, where it is deposited in bunkers and is taken thence by our contractor, Mr. Bohlman, at stated and regulated prices to different portions of the company's property as needed.

Q. What is the distance from the nearest railroad stations to this point on the mine where we are now taking testimony?

A. About two miles.

Q. How many different railroads from San Francisco and San Jose have stations at a distance of two miles from this point or a little over?

A. Two different railroad systems. They have regular daily passenger and freight trains on both lines.

Q. What quantities of ore are annually transported to the furnaces from the different portions of the mine?

A. About 40,000 tons per year.

Q. Calling your attention to election and political matters, state whether or not during your term of office, Mr. Randol, the Manager, has ever communicated to you any directions, instructions or requests, or officially dictated to you with regard to how you or any of the employees of the mine should vote at any election for national, State or local officers?

A. No.

Q. During that time have you ever given any directions, instructions or intimations to any of the officers or employees under you as to how you or the Manager wished any one to vote at any election for national, State or local officers?

A. No.

Q. Who alone has power to discharge men?

A. I have the absolute supervision of the discharge of all the men.

Q. Since you have been Superintendent of this mine has any

man ever been discharged from the employ of the company on account of the manner in which he had voted or intended to vote, or on account of any political reason?

A. I have never so discharged a man.

Q. To what party does Mr. Randol belong?

A. Mr. Randol affiliates with the Republican party.

Q. Where had Mr. Randol been from the time of the political conventions up to the election held in November, 1886?

A. He had been in the East, out of the State entirely.

Q. How long had he been back at the mine before election day?

A. I believe he returned here the day before the election.

Q. Did you have any political talk with him the night before election?

A. Yes, we always discussed politics in a personal manner, humorously, in which connection, the night before election, he told me he thought there were very few important issues involved in the election, and it was very immaterial to him how the election went.

Q. With what party do you affiliate and with what party have you affiliated in the past?

A. The absorbing nature and responsibilities of my duties here have prevented me from even the possibility of taking much interest in politics. Just before election I read the papers on both sides, and unfortunately I see that one partisan paper will make one man a villain and the other partisan paper will make the other man a villain, and it is very annoying and trying to me to make up my mind as between villains, though in truth they may be all most honorable men. The place of my birth, Kentucky, gives me a kind of leaning towards Democracy, but I also graduated at Harvard University which is thought to be a kind of hot bed of the Mugwumps, and so I may be perhaps a little tainted that way myself. I have scratched unmercifully. I fear that my individual politics had very little weight at the election of November, 1886. I know it as a positive fact that my main political idea had but little weight here then. I know it from the fact I cast at this precinct the only vote for the head of the American party ticket.

Q. Have you any knowledge of any individual or official efforts being made by any officers of this company at the election of November, 1886, against Mr. Sullivan personally?

A. No.

Q. What do you know about the politics of Messrs. Derby and Lowe, who have been attacked in this contest?

A. Mr. Lowe is a Republican and Mr. Derby a Democrat.

Q. There has been some evidence given on the part of the contestant, tending to show that you were about the polls a good deal of the time that day; state the facts in regard to that matter.

A. In fact, as far as I know, I was very little at the polls, but in order to go from my dwelling to my office I had of necessity to pass the place, as the sidewalk leading thereby was the only way of getting there. I probably thus passed the polls two or three times during the day, and once in company with Mr. Randol; I believe that is the time the witness testified seeing me; altogether I suppose I must

JUSTICE'S OFFICE AND VOTING PLACE, HACIENDA.

have been about the polling place a half or at most three-quarters of an hour during the day.

Q. Did you, yourself, or did Mr. Randol in your presence, do anything to influence, control or coerce, or intimidate any voting employee at that election ?

A. No.

Q. How were the members of the election board of that election appointed ?

A. In the usual manner prescribed by the Code.

Q. What is the distance by the road, approximately, from the English and Mexican camps to the polling place ?

A. I should estimate over three miles to the Mexican camp, and two miles and a half to the English.

Q. What means were provided for such employees of the company as desired to vote, to travel from the Mexican and English camps to the polling place ?

A. The men were brought down in stages from the Hill to near the polls.

Q. What is it to the men themselves to be brought down and returned in stages ?

A. That they thus had an opportunity of all voting and returning to the occupation at which they are ordinarily engaged.

Q. What would be the effect on the ability of the men to perform further work that day if they walked down and up the Hill instead of riding ?

A. I do not think they would be in as good a condition for work as if they had a conveyance, nor could they do it in as quick time.

Q. State what was the position where the Great Register hung on that day ?

A. It is right near the edge of the bridge towards the store, nearly 40 feet from the 100-foot limit, outside of the limit.

Q. Some testimony has been given concerning Mr. Bulmore having a book about the polls in which he wrote. State what you know about that book ?

A. Mr. Bulmore's book is an alphabetical list containing the name of every voter in this precinct with his register number. Mr. Bulmore so far as I know, had no reason for having this book other than to facilitate the voting of the men as they came down, or came about the polls.

Q. How was that a convenience to the men for him to have a book alphabetically arranged, with the Great Register number of each voter opposite his name ?

A. They could find their names quicker in this book than they could from the Great Register. Some Mexicans also are not able to read English, and required assistance in this matter.

Q. Some testimony has been offered in this case by Mr. Kennett. Did you know Mr. Kennett ?

A. Yes.

Q. Did he quit the employ of the company after you came here ?

A. Yes.

Q. Do you know whether or not he has applied to the company for employment since that time ?

3

A. I do.

Q. What evidence have you which you can present concerning that matter?

A. I have three letters, originals, which I desire to read. The first is dated:

ALAMEDA, Cal., May 13, 1885.

To J. B. Randol, Esq., Manager—DEAR SIR: Can I obtain employment with you at New Almaden or elsewhere.

Very respectfully,

F. B. KENNETT.

The reply was:

SAN FRANCISCO, May 14, 1885.

F. B. Kennett, Esq., Alameda, Cal.—DEAR SIR: Replying to your note of yesterday, I regret that it is impossible for me to give you employment at present. Yours truly,

J. B. RANDOL.

The next is dated:

ALAMEDA, May 17, 1885.

J. B. Randol, Esq., Manager—DEAR SIR: Your favor of 14th received; I desire to state that in the event of your requiring my services I will be pleased to engage with you for as long a term as you may desire, and pledge myself to a careful attention to your interests.

Very respectfully,

F. B. KENNETT.

Q. Was all of that correspondence subsequent to that date when Mr. Kennett was last in the employ of the company?

A. Yes, I have before stated that I took the position of Superintendent here in September, 1884, and Mr. Kennett left I think the latter part of the same year.

Q. James Reedy has given some testimony in this case in which he states that he was discharged by Mr. Randol from his position as coachman for political reasons. Will you state what you know about Mr. Reedy's discharge and the cause of it?

A. I know about the cause of his last discharge, but I understand that there were numerous discharges he claims to have had here, but I know about the last. That was soon after taking my present position here, Mr. Reedy, as I understand it from Mr. Randol and others, bought a horse for The Quicksilver Mining Company, or at least aided in the purchase of a horse for The Quicksilver Mining Company, known as Dixie; this horse was finally thought by Mr. Randol, and for good reasons, to be tricky and dangerous, and Mr. Reedy had never informed him of the nature of the animal, although he drove Mr. Randol's little children and wife out with it. After discovering the nature of the horse Mr. Reedy was discharged, and the subsequent career of the horse was such that there could be no doubt about its disposition. He was put into a four-horse team and started the whole four horses running away and some portions of the wagon were injured and one or two of the horses hurt; in fact Dixie himself was so disabled that he was sold for half the original price paid for him.

Q. In what capacities was Mr. Reedy employed about the mine after that?

A. Mr. Reedy had a very large family here, and appealed to our sympathy, and was allowed to remain in the company's house after he had obtained employment of Mr. Frank Bohlman, the contractor for the teaming here, and I believe drove his team, but had some trouble with Mr. Bohlman which I do not know personally. After the trouble with Mr. Bohlman he left the camp owing the company for house rent $26. He never paid that rent to this day.

Q. Did his family remove from the property immediately after his discharge?

A. No; his family remained here until he had sought employment elsewhere; until he got a house in San Jose for them.

Q. Some testimony given on the part of the contestant seems to be an attack upon you personally and your conduct in connection with the property. What have you to say in regard to that matter.

A. I desire to say here, that, feeling conscious of my integrity and good purposes, and feeling sure that any of my personal acquaintances, whose good opinion I would care to keep, would not believe such statements of me, from such unreliable sources. I do not care to make any further defense against such scurrilous attacks; and those who do not know me who examine the testimony introduced, will, I believe, be satisfied that that testimony refutes itself.

Q. Mr. Jennings, what statement do you desire to make in regard to the general character and purposes of the management of this mine.

A. I desire to state here and rather generally that I know of no branch of mining industry that has been carried on on this coast on such purely industrial grounds as this one, and which has attempted to administer so largely to the wants and affairs of their employees as this; that the purpose and intention of the management has been kindly towards its employees.

Q. State whether or not the local management has been in any way interested in, or dealing in the stocks of this company, or whether the management has been conducted with any reference to affecting the values of the stocks, irrespective as it should naturally result from the industrial management and profits of the mine?

A. I am of the firm belief that J. B. Randol, as Manager, has never in any way, with the reports or published statements, or otherwise tried to influence the stock values and that the management though conservative has been generous in its official reports to its stockholders, and to those who have a right to know its business. It has heretofore thought it good policy to keep much of its business and its policy to itself, but such widespread notoriety has been given to the attacks of the contestant upon this management, that as men, and also to make a right showing before some of their stockholders who may not have ready access to all their records here, the foregoing plain statement of the facts of the business of this company has been given to the world, and I think very liberally.

TESTIMONY OF DR. W. S. THORNE.

By Mr. Cross:

Q. Where do you reside?

A. In San Jose. I am a physician and surgeon. I am 46 years old. I have resided at San Jose or in its vicinity since 1858.

Q. How long have you known the New Almaden Quicksilver Mine?

A. I have known the Almaden Quicksilver Mines since that time. I came here first to this mine in 1858.

Q. Have you any idea as to the number of people resident upon this property at that time?

A. Between 1,500 and 1,600 people. Approximately the same number of population there is now.

Q. State what was the social and industrial condition of the people upon this property at that time.

A. I can speak of the mine from my own personal knowledge since the first day of May, 1869. The social condition of this mine at that time was very bad.

Q. What was the general reputation of the class of people who resided here at that time?

A. Exceedingly bad. As to their morals and their reputation for good order, they were largely a turbulent, criminal class of people in those days.

Q. State what changes and improvements have been made in the social condition of the people residing upon the grant since the time Mr. J. B. Randol has been manager?

A. I have been visiting this mine for the last eighteen years; it will be eighteen years the first day of next month since I began to visit this mine as a physician—visiting physician—coming regularly; the rest of the time I have done a consulting practice there with the local medical incumbents, or making medical visits as occasion required, and knowing the people intimately as I do, I can state from my own personal knowledge, that there have been noticeable progressive changes in the character of this population from that day to this. With reference to the medical department, I can say that these people in old days when I came here, were at the mercy of chance or accident. When they met with accidents here they generally died for want of medical care, they were too poor to send to San Jose to get a competent surgeon, and I know of my own personal knowledge that many in cases of accidents and disease died here from

WOOD PACKERS.

lack of medical care; the medical men could not come so far without remuneration, and these people were unable to pay them, and the consequence was that under the old regime these people died of disease and accidents which occurred to them in the mine, for want of proper medical and surgical treatment.

Q. State what improvement has been made under Mr. Randol's management, and by what means in that regard?

A. Shortly after Mr. Randol became manager of this mine he secured the services of a very competent physician who became the local medical attendant to the mine, and who was extremely conscientious and intelligent in the discharge of his duties as physician to the mine; I was frequently in consultation with him and I know that from that time the men had very careful and skillful attention. Doctor A. R. Randol, Dr. Hopkins, Doctor Cochrane, myself and Doctor S. E. Winn have been successively the resident local physician of the mine. Doctor Winn came to this mine about September, 1879.

Q. What have you to say as to the qualifications and character of Doctor Winn for the position?

A. Doctor Winn is one of the most competent physicians within the circle of my medical acquaintance, which extends all over the State; I know all of the prominent physicians in San Francisco. I know all of the prominent physicians in all the towns of the State. As president of the State Medical Society of California, I know all of the most prominent medical men in the State from its southern extremity to its northern confines and can conscientiously say he is one of the most competent men I know of.

Q. Doctor, during the period of time that you speak of when yourself, Dr. Cochrane, Dr. Hopkins and Dr. Winn held the position of resident physician and surgeon at this mine, what method has been used to compensate the regular physician for his services to the miners and their families?

A. The position is sustained by what is called a "Miners' Fund," which arises and is sustained by voluntary contributions from those actively engaged in the employment of the mine.

Q. Doctor, from your experience and observation of such matters, what would you say as to the economy or reasonableness of the medical attendance to the employees and their families, at the rate of $1 per month for each employee and his family?

A. I would consider it extremely economical and advantageous, and consider such an arrangement extremely beneficent in its operation to the members who contribute to the fund?

Q. In underground mining operations are there frequent occasions for the employment of surgical skill?

A. Yes.

Q. What would you say as to the uniform charge of $5.00 as provided by the rules of the "Miners' Fund" in cases of accouchment?

A. I should say that was one-fifth of the minimum charges usually charged.

Q. Doctor, from your acquaintance with the employees of this mine and your observation at their homes and with the ordinary laboring classes of other communities of California with which you are familiar, what would you say as to the comfort, intelligence and local surroundings of the employees here as compared with the same classes of laborers in other communities that you are familiar with?

A. They are the best that I have ever seen, and I have been acquainted with mining camps in California and Nevada for the last thirty years.

Q. What would you say as to their comfort, their homes, clothing and food, as compared with the laboring classes of other communities with which you are familiar?

A. It is the best I have ever seen.

Q. During the time that you were physician for the mine and since the Miners' Fund was established what can you say, if anything, with regard to what other classes of disbursement were made from this fund besides the disbursements for medical attendance?

A. Well, co-eval with the establishment of this fund, they established on the Hill a first-class apothecary shop to dispense the remedies to the people. The quality of the drugs and prescriptions dispensed at that dispensary were the best that could be had on this Coast, and during my time they charged nothing for them.

Q. What effect upon the number of cases of salivation and the degree of those cases was effected by the improvement in the furnaces by Mr. Randol?

A. I can answer that in a general way, that salivation became very much less, and during the last few years it has almost become extinct, except in cases of utter carelessness, without the fault of the furnace or the management.

Q. In your early acquaintance with the mine and the people resident upon it, what were the principal nationalities employed at the mine?

A. Mexican, Cornish or English miners, with a sprinkling of American and other nationalities, including Irish, and in former times they used to employ some Chinese. During Mr. Randol's administration I think that there has been a very large increase in the white, and the Mexican element has decreased.

Q. At the time you came to the State in 1858, was not the condition of society socially, and so far as the labor interests were concerned in California, very much more crude and less developed than at present, Doctor, throughout the entire State so far as you yourself were acquainted, and very much lower in its condition than at present?

A. It is my impression from my knowledge of California—I came to this country in 1857, and went to the mines after remaining in San Francisco three months. I worked in the mines, and it is my impression that in the early days of California, the very best labor element that this commonwealth has ever seen was then in the field, both intellectually and every other way; I met doctors and lawyers and statesmen and judges, men who subsequently became distinguished in the law, distinguished in politics, men who afterwards went to Congress, were all co-laborers in the mines; men who become distinguished judges, were laboring with their hands in the mines, and your distinguished witness was there laboring also.

Q. Then as I understand you, Doctor, the Almaden Mine at that time was an exception to the rule as you found it, and had a much

MEXICAN CAMP FROM UPPER ROAD.

lower class of labor and population within its boundaries than any other mining establishment that you were acquainted with ?

A. It did most emphatically.

Q. Why was that so far as you are able to determine or now can state?

A. Because they had a class of Spanish peons here, and many of them renegades from justice; they were murderers and thieves, and Almaden at that time was a rendez-vous for the worst elements of this State. They came here in hiding from every part of the State, and if any man knows what a Mexican peon is he knows that the word means slave; that is what those people were, and they were in those days the chief controlling labor element of this mine.

Q. Was Santa Clara County in its condition as to labor and sociability at that time as far advanced as at present?

Q. (By Dr. Thorne): Do you mean as to the men who labored with their hands in those days ?

(By Mr. Cross) : No, the general condition, the social atmosphere and the surroundings and conditions of the labor element.

Q. Then, as I understand you, there was somewhat of a chaotic condition, socially, and as far as the labor interests were concerned at that time, as compared with the present in Santa Clara county?

A. In Santa Clara county in those days, so far as I know—I was a boy in those days and I was more interested in my rod and gun and horseback riding than I was in society—something I never knew anything about—but I know there were very respectable people and wealthy people lived in the country. I never attended a party in those days or social gathering. I know we had good law and good order in the county; our distinguished friend John Murphy was sheriff, and if John could not kill a fellow by hanging him he would drink him to death, but I can only say that we had good society and very respectable people in the county in those days, but of course society was not stratified as it is in these days, and it takes a long time to make a thoroughly civilized and polite community.

Q. What, as you now remember, Doctor, were the moving causes on Mr. Randol's part to improve the condition of the miners?

A. I believe that they resulted in accordance with the character of the man. He is a progressive man; he is a man the whole tendency of whose business life, so far as I am acquainted with him, so far as my experience goes, has been to systematize, to produce order out of chaos, and institute good order where formerly there existed extravagant waste and bad management. I believe I have never had any conversations with him on the subject, but I believe they resulted on his part purely from humanitarian motives. If there is any doubt I would give him the benefit of that doubt.

Q. Then, as a matter of fact, I gather this inference from what you state, that salivation has not been a chronic trouble at this mine?

A. No, I cannot say that it has been. I have seen some very bad cases of salivation here; very bad; the worst that I ever saw; but in those cases which I treated they were cases where the men had done things that they were not required to do, and foolish things, and in fact things that they knew they ought not to do, and we put a stop to it.

Q. So far as you have observed it is kind of natural when a candidate for political office has been defeated to lay it to something else besides the fact that the people did not want to elect him—is it not so?

A. Well, I am not sufficiently acquainted with political candidates to answer that question. I have had very little to do with politics or politicians.

Q. So far as you have observed has it not been kind of customary for candidates for office in Santa Clara County and elsewhere to wrestle pretty lively for votes about election time?

A. That has been my experience, my limited experience.

Q. Now Doctor, you were speaking about your experience here with a class of diseases and accidents that have required treatment and the kind of patients that you have treated. Have you in your experience or observation here, known of any defeated candidate for office, except Mr. Sullivan, seeking a quicksilver mine to obtain mercurial treatment for a political sore?

A. No, I will answer that in the negative.

Q. Would you from your medical experience and knowledge of this locality suggest that a candidate under such circumstances could work in the mine on the Hill or about the furnace at the Hacienda?

A. I do not know. I would recommend him to try again and not try medicine at all. Just try the open air—I am not much of an advocate of medicine although I am a practitioner.

Q. Would you suggest that when he tried twice and got defeated, and become satisfied that he could not get in by the votes of the people, that he had better try it by a contest?

A. You are asking me questions that I am not able to answer.

Q. Doctor, from your knowledge of this mine, the people living upon it, and its management, and the rumors that you have heard, and the sources from which they came, what is your belief as to whether or not the voters of Almaden precinct at the last election were affected by coercion or intimidation, or other improper influences on the part of the management of the mine.

A. You ask me for my personal belief in this matter? In my own opinion I do not think it was. My opinion is, as I was discussing with a gentleman in my house some months ago, respecting the same matter, I maintain that view, and in my intercourse with the people of this mine for the last eighteen years, I have never to my own knowledge seen the slightest intimation of anything of the kind, and indeed I have made some inquiry of the people at this mine within the last twelve months respecting that matter, and I have never yet found a man who said he was coerced or influenced, and I know that some of them were men who voted the Democratic ticket.

Q. So far as you know those who have claimed that there were any intimidation of voters here were either disappointed candidates or those who sympathized with Mr. Kearney at that time?

A. Yes; I have met people for the last 18 years who have been discharged from this mine and one that I know was extremely vituperative, he charged Mr. Randol and the management with all sorts of things, but he never charged that there was any political corrup-

TESTIMONY OF DR. S. E. WINN.

By Mr. CROSS:

Q. What position do you hold at the Almaden Mine?

A. I am resident physician and surgeon, since the first day of September, 1879. It is a salaried position—$400 a month, paid out of the Miners' Fund.

Q. How is that fund made up?

A. By contributions; each employee of the company on the pay roll is required to pay one dollar a month into the general fund known as the Miners' Fund, and out of that my salary is paid with other expenses. The druggist gets a salary out of it, and it is then applied for the buying of medicine, and also for the relief of the indigent poor, and also when men are hurt in the mine. When they are wounded and injured in various ways at the mine, if they are not able to pay their board, their board is paid out of it, and all their supplies are furnished them and paid for out of that fund. It also furnishes two hospitals for those who are injured in the mine, one in the Mexican camp and the other in the English camp on the Hill. I have held the position of resident physician since the first day of September, 1879.

Q. State what your duties are, and what services you perform as resident physician, for this pay of $400 per month.

A. I am required to reside at the mine. I reside on the Hill from the fact that by far the largest part of my work is there (the greatest number of inhabitants), and more accidents happen there, and I am required to be here in readiness to attend to all calls, whether for injuries or disease. In the morning I remain at home until eight o'clock, in order to receive messages from different families that may need me throughout the day. It is generally understood that they send for me at that time, so that I can lay out the work and accomplish it with more success and with better results to them. After eight o'clock I spend the hours from that until eleven, in visiting the patients on the Hill. From eleven to twelve each day I have an office hour on the Hill, and there I receive all of those that come for treatment to the office, and if longer time is needed than the hour, I remain longer, but in the main try to get through within the hour, if possible, and have other cases to wait there, because I have an office hour at the Hacienda from half-past twelve to half-past one, so as to be here at least a half hour while the men are off duty, so that that they can consult me at the office here. I devote my time ex-

PART OF ENGLISH CAMP, HILL.

clusively to this employment, except rarely in cases of emergency, as a matter of humanity.

Q. You speak of some portion of the fund being devoted to supplying indigent persons with means and with necessaries. Who determines who should be supplied with those things ?

A. Soon after I came here Mr. Randol told me he wanted me to look after that matter and see that there was no actual want at the mine among the employees or the inhabitants here. Wherever I have found such actual want I gave orders for supplies to the amount that I think necessary to meet the needs of each particular case. It was left to me to judge as to the merits of the cases; since that time I have given orders. There is hardly a week but what I give orders for provisions and supplies—very few weeks if any, and sometimes a number of orders in one week for supplies to persons that really need it; and those orders are honored and paid by order of Mr. Randol, trustee of the fund. I keep records and they show over 5,000 professional calls and consultations per year. There is hardly a day but what there is more or less surgery to attend to; men are getting injured every day, for instance during the last week I have had one case of a man that run a drill through his foot, and another that run the sharp end of a crowbar through his hand, and another that had a thumb mashed off at the first joint, and a number other cases such as scalp wounds and fractures resulting from accidents incident to the business of mining.

Q. State whether or not, Doctor, during your term of service here upon the mine you have become familiar with the condition of the people of the mine as to their methods of living, their economic arrangements and household affairs and domestic matters.

A. I am at the house of almost every one in the camp. During the seven years and a half or more that I have been here, I have been called, I suppose, in all the families that are here, unless some very recent ones. As regards the houses in which they live in the English camp I think that the majority of the houses are owned by the employees, they pay a ground rent, as I have heard, as a protection to the company and their property, more for that than for any gain out of it, and a man who builds or buys a house that is on the ground, that house is his property, which he can sell when he leaves or dispose of it any way he likes, and the majority of the English people live in their own houses that way, and they keep them in the main in good repair; and I have been frequently present when their meals were served, they seem to live on good food; they attend church, they are great church-goers and they are well dressed—there do not seem to be any wants in that regard. I think you will find the people who attend the church on the Hill about as well dressed as you will find them in any town of this size, at any rate in any town that I have lived in—of course this is speaking of the English people; the Mexican people are not as provident as the English people; do not make as good use of their earnings; the houses are very good for this climate; there are some private parties that own houses there and these houses are not kept in as good repair as the company's houses; and as regards their living in comparison with the populations of the same class of other localities

I think they live as well. That is the English people; the Mexican people, as I said before, are not as thrifty on the same amount of earnings; I have never lived in a community where there was a Mexican population before, and it does not come up to the way of English living because they are not as frugal and as careful of what they make.

Q. Doctor, have you made any photographic views of objects in the New Almaden Mine?

A. Yes; made quite a number of them during the last three or four years. I made all of the negatives myself. (Dr. Winn here presents a volume of fifty views of improvements, localities, machinery and works at the mine, including underground mining views taken by artificial light.)

Q. Doctor, have you ever voted at this precinct?

A. I have.

Q. How many years?

A. Ever since 1880.

Q. Doctor, have you ever seen anything going on here at elections like intimidation or coercion, or the exercise of undue influence with regard to how the vote should be cast?

A. I come to the polls cast my vote here and go back to my business, so I can only speak for myself. I have never had any intimidation offered me, and I have never had any person ask me to vote one way or the other.

Q. So far as you are concerned you have always been independent of any of the managers of the mine?

A. Entirely so, entirely so; not even one man has asked me, or suggested to me that one man would be a good man for the mine to vote for; never had any influence of that sort exerted or attempted.

Q. With what political party do you usually act?

A. I vote the Democratic ticket. Since I have been here I have voted for Hancock, for Cleveland, for Stoneman and Bartlett, for Tully and for Sullivan.

Q. In the main, you vote the ticket of that party?

A. Yes, but there are some local and judicial officers that I vote for on the other side.

Q. You exercise you personal preference?

A. For instance, I voted for Belden and Spencer for Superior Judges because I knew them and did not know the other men, and I knew they were able men. In several instances I have voted for other Republicans for county office, but they are always my preference.

Q. In local matters you have exercised your personal preference without reference to politics.

A. Yes.

Q. But where party issues are important, there you ally yourself with the Democratic party in main?

A. I voted for Mr. Sullivan at the last election.

PART OF ENGLISH CAMP.

TESTIMONY OF CHARLES F. O'BRION.

By Mr. CROSS:

Q. What is your name, age and occupation?

A. Charles F. O'Brion, 53 years of age, my present occupation is surface foreman on the Hill. I came to the mine in March, 1865, five years before Mr. Randol arrived.

Q. You may state what your occupation has been, and the positions you have held since that time.

A. I commenced to work for The Quicksilver Mining Company on March 23, 1865, at anything that offered, at $2.50 per day; was soon appointed night-watchman at $3 per night, which position I filled for about three months, when I was requested to accept the position of chief weigher and receiver of all ores taken from the mine. I filled this place for about two months. I was then promoted to the position of foreman at the main planilla, that being the principal exit of nearly all the ores taken from the mine in 1865.

Q. What are the duties of the surface foreman?

A. Collecting the house and ground rents on the Hill, keeping in repair all the company's dwellings, have charge of nearly all the men working on the surface and keeping their time, and keep all wagon roads in repair, and attend to the cleaning, recording and shipping all the ores extracted, attending generally to the ordering and issuing all the material used, in the mine except coal, wood and timber which is contracted for at the company's office in Hacienda; also looking after the sanitary condition of the Hill, such as disinfecting the camp monthly in the summer and oftener if necessary, with corrosive sublimate; the cottages are well built and comfortable; they are furnished and provided inside in very good order, they have every comfort almost, carpets and curtains, and everything that way, and furniture.

Q. The Mexicans coming from warm climates, do they take as much pains in the matter of furnishing and keeping their houses as the people whose ancestry comes from colder climates as you have observed?

A. No.

Q. What can you say as to the quality of the food which they consume?

A. They get their food at the same place that I get mine, and I do not suppose there is a store in the county that has got any better assortment of food than the store on the Hill.

Q. What can you say as to the manner in which they are clothed as compared with the same grade of labor in other localities that you have been acquainted with as to being well clothed or otherwise?

A. I think they are as well, if not better.

Q. What can you say as to these miner's cottages having about them little flower gardens and vines and the like?

A. I consider they have been very fortunate in that respect. Within the last three years Mr. Randol has taken particular pains to send up flowers, roses and everything that he could spare from his garden down here. Within the last two years I think I have distributed at least 1,500 rose bushes amongst the people; that is done at the company's expense.

Q. You speak of being distributed by Mr. Randol. What facilities has the company for furnishing these plants?

A. They employ here at the Hacienda a gardener whose purpose it is to raise all these different kinds of plants. They have hot houses and every facility for raising flowers, and the assortment is very good.

Q. Since Mr. Randol became Manager here, have you ever seen anything like interference with the personal liberty of the employees of the company on the part of the management?

A. No, I never did. On the contrary I think that he is quite free from anything of that kind.

Q. What was the social and moral condition of the people living upon this mine at the time that Mr. Randol came here to take charge?

A. In former years Almaden was known as the free retreat of cutthroats, gamblers and all sorts of thieves and bad men and women; when life was in continual jeopardy, with scarcely no law to prosecute the guilty, and murder was frequent; to-day, there is no place with a population of 1,500 to 1,600 souls where more respect is held for the law of the land and less crime is known to exist; this has been brought about by the influence of both Methodist and Catholic Churches in a measure, but the principal causes spring from the fact that our Manager, J. B. Randol, immediately upon assuming control of this property in 1870, made strenuous and untiring efforts to purify and rid this place of all its bad influences and elements, aiding the officers in executing the laws, throwing no obstacles in their way, and as a result of this direction of his sixteen years management, life is as secure here day and night as in any town in California.

Q. What has Mr. Randol's management done with regard to excluding from these properties that class of idle and dissolute people?

A. It seems to have been his purpose from the commencement to let them out as fast as it could be done, and he has accomplished it very well; drunkenness on the grant during late years is broken up.

Q. What is done with reference to giving employment to men who have become old and broken down, or ineffective in the employment of the company?

A. A great many, particularly of the Mexican population have been here fifteen, twenty, twenty-five and thirty and more years, and have worked in the mine, and have worn themselves out here until they are hardly capacitated to go away from here and earn a decent living, and where men have been faithful, and used up their vitality here for the benefit of the company, the company in return help them in any way, shape and manner as they can; if a man is incapacitated from work in the mine, they try to find something for him to do on the outside; some light employment where he can work.

Q. Do you know Dr. Winn personally?

A. Very well acquainted with him.

Q. Had occasion to employ him in your family?

A. Yes; have had him attend to my family occasionally, he also has attended me.

Q. What can you say as to your being fully satisfied or otherwise with Dr. Winn and his attendance upon your own family?

A. I am well pleased.

Q. What is your opinion, Mr. O'Brion, from your experience here, from before and since the Miners' Fund was established, as to its being really beneficial or otherwise in contrast with the system of requiring miners and their families to depend upon such physicians as they might obtain without any system?

A. I should consider that entirely a one sided question. There is hardly any comparison to be drawn. It is all one sided in favor of the present system.

Q. What do you say with regard to your own politics?

A. Relative to my politics, in the main I have affiliated with the Democratic party, but as I grow older, I am becoming more and more convinced that to have the purest and most efficient administration of our laws, it can only be done by selecting from our county, State and national ticket, the ablest and best men that allow themselves to go before the country as candidates; consequently with such views, I naturally scratch my ticket on election day; I voted for Tilden, Hancock and Cleveland, and also for Mr. Sullivan, the present contestant, the first time he ran but not in November last; also for Governor Bartlett and mainly the balance of the ticket. I have no animosities against any race, respect a man if he be one, no matter what nationality he may spring from. Since my residence in New Almaden, I have had little or nothing to do with politics. I was a State delegate to the Democratic Convention in Sacramento when H. H. Haight was nominated for Governor.

Q. State Mr. O'Brion, whether in your experience here during Mr. Randol's administration anything has been done, to intimidate, coerce or unduly influence your vote?

A. I have been connected off and on with The Quicksilver Mining Company for over 22 years and have always been during Mr. Randol's 16 years of successful management of the mine, well and kindly treated by him and was never coerced, intimidated, bulldozed, or even requested by him to vote any particular ticket, and the same I may say of Mr. Jenning's administration; I have always voted as my conscience dictated in every election and calculate to enjoy that blessed privilege in what few elections I may yet attend.

Q. Have you ever seen anything indicating that undue influence was being used by the management or the officers of this company in the matter of how men should vote?

A. No; never have.

Q. Have you ever seen anything to cause you to believe that men were discharged from the service of the Company, or likely to be discharged from the service, on account of their political views or the way in which they voted?

A. No; I did not.

Q. Have you ever seen anything to indicate that the employees of this Company did not exercise the elective franchise just as freely here as other men do in other places?

A. I know that I always have, and I do not know any reason why the other people should not have the same privilege.

Q. Have you ever seen anything to indicate that they didn't ?

A. No.

Q. What would you say as to the party with which the Cornishmen naturally affiliate?

A. My opinion is that they in a large majority affiliate with the Republican party.

Q. Naturally so ?

A. Yes.

Q. What can you say with regard to the Mexican population?

A. I think that they are inclined to vote that ticket also.

Q. Naturally inclined that way ?

A. Yes.

Q. State what you know as to the manner in which the men are brought to the polling places at election time from the English and Mexican camps?

A. It has generally been the custom of the officers of the mine at the Hill to notify them the day before that there would be an election at the Hacienda and they would like them all to congregate at the store early in the morning where there would be conveyances to take them to the polls and take them back again so that they would lose as little time as possible from their labors?

Q. How is it a benefit to these men to have an opportunity to ride down to the polling places and back on election day ?

A. A benefit in this way, to come down the hill on foot and then walk back they would lose half of the day at least, and by riding down and being carried back, they are almost as fresh as when they left their homes in the morning, and go back to their work.

Q. Who owns and conducts the stores and store business in the mines ? I am not speaking of the ownership of the building, but of the stores ?

A. They are conducted and the contents of the stores are owned by Mr. Derby and Lowe.

Q. State whether or not you are in the habit of trading in their stores ?

A. I do all my trading there. So far as experience goes, I have been always treated very well by them.

Q. What has been your observation of Mr. Randol's conduct towards the employees of the company?

A. Well, I do not see how it could be any better. He of course has rules and regulations by which everything is done, and as long as men comply with these rules and regulations, they will never have any trouble with him.

Q. Those rules apply to the industrial management of the business, do they?

A. Yes; and he steps outside of that and often takes a great interest in their social matters and helps them in a great many ways, he is very liberal in giving them occasional days of recreation and so forth.

Q. Treats them with kindness and consideration does he as an employer ?

A. Yes.

Q. What can you say as to the feeling and sentiment of the men in the employ of the company towards Mr. Randol?

A. I think that with very few exceptions — probably not any exceptions—a good feeling exists (of course in a large business like this you cannot please everybody), but my experience has been that Mr. Randol has generally had a plan, a course laid, out which he thought and believed was justice not only to the company he represents, but to the men themselves, and he has followed it; when they become dissatisfied they are at liberty to quit.

Q. State whether or not in your judgment, in carrying on an establishment of this size it is necessary to have such rules?

A. I should say decidedly so; there must be a head, and a firm one, to make this business prosper.

Q. Is there in these rules and regulations which you speak of, in your judgment anything harsh or oppressive, or needless to the prosperity of the business enterprise?

A. There is nothing in those rules but what any man who seeks employment can justly comply with.

Q. State what you know with regard to the men who have been employed here, who have quit and went away, coming back and seeking re-employment?

A. It is a very common occurrence. I am a little illustration of that myself. I have been away, and this is the third time now that I am working for this company, and I have never made anything by going away. I ought to have stayed here all the time; it is a very common occurence for men to go away, to get dissatisfied, or think they could do better, and go away like myself and come back—go away and get rid of what they have saved and spend it, and come back and try it again. One of the most sensible men that I know of is a gentleman by the name of Mr. Carrol, he went to work about the same time that I did and has never left yet.

Q. Staid with it?

A. Yes; staid right with it, and voted the Democratic ticket ever since he came here, without a scratch.

Q. That vote has been well known, has it?

A. I suppose it has. I feel very well satisfied of it in my own mind.

Q. So far as you know no attempt at concealment of the fact?

A. No.

Q. Have you ever seen anything to indicate that Mr. Carroll's relations with the company have been in any way affected by the fact that he voted the Democratic ticket, and that it was known?

A. No; they found that he was the right man, and they got him in the right place, and they kept him, and they will keep him as long as he will stay.

TESTIMONY OF JAMES CARROLL.

The WITNESS—Before I commence there are three things that I could prove, and I can prove them here or any place else.

By Mr. CROSS:

Q. What are the three things Mr. Carroll?

A. I am working here 22 years now for the company this month, and during that time I voted at every election and generally voted the Democratic ticket, never was hindered in any way, shape or form, never was told that I should vote one way or the other by any man; always was treated well. I found the manager to be a first-class man and a gentleman to me in every way. I have no complaint whatever to make.

Q. What is your age, occupation and residence?

A. About 50 years old. I take care of a stable, and dump cars as they come out of the mine on the Hill. I reside on the Hill at the New Almaden Mine. I was born in the old country. Came to America in 1851. I came here to the mine in 1865.

Q. Were you here when Mr. Randol came?

A. Yes and long before.

Q. What changes have taken place in the condition of the people here on the mine under Mr. Randol's administration?

A. I believe there have been pretty good changes for the better. Better for the people working at the mine and their families.

Q. Have you ever seen anything in Mr. Randol's management or the management under him like oppression or hard treatment or undue interference with the affairs of the people here?

A. He never acted so with me.

Q. Have you seen him act with anyone else?

A. No. When I ask a question of a man in regard to his getting along he says: I will go to Mr. Randol and he will make it all right, and generally did so.

Q. That is if any one feels dissatisfied about anything and has good cause and goes to Mr. Randol he makes it right?

A. That is the general opinion and that is the feeling here.

Q. Have you ever known of any case, any man who had a just cause of complaint about anything here at the mine that could not get a hearing from the management?

A. No, never. They always got a hearing.

Q. During the time that Mr. Randol has been here as Manager have you ever seen anything like intimidation or coercion or undue influence on the part of the management with regard to the voting?

A. If there was anything said to other people, I don't know it, but I am certain there was never anything said to me.

Q. Never been any attempt on the part of the managers of the mine to interfere with how you should vote?

A. Oh, no, neither of them; neither of the officers of the mine ever said anything to me.

Q. What do you think of the Miners' Fund?

A. I am sure, I do not know anything about that.

Q. Do you think the Miners' Fund is a bad thing or a good thing?

A. I think it is a good thing for me.

Q. Has there ever been any trouble here at the mine about the men getting their pay for their work or their contracts?

A. No, never that I know of. Pay-day comes regularly, and they get their pay; they must take it. The company won't keep it.

Q. Have you been around the polls from time to time on election day?

A. I come here and vote and go back to my work.

Q. State how the men at the mine feel towards Mr. Randol and Mr. Jennings.

A. Very well, I believe. They respect them.

Q. During Mr. Randol's administration have you ever known of any man being discharged on account of the way he voted?

A. No.

Q. Have you ever known of there being any feeling amongst the men that they had to vote the way the Manager wanted them to or they would lose their places, or anything like that?

A. I never heard of that.

TESTIMONY OF REV. J. L. TREFREN.

By Mr. CROSS:

Q. Where do you reside? What is your age and occupation?

A. I reside at New Almaden. I am 59 years old. I am a clergyman of the Methodist Episcopal Church, and a member of the California Annual Conference of that church. I reside at New Almaden and am the regular minister at that place.

Q. Please give a statement of the kind and reasonableness of the cost of such a church, as near as you can.

A. It is built of wood, rustic outside, ceiled inside, with basement rooms, audience room above, well finished, corner tower and of good style. I should say a fair price for the cost of it ordinarily in such cities and towns as I have lived in, would be, say $3,500 to $4,000.

Q. What places have you served in as clergyman, in the State of California?

A. I have served in Napa, Petaluma, the City of Sacramento, Grass Valley, Chico, Vallejo and Santa Cruz.

Q. How large a church membership have you at New Almaden?

A. About fifty. My average congregation is about 200. There is a Sunday School connected with my church, with an average attendance of about 165.

Q. What is the business principally of your congregation and the membership of your church?

A. They are miners at the New Almaden Mine.

Q. What is your annual salary in this church?

A. I receive $1,000 and the house in which I live, making $1,120.

Q. What can you say, Mr. Trefren, as to the general appearance of your present congregation as to the average intelligence and appearance of the people who attend your church here?

A. Comparatively, they would compare very favorably in every respect, as to intelligence, dress and general appearance, with other congregations I have served. I have never preached to a better, more intelligent appearing, better behaved congregation, better dressed, and apparently better fed; our Sunday School is an extra Sunday School, if you please; the children are well officered, they have good teachers; it is very regularly and well attended, and they are better versed in the Scriptures than is usual in Sunday Schools even.

Q. What would you say as to the general intelligence and appearance of the children both at church and on week days as you see them?

A. They are smart, bright, well-clothed and comfortable.

Q. Week days and Sundays as well?

A. As well as children usually are.

Q. Is there any place where you hold services on the grant of The Quicksilver Mining Company, except at the church on the Hill that you have described?

A. Yes; at the schoolhouse at the Hacienda; we hold religious services there twice on each Sabbath; we have three local preachers and we have a plan for the local preachers to act a part of the time, and the local preachers come here a part of the time. I come here usually on Sabbath morning, the local preachers at night; we maintain a regular service at both of those places, there is also a Sunday School.

TESTIMONY OF FRANCES MYERS.

By Mr. CROSS:

Q. What is your name, age, residence and occupation?

A. Frances Meyers; I am going on 75; I have been a mechanic, when I was actively engaged in business; I resided at the Almaden Mine on the Hill.

Q. When did you first know the Almaden Mine?

A. I came here in the month of November, 1854.

Q. Who had charge of the mine at that time?

A. A man by the name of John Young was the head officer of the mine; I first became employed at the mine at that time; I worked here at the carpenter business off and on until 1877, for the com-

M. E. CHURCH, HILL.

pany; I built the big house the first work I did where the manager resides now; General H. W. Halleck was the manager of the mine at that time; he was then called Captain Halleck, but afterwards became General Halleck; there was heavy litigation about the ownership of the mine for years.

Q. Who came after General Halleck?

A. When he left there was a compromise made in the lawsuit, that had closed the work for a long time. Different parties were contending for the ownership of the mine in that litigation. I think Mr. Samuel F. Butterworth was the next manager of the mine, and he had superintendents under him the same as Mr. Randol has superintendents under him. Mr. Butterworth remained as manager until Mr. Randol became manager.

Q. Mr. Meyers, what will you say as to Mr. Randol's general conduct as you have observed it towards the employees of the company during the time that he has been manager?

A. I have always found him a very upright square man in his dealings with his men, disposed to do what was right as near as I could tell.

Q. Have you ever seen anything on his part like tyranny or harsh treatment of the men?

A. No.

Q. State whether or not there has been any improvement in the class and condition of the people living on the mine from about the time Mr. Randol took charge up to the present, in your judgment?

A. Yes; I think there has been an improvement; there have been more families and more children, more churches and school houses.

Q. What would you say as to the comparative morality of the people occupying the grant now as to what it was in early days, or when Mr. Randol came here?

A. It is better than it was.

Q. What will you say, Mr. Meyers, as to the way in which the employees of this mine are housed?

A. Most of them have comfortable houses to live in. They are cheap houses; not costly houses; but generally comfortable, and the people generally, particularly those of the Caucasian race, are neat and cleanly and take pains to have everything nice and clean about their houses and their children; they are a neat set of housekeepers as a general thing, the English people particularly.

Q. What will you say as to the manner in which the employees of the mine and their families are fed and clothed. You can speak of it comparatively if you choose?

A. I think that they are well as a general thing. They are well clothed, as the witness who just preceded me stated, in his congregation, they make a very genteel appearance; a person who knew nothing but what he could see, would not know whether he was in a church at Almaden or in Grace Church on Broadway, New York; they appear to be as elegantly dressed, and have as nice and genteel an appearance as a congregation would have anywhere.

Q. What, so far as you have observed it, is the feeling and manner of the employees of the mine towards Mr. Randol?

A. They are respectful.

Q. Have you ever seen anything to indicate that there is any feeling towards him as though he were a hard task master, or any unkindly feeling towards him on the part of the men?

A. No. I have never known anything of the kind.

Q. How long have you been a voter of this precinct?

A. I have always been a voter ever since I have lived here. I am a native born American.

Q. With what party do you affiliate, and have you since Mr. Randol has been here?

A. I have always voted the Democratic ticket.

Q. Have you ever been connected with the Election Board of this precinct?

A. Yes, frequently.

Q. Were you a member of the Election Board at the election in November, 1886?

A. I was. I was Inspector of Election.

Q. Since Mr. Randol became Manager of this mine have you ever known of his interfering in any way with the way in which the employees voted at any election for officers national, State or county?

A. I have never known him to take any active part, personally.

Q. Have you, during that time, known of any intimidation, coercion or undue pressure or influence being used towards the employees of the mine as to how they should vote?

A. No; of my own knowledge I know nothing of the kind. I know how far my own vote was concerned in the matter.

Q. What has been done, if anything, by the management of the mine looking towards the controlling or influencing of your vote during that time?

A. Never any attempt has been made to influence my vote, and it was always known by the Manager, I suppose, and everybody else that wanted to know, that I voted the Democratic ticket. I never tried to conceal it, and always voted it publicly. I am not aware that it has injured me in any way. I have never seen anything to indicate that my chances for employment, or of preference or advancement at the mine, were in any way affected by my political views or the manner in which I voted. None in the least.

Q. Did you see anything in any way connected with the election of 1886 that indicated that any one who voted at this precinct was coerced or intimidated or unduly influenced in the exercise of the elective franchise?

A. I do not know of any. There are always certain parties at all elections, I suppose, and in all precincts, who take an active interest in politics and try to get all the votes they can for certain candidates; that has generally been done here.

Q. The same as in any other precinct so far as you could see?

A. That is done everywhere, I think. Electioneering and working to get votes for candidates. There is a large number of voters here who have really no choice.

Q. Have you ever seen about this mine since Mr. Randol has been manager anything like slavery or serfdom or peonage upon the part of the employees of the mine?

A. No; not at all.

HILL SIDE COTTAGES, ENGLISH CAMP.

Q. About the houses, the homes of the miners here, by whom are the most of their homes owned so far as you are advised?

A. Most of the houses belong to the company. I know a good many families that own their own houses, but I can't say how many. I own some houses on the grant, and I rent them to employees of the company.

Q. Do you know Mr. Jennings?

A. Yes.

Q. Have you ever seen anything on the part of Mr. Jennings tending to indicate that he was trying to intimidate or coerce or to control the vote of the employees of the company?

A. I never have.

Q. Have you been pretty generally acquainted with the miners on this grant, of Cornish descent?

A. Yes sir, I know them all by sight. I do not know the names of all of them.

Q. What party do they generally vote with?

A. My impression is, they generally are Republicans in their party affiliations.

Q. What do you know as to the Mexican vote in that regard, anything?

A. I don't think they have much choice. They don't care much about it. Some years ago I remember there was an impression among the Mexicans that the Republican party meant the party in favor of a republican form of government, and the Democrats they supposed were opposed to the republican form of government, and as they came from a republican form of government, Mexico, they are in favor of the Republicans from the name, nothing else; they didn't know the difference. They were in favor of a Republic and they thought Republican meant that.

Q. Did you hear or see or know of anything being done at the election of 1886 by the management of this mine or its officers with reference to the defeat of Mr. Sullivan and the election of Mr. Felton?

A. I do not know of anything; the election was conducted as they have always been; for the accommodation of voters conveyances were sent upon the Hill to bring them down and take them back again; I do not think there is a precinct in the State where a greater disposition is shown than there is here to conduct everything fairly, legally, honestly and justly; there used to be an impression that they thought if the vote was not cast as some wanted it to be, it was doctored in the counting, but so far as I had anything to do with the elections I have never known any attempt or any disposition shown to do anything but what was fair and honest and just and legal.

Q. How has the Election Board of this precinct been appointed?

A. By the Board of Supervisors of the County.

Q. Has the Board here, so far as you have known, been divided between the different parties?

A. Yes.

Q. State whether or not at the election of 1886 you saw anything tending to show that the 100 foot limit provided by law, was not respected?

A. I thing it was respected; I think we attended to that.

Q. How long has this same place been used for the purpose of the polls?

A. It has been used many years for that purpose.

Q. So far as you know is there anything objectionable about having the polls located at this place?

A. Not that I know of.

Q. How is it for the convenience of voters of the precinct?

A. It is about as central and convenient a place as we could get; a great many of the voters of this precinct live in the valley, and perhaps more at the mine than any other part of the precinct. One object in locating the polls here, is the building belongs to the company, they never charge us any rent. I notice in other precincts the Board of Election has to rent a place to hold the election in, and the county pays for it, here they never pay anything.

TESTIMONY OF PROF. G. E. LIGHTHALL.

By Mr. Cross:

Q. What is your name, age, place of residence and occupation?

A. G. E. Lighthall—My age is 53, occupation school teacher, my residence is New Almaden.

Q. How long have you resided at New Almaden?

A. Nearly six years; came here in 1881.

Q. What has been your occupation during the time that you have resided at New Almaden?

A. I have been a school teacher.

Q. How many teachers are there teaching in the public school on the New Almaden grant?

A. There are now six employed.

Q. How many male and how many female?

A. One male and five female.

Q. How many teachers have you directly under your charge?

A. I have three under my charge.

Q. What number of pupils are enrolled in the school of which you have charge, consisting of yourself and three other teachers?

A. Last year we had 253 enrolled and there is about the same number enrolled this year.

Q. What is the average daily attendance, or about the average daily attendance at your school?

A. The average daily attendance so far this year is 169.

Q. How many school buildings are there on the grant?

A. There are three on the grant, one at the Hacienda, and two on the Hill; there are two separate school districts—Hacienda and the Hill, one schoolhouse in the Hacienda School District, and two in the Hill School District.

Q. What can you say of the quality of these buildings and their adaptability to the use of the schools and so forth.

A. The buildings are in very fine condition and well supplied with everything that they require; I have complete control of that myself. If I need anything I get it. The trustees have left that matter in my hands entirely.

Q. State whether or not these schools are governed by a board of trustees which constitutes a portion of the public school system of the State.

A. They are; organized and conducted on the general plan of instruction.

Q. How long have you been engaged in the business of teaching?

A. I do not exactly remember. I have been engaged in teaching in Santa Clara county for over eighteen years. I have taught over twenty years in the State of California.

Q. What schools have you taught in Santa Clara county besides the schools here?

A. I taught in Orchard District, in San Antonio, in San Jose I taught in the Reed-street, the Fourth Ward and the High School, and I have taught here at the Hacienda and Hill Districts.

Q. What have you to say as to the intelligence of the children in these two school districts, having their buildings on the mine, as compared with the intelligence of children which you have seen in other schools?

A. I think the children are just the same as all others; fully up to the average of intelligence.

Q. Are these children in these schools mostly of a parentage employed by the mining company?

A. Nearly altogether.

Q. State what number of pupils, if any, graduated during the last year in your district?

A. In my district I had three graduates, and they received grammar school diplomas from the County Board of Education.

Q. What test is applied for the purpose of determining who shall have those diplomas?

A. The County Board furnishes the examination papers, and diplomas are given if they are up to the standard.

Q. What rights do these diplomas give to those who receive them?

A. They are entitled to admission to any High School or to the State Normal School without further examination.

Q. What became of those three graduates?

A. They still reside on the Hill. The two young men are learning the trade of blacksmithing in the shops of the company, and the girl is stopping at home with her people.

Q. What can you say as to the clothing and appearance of the children who attend the public school here, as compared with the children of laboring people in other communities in which you are acquainted?

A. The children are very neatly and well clad, keep in a very cleanly manner and compare favorably with school children anywhere.

Q. Anything to indicate that their parents are in want, or anything of that kind?

A. No; all appear to be well to do, from the appearance of the children.

Q. How do these children, as to clothing and appearance, compare with the school children of the farming districts in this portion of the State, so far as you have had opportunity to observe them?

A. They compare very favorably. They are fully as well clad and appear to be as well kept in every way.

Q. Have you, during your residence here, had occasion to come in contact considerably with the people who live upon the grant and who work for the company?

HILL SCHOOL.

A. Yes; of necessity I have seen all the miners and others.

Q. What would you say of the employees of the company as to intelligence as you have seen them ?

A. They are fully up to the average of laboring men anywhere.

Q. What would you say as to the manner in which they seem to be clothed and provided for ?

A. They all appear to have a sufficiency of clothing and very good too; when they turn out for holidays; of course in their ordinary labor they have clothing suitable for the mines.

Q. You stated that you had taught at San Jose a good many years; when you lived at San Jose did you ever hear talk about this mine and the management of it ?

A. I did.

Q. What did you use to hear about that mine ?

A. I could hardly say; men have very strange ideas; rumors of one thing and another about the management of the mines the same as I hear now when I go into San Jose, talk rather against the method of conducting things here and the way in which people live.

Q. Did you have that impression before you came here to reside ?

A. I had somewhat of that impression. Had imbibed it owing to the stories which I had heard.

Q. What effect upon your opinion in regard to that matter has your residence and experience here had ?

A. It has removed it altogether; I see that there is no foundation at all for the stories. I found those rumors to be utterly unfounded.

Q. Do you when you visit San Jose sometimes hear the matter remarked about still ?

A. I do, rumors as usual, which I do not pay any attention to, now knowing better.

Q. From your experience and observation here do you find anything as a foundation for the rumors that the miners here are illtreated or deprived of their personal liberty or overridden or tyrannized over or anything of that kind ?

A. I have never seen anything of the kind; on the contrary I think that they are very well used; there are many things going to show that here.

Q. Mr. Martin Corcoran of San Jose has given some testimony in this case; he says while he has not visited the mine that he has heard a great many rumors about men being compelled to vote and being deprived of their liberty of action and that kind of thing. What do you think would be the effect upon his views of those matters if he would come here and stay a while at the mine ?

A. I think he would quickly become disabused of those prejudices.

Q. From what source do you consider that these false impressions arise mainly, these false rumors ?

A. I can hardly say; it is hard to follow up a rumor as to how it originates. Disappointed candidates, men discharged from labor and various things would cause men to talk about the mine and these things being repeated again would assume larger proportions, as any scandal or rumor would. Perhaps some men might be dissatisfied because Mr. Randol does not permit them to manage the mine in their way.

Q. Have you had any experience on Election Boards of this precinct ?

A. I have been a member of every board since I came here in 1881.

Q. How have the boards been appointed at all those elections ?

A. By the the Supervisors of the county; in the usual manner.

Q. Has there at any of these elections, so far as you know, been any tampering of any kind with the ballots or the counting or the conduct of the Board ?

A. Nothing.

Q. Has there ever been any discord in the Board growing out of any party questions ?

A. No; nothing concerning any party question ever; there never was any discord in the Board; we have sometimes held a consultation as to what we should do with certain ballots, but we always arrived at a unanimous conclusion; it would be purely a question of law as to how ballots should be counted or whether the ballots should be received or something of that kind: it is very difficult to determine exactly what to do with certain ballots, and we have held a consultation on the point and arrived at a decision in each case; there has been no wrangling whatever.

Q. And you say those decisions have been unanimous ?

A. Yes. I do not remember that we ever took a test vote on it.

Q. Has there ever been so far as you know, anything like crookedness in the conduct of the Board of this precinct since you have been a member of the Board?

A. No; nothing.

Q. Have you ever at any of those elections witnessed anything like intimidation, coercion or undue influence exercised upon the voters of this precinct or the employees of the mine ?

A. I never did.

Q. Have you ever seen any electioneering or work for the candidates or tickets in this precinct different from what are commonly practiced in other precincts?

A. I never did. I have seen a little electioneering by both parties, but it has been in the usual manner, nothing unusual about it.

Q. Have you ever seen anything to indicate that the managment or officers or those having charge of the work of this mine have bulldozed, intimidated, coerced or otherwise abused the elective franchise of the employees of the mine ?

A. I never did.

Q. Have you ever seen any scarcity of the tickets of the different parties on election day ?

A. I do not know anything about that. I think there has always been a sufficiency of tickets.

Q. Has there ever been an election when you have not found a good many Democratic tickets in the box ?

A. We have always found about the same number of Democratic tickets at the three elections. So far as I could judge by the ballots, the Democrats voted the Democratic ticket, and the Republicans the Republican ticket. I think that I could come within three or four of telling how many Democratic ballots there would be in the box if an election were held to-morrow, judging from what I have known heretofore. The ballots have been very uniform, showing the party lines very plainly.

Q. Been more or less scratching, has there not?

A. More or less scratching. I have witnessed the fact that there were candidates who were favorites with the voters in this precinct, some candidates have run ahead of their tickets.

Q. That happens at other precincts as well as New Almaden, does it not?

A. I presume so.

Q. You exercise the privilege of scratching your ticket if you see fit?

A. I do.

Q. Has there ever in this precinct been any attempt to intimidate r coerce or influence your vote?

A. Never has.

.Q. What can you say as to the relations between Mr. Randol and the employees, so far as you have observed it, his manner towards the employees and their manner towards him?

A. It has always been respectful.

Q. Have you ever seen anything in Mr. Randol's conduct towards the employees like tyranny or oppression or hard usage?

A. I never did.

Q. Where do you board?

A. At the boarding house on the Hill.

Q. How long have you boarded there?

A. A little over two years; two or three years.

Q. What can you say as to the quality of board provided there?

A. It is of good quality and well prepared. I have not heard of any complaints at all of any kind.

Q. What office do you hold in this township?

A. I am Justice of the Peace.

Q. How long have you been Justice of the Peace?

A. I think that it was in 1882 I was first appointed to fill a vacancy, and then was elected afterwards twice.

Q. What can you say as to the peace and good order and observance of the laws on this grant?

A. I think at the present time the peace and good order is remarkably good.

Q. What is about the population of this township in which you are Justice?

A. From 1,500 to 2,000; somewhere along there.

Q. What number of criminal complaints have you lodged in your court this year?

A. I think that I have had six this year since the 1st of January; there is a very decided improvement since I came here on the Hill with regard to observance of the law among the Mexican population; our principal complaints came from them and now they are getting to be very orderly; we have but very little trouble now with them; they are almost abandoning the use of weapons which they were formerly very free to use.

Q. Did you know the reputation of this community in those regards a few years ago?

A. Yes, in common with other places I have heard Almaden mentioned.

Q. What was 'the reputation of this community in former years in regard to the state of society and morality here?

A. About as bad as it could be. This was noted as one of the bad places of the State—one of the worst.

Q. What class of people tendered to give it that reputation?

A. Principally the Mexican portion—the old settlers formerly.

Q. What social condition, if any here, do you think has had any influence upon the people resident on the grant?

A. Aside from the churches and school, I think that the "Helping Hand" has done as much as anything to aid in keeping good order.

Q. How long has that organization been in existence?

A. I do not remember; it has been over a year ago.

Q. Will you state how that organization operates, what it does and what you think it works in the community?

A. It is an organization to give the men an opportunity to meet and converse with each other in a good, comfortable room, playing little games they may wish to play, cards or checkers or anything of that kind. Attached is also a reading-room, with a good selection of monthly, weekly and daily papers and magazines, and also a nice library of miscellaneous reading matter. I think the tendency has been that men after their suppers, instead of going to the saloon on the Hill, would naturally fall into the habit of going to this room and get engaged in a game of cards and remain there until it was time to go to bed.

Q. Do a good many read at those rooms?

A. Yes; quite a number. I go in there quite frequently, and almost always find a large number in the reading-room, busily engaged reading the different papers, magazines and the books there. I think that that has had a very good effect on the population and a tendency to produce social good order and pleasant social relations. The reading-room is distinct from the general amusement and conversation room.

Q. What else is there connected with this establishment besides the reading-room and general conversation room?

A. There is also a cook-room, and a cook employed there who furnishes to any one who wishes light refreshments, and at very low rates; too low for profit.

Q. Are there any entertainments given at the Hill—any public entertainments?

A. Yes.

Q. What is the character of those entertainments generally?

A. Something light to keep the people amused; occasionally when they can do so they have something more solid. Most of the amusements are gotten up by the residents, or when they can get outsiders to take part in it they do so; these entertainments are free; there are sometimes dramatic entertainments given by outsiders at which an admission is charged; the main hall or auditorium is fitted

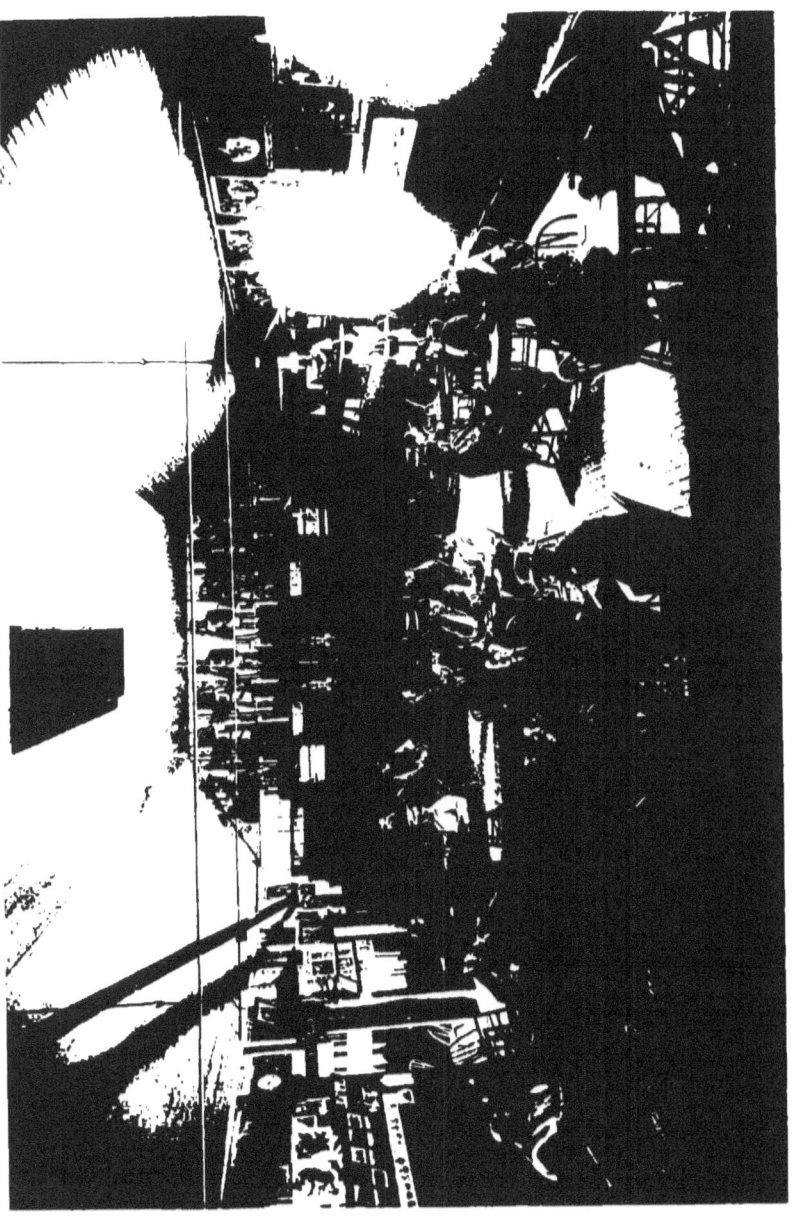

"HELPING HAND" CLUB ROOM, HILL.

with a very nice little stage, with good scenery, so that it is possible for small companies to render plays there.

Q. State whether or not the management of the mine has taken any hand in organizing and fitting up and assisting this Helping Hand Society.

A. Yes; they have taken a very deep interest in it, in fact it is almost wholly conducted by the mine management, and the different members composing it.

Q. Due to their efforts that it was organized and maintained?

A. Entirely to their efforts. Mr. O'Brion is the chief of that institution; he is very enthusiastic; he takes a great deal of interest in the Helping Hand, preserves proper order and keeps everything going along smoothly. He takes a very great, deep interest in it.

Q. What musical organizations if any have they on the Hill.

A. There are two brass bands, one in the English camp and one in the Mexican camp. There are also the church choirs.

Q. State whether or not there is a public library connected with the schools.

A. Yes, we have a very good public library connected with the schools on the Hill and also at the Hacienda.

Q. Can you give any statement of the number of volumes in those libraries?

A. I think that we have about 500 volumes now in both libraries.

Q. Who has a right to the use of those books?

A. All who reside in the district. It has been entirely free, no charge. They are allowed to take books from the library and keep them a stated period and return them. We encourage children all we can to take books home, and they very frequently take out books not only for themselves but for their parents; we encourage them all we can in that.

Q. What is the general character of the books composing the school library?

A. Miscellaneous. We have a few reference books for the use of those who wish to find anything that they cannot get readily otherwise, and then we have quite a number of small books suitable for the children; well, for all objects, the books are selected— histories, works of science, works of fiction and children's story books.

Q. What would you say of the class of books contained in the Helping Hand Library?

A. They have a large number of books of fiction in paper covers, also Dicken's Works and various other standard works—a miscellaneous collection of books, including works of art, science, history, and biography.

Q. Are those books allowed to be taken from that library, or are they to be read at the reading room?

A. People are permitted, I believe, to take books from that library by making a deposit to insure the return of the book; the books are free, but a deposit is made to insure the safe return of the books of the library.

Q. What magazines and papers, that you can recall, are taken regularly and read in the reading room of the Helping Hand Club?

A. The Century, Harper's and other popular magazines, the principal daily and weekly San Francisco and San Jose papers, in English and Spanish, also the principal Eastern pictorial papers.

Q. State generally, whether, so far as you have observed, the people of this community have exercised as much freedom of action and opinion as any other communities that you are acquainted with?

A. I think they do, and I know of no reason why they should not. Never observed anything that interfered with it.

Q. As to their labor, they are required to do their work and observe the industrial rules of the company, I suppose?

A. I presume so, that would be necessary in the management of a business of this extent; it would be absolutely necessary that there should be rules and regulations governing the mine, but so far as interference with them outside, I do not know of any—outside the mere industrial conduct of the business.

BRIDGE ACROSS SLAG DUMPS, HACIENDA.

TESTIMONY OF WILLIAM STILES.

By Mr. CROSS:

Q. What nationality are you?

A. I am an Englishman.

Q. How long have you been at this mine?

A. Thirteen years. I have worked by the day, by the month, as tributer, and for six years last past I have been furnace foreman; my wages have varied from $2.50 per day to $120 per month on contracts; I made from $80 to $117 per month; I have seen contract systems in other mines.

Q. Which do you think is the best system, having seen different kinds?

A. I think that the contract system here is more fair for a man.

Q. Do you think that system as used here is fair to both parties, both to employer and employee?

A. Yes.

Q. About how many men are under your charge generally?

A. From thirty-five to fifty.

Q. What do those men do?

A. Those men have to charge the furnaces, fire and discharge the furnaces, and keep everything clean around the furnaces; some of them attend to the quicksilver; their wages vary from $1.25 per day for boys to $85 a month for men.

Q. In what manner has Mr. Randol treated you?

A. He has treated me very gentlemanly; never been unkind towards me; always done what I think is perfectly right.

Q. What can you say as to the treatment of the men employed here as compared with the men you have seen employed in other places?

A. I think the men are treated as well in this mine as in any mine I have ever seen, and, in fact, there are very few places where men are so well treated as they are here.

Q. How does Mr. Jennings seem to feel towards the men, and how does he treat them?

A. Mr. Jennings has great sympathy for the men. He has ofttimes given me instructions to be very careful and look after everything, so that the men shall not be injured by any of the fumes or anything of the kind, and, in fact, Mr. Jennings is very favorable towards the older class that have worked here for many years.

Q. What do you know about voting here at the mine?

5

A. I voted here. I do not know anything different here from any other place.

Q. How many years have you been a voter here?

A. I think I voted first for President Garfield, and I attended all the elections since then.

Q. Did you vote the Republican ticket since that time?

A. Yes.

Q. Do you generally vote the Republican ticket?

A. Generally do.

Q. Ever scratch it?

A. Sometimes I have. If I see that there is a man I want to scratch for a man on another ticket I have occasionally scratched off and put another man down in his place, where I thought I had good reason for it.

Q. How do the English boys, or, as we call them, the Cornish boys, mostly vote? What party do they like the best?

A. As a general rule I think they are Republicans. I think if one should go around and inquire he would find they are nearly all Republicans.

Q. What have you ever heard Mr. Randol or Mr. Jennings doing about the voting?

A. Never heard anything at all.

Q. Did they ever try to direct you how you or the men should vote?

A. No officer ever gave me any direction how I should vote, or which way I should vote; in fact never inquired what my political views were.

Q. Ever give you any instructions or directions what they wanted the men to do about voting?

A. Not at all.

Q. Did you ever have any directions from Mr. Randol or Mr. Jennings, or any of the officers of the company, as to what you should do or what the men should do about voting?

A. No; never spoke to me on the subject.

Q. Did you ever hear the men talking amongst themselves as though they had to vote a certain way or they would be discharged or not get work?

A. I never heard any such a thing.

Q. Have you ever known or seen any intimidation or coercion or pressure used here by any one connected with the mine, concerning how men should vote?

A. No; I never saw anything of the kind; never heard of any such thing, in fact I could always vote which way I liked. I had three different kinds of tickets in my possession last time; could vote any one of them.

Q. So far as you know now, how does each man vote here?

A. I think that they are mostly Republicans, I think so, but then I suppose they are like other people, if they want to scratch they do so. Vote as they please as far as I know.

Q. What do you know about the store? Do you buy goods at the store?

A. Yes; I am very well satisfied with the quality of goods I receive at the store. I go there and order my things or my wife sends my daughter down and gives an order and it is delivered at my house.

Q. Do you buy most of your supplies at the store?

A. Yes.

Q. Did you ever have any boletos?

A. Yes.

Q. What are the boletos good for after you get them?

A. Just as good as money.

Q. Have you ever used them?

A. Yes; when I came here to the mine first, like a good many others, I was not very flush with money and of course I would have to wait for my money until regular pay-day, and I was told that I could go the store and get some boletos, which I did, and I found them to be of much advantage to me at that time.

Q. Is there any rule or custom requiring a man working at the mine to take boletos?

A. I never knew of any such a rule; never heard of any.

Q. Did you ever hear of any man being discharged on account of not taking boletos, or not buying at the store or anything like that?

A. No; never heard of such a thing. In fact we have had men working in the yard who never took any boletos, and they continued to work right on, the same as others.

Q. When are the men paid?

A. They are paid regularly every pay-day, once a month.

Q. From whom do you rent a house?

A. I rent the house from the company.

Q. What rent do you pay?

A. I pay six dollars a month.

Q. How many rooms in your house?

A. Six rooms; it is a comfortable house.

Q. What do you do about rules when men come and go to work for the company, new men?

A. It is the duty of Mr. Bulmore or myself to call attention to and read over the rules before they start to work, and of course, if they like to abide by the rules, they go to work, if not they would not go to work.

Q. Did you ever know a man to quit work on account of a rule?

A. Never have known one.

Q. State whether or not the men that came here to work under you generally remain a pretty long time, or whether they go away pretty soon?

A. We have got men that were working here when I came and they are working here yet, and as a general rule they remain here a long time.

TESTIMONY OF GEORGE CARSON.

By Mr. CROSS:

Q. Are you in the employ of The Quicksilver Mining Company?

A. Yes.

Q. What position do you hold?

A. I occupy a position as clerk; also as telegraph operator and am postmaster.

Q. What political party do you belong to?

A. I belong to the Democratic party.

Q. How many elections have you attended in this precinct?

A. Every election since I have been here.

Q. Ever been on the Election Board?

A. I have always served on the Election Board at all principal elections as clerk.

Q. Have you ever known an Election Board that did not have Democrats on it as well as Republicans, at this place?

A. Since I have been here I have always served as one Democrat, and there has always been a Democratic Judge or Inspector as well.

Q. What ticket have you voted at elections since you have been here?

A. I have always voted the Democratic ticket.

Q. Do you scratch sometimes?

A. Very little, occasionally.

Q. Has that fact been well known here at the mine?

A. Yes, I have made no secret of it whatever.

Q. Do you know whether or not it has been known to the officers and managers of the company?

A. I think so, certainly. I know that it has; they know that I am a Democrat and a strong one.

Q. Did you vote at the election of 1886?

A. Yes.

Q. Did you vote for Mr. Sullivan?

A. I did.

Q. Did you do any work for Mr. Sullivan?

A. I tried to influence what people I could to vote for him.

Q. That was before election day?

A. That was previous to that election day.

Q. Did you do that secretly or openly?

A. I did that openly, sir; openly.

Q. Did anybody in any way connected with the company ever object to your political course?

A. They paid no attention to it whatever.

Q. Have you any reason to think that it has in any way affected your relations with the company or your prosperity or advancement in the business?

A. I am almost sure it has not.

Q. Ever have any difficulty in getting a Democratic ticket to vote since you have been here?

A. No; always plenty of them about.

Q. Have you ever seen any interference with elections here by anybody?

A. I have not; no.

Q. Ever seen anything to indicate intimidation, coercion or pressure by those who have charge of the mine and the men in regard to how they should vote?

A. No; none whatever.

Q. Do you know whether there have been other Democrats employed here at the mine since you have been here?

BRIDGE. HACIENDA.

A. Yes; there are others.

Q. Has that fact been well known?

A. Yes.

Q. Did you see that it made any difference in their employment or preferment, anything of that kind, with their relations with the company?

A. No.

Q. What is your judgment as to whether it did or not?

A. I do not see that it has interfered with them in any way, shape or manner.

Q. Have you ever seen anything like coercion, intimidation or undue pressure on the employees of this company in regard to voting?

A. No; I think persons can vote just as they please. Just as freely here as anywhere.

Q. Does the fact of men getting boletos or not getting them have any influence whether the company gives them work or not?

A. None whatever.

Q. Whom did you first vote for, for President?

A. The first President I voted for was Tilden. I afterwards voted for Hancock and all the Democratic candidates since in succession right through.

TESTIMONY OF ANDREW DAHLGREEN.

By Mr. Cross:

Q. How long is it since you first came here to the mine?

A. Fifteen years. Have worked here ever since.

Q. What salary do you get as watchman?

A. $85 a month.

Q. What nationality are you?

A. A Swede.

Q. When did you vote first?

A. The first vote I put in was for President Garfield.

Q. How did you vote at the last election?

A. I voted the Republican ticket. All the time I do that.

Q. Did you vote for any Democrats that time?

A. No. I vote just a straight Republican ticket.

Q. Anybody ask you how you were going to vote?

A. No, nobody.

Q. Anybody tell you how to vote?

A. No; nobody at all.

Q. Anybody connected with the company say to you that they wanted you to vote a certain way?

A. No.

Q. Who did you get your ticket from?

A. Mr. Stiles gave it to me. I knew it was a Republican ticket.

Q. What do you think about the Miners' Fund?

A. Pretty good; very good; I got lots of sickness in the house sometimes, and I only pay a dollar a month and I get the doctor free, it is a very good thing.

Q. Do you ever get any boletos?

A. Yes; sometimes I take them if I feel like it; sometimes I take so much a month, and then if I do not feel like it I pay silver, and it is all the same thing.

Q. Does it make any difference in the price of goods?

A. No; no difference at all. Get the same thing if I give a dollar in boletos or a dollar in silver.

Q. Did you ever hear of any rule that a man must take boletos or he would get discharged?

A. No, I never heard that; and I never heard a man being discharged for that.

TESTIMONY OF JOSE GONZALES.

By Mr. CROSS:

Q. How long have you worked here?

A. About six years.

Q. When did you vote for the first time?

A. I voted in 1876 in San Francisco the first time.

Q. Whom did you vote for, for President?

A. For Hayes.

Q. What ticket did you vote?

A. Republican ticket.

Q. Was that before you ever came to the mine to work?

A. Long before I ever came here.

Q. What ticket do you generally vote?

A. Vote the Republican ticket.

Q. Were there any names scratched on your ticket the last time you voted?

A. Yes. A friend asked me if I would like to vote for them, they were very good men. I told him all right, if they were good men, I would like to vote for good men.

Q. Did you ever vote any other ticket except the Republican ticket?

A. Yes, I voted one Independent ticket.

Q. Who did you vote for at that time?

A. I voted for O'Donnell. I read an article that he said something against a Chinaman, that suited me, and I thought that I would give him my vote.

Q. Did Mr. Randol or Mr. Jennings ever tell you how to vote?

A. No.

Q. Ever ask you how you were going to vote?

A. No, nobody here in the mine asked me. Always voted just as I pleased.

Q. What country did you come from?

A. Central America.

Q. Are you a good deal acquainted with the Mexican people in California?

A. Some of them, yes.

Q. What ticket do they generally vote?

A. They generally, so far as I know, vote the Republican ticket.

Q. Do they like that ticket the best generally?

A. Yes, so far as I know.

Q. What ticket do the people of Spanish descent vote in the United States?

A. So far as I know, the Republican ticket.

Q. Do you know Mr. Pacheco?

A. I do. I saw him and got acquainted with him once. He was a Republican. He was elected Lieutenant-Governor and to Congress.

TESTIMONY OF GOTLIEB STOLTZ.

By Mr. CROSS:

Q. How long have you worked here at the mine?

A. Nine years.

Q. What countryman are you?

A. German.

Q. What ticket did you vote last November?

A. Republican.

Q. Who told you how to vote?

A. Nobody.

Q. Who asked you how you were going to vote?

A. Nobody.

Q. How did you happen to vote the Republican ticket?

A. I was a Republican before I got my papers, before I was a citizen.

Q. Do you prefer that party?

A. Yes. I like that party the best.

Q. How did you happen to be a Republican?

A. I don't know. I like that party better, I think that it is good for the country.

Q. Has there anybody here at the mine ever tried to interfere with your voting?

A. No.

Q. Anybody ever try to prevent your voting the way that you wanted to?

A. None whatever.

TESTIMONY OF CHARLES HIGGINS.

By Mr. CROSS:

Q. What is your full name?

A. Charles Higgins.

Q. What is your business.

A. Blacksmith.

Q. How long ago did you first come to this mine to work, Mr. Higgins?

A. About twenty-six years ago. I have been away five years of the time.

Q. How much of a family have you?

A. Six children, myself and my wife.

Q. Do you rent a house from the company?

A. Yes.

Q. What rent do you pay?

A. Seven dollars.

Q. How many rooms are there in your house?

A. It is quite a large house; I think there are about eight rooms.

Q. You are employed here as a blacksmith, are you?

A. Yes; working in the shop at $3 per day.

Q. How do you get along with Mr. Randol?

A. I could never find any fault.

Q. What use is it to have the boletos?

A. It is very accommodating from one pay-day to the other to get boletos the same as you would get a silver dollar. The boletos are just as good as the money.

Q. What nationality are you?

A. I am Irish descent; I was born in Ireland.

Q. How long have you been a voter?

A. The first President that I voted for was Buchanan.

Q. What ticket have you voted ever since?

A. Democratic ticket.

Q. Do you ever scratch?

A. Sometimes. Very little though. If I want to scratch I do so; very little scratching I ever do. I like it pretty straight.

Q. Did anybody here at the mine ever try to interfere with your voting?

A. Not at all.

Q. Anybody ever try to dictate to you how you should vote, anybody connected with the mine in anyway?

A. Not at all. There would be some electioneering that would not amount to anything.

Q. Has it been well known here at the mine all the time that you were a Democrat and voted the Democratic ticket?

A. I think so. Never concealed it at all.

Q. Can you see that it ever made any difference with your employment or pay, the fact that you were known to be a Democrat?

A. I could never see any difference.

Q. It don't influence matters at all?

A. Not at all.

Q. Who did you vote for Congress last time?

A. I voted for Mr. Sullivan.

Q. You sometimes have occasion to ask a little favor of Mr. Randol, he being the manager of the mine?

A. Yes; many times.

Q. What has been the result?

A. Always granted.

Q. Have you worked for other parties, other people, in California?

A. Oh, yes.

Q. What can you say as to this as a place for a man to work, as compared with other places that you have worked?

A. I must say that I have never worked so long in any place in California or that I liked so well as Almaden.

MEXICAN CAMP, SOUTH SIDE.

Q. Did you ever have any trouble about the rules here at the mine?

A. Not at all; I never had any trouble.

Q. Did you ever see anything about the rules that you thought was not fair and correct?

A. They suited me; if I did not think they suited me I should stop working.

Q. What do you think about the Miners' Fund as to whether it is a good thing or a bad thing?

A. I think it is a very good thing.

TESTIMONY OF ADOLFO BANALES.

By Mr. CROSS:

Q. How long have you been here at the mine?

A. Twenty-three years.

Q. How much of that time have you been at work?

A. All the time with the exception of a few days now and then; I repair flasks.

Q. What nationality are you, originally?

A. I was born at Los Angeles of Mexican parentage.

Q. When did you first vote?

A. I voted first in 1872 for President Grant.

Q. What ticket do you generally vote?

A. The Republican.

Q. Ever scratch it any?

A. In very few cases; sometimes just to vote for a man that I particularly knew, who was on the other ticket, and that I wanted to vote for.

Q. How did you happen to vote for Grant at that time?

A. I had just come of age, and he was running for a second term, and I had read a good deal about the man, and I was very glad to have a chance to vote for him. He was my choice, from what I had read and heard about him.

Q. Did you know something about his history; what he had done for the country and so on?

A. Yes; that was the reason I voted for him.

Q. You say that you are of Mexican descent. Are you acquainted with a good many people of that descent in California?

A. Yes, I have always been more or less acquainted with the Mexicans living around where I live.

Q. What ticket do they generally vote in California?

A. They generally vote the Republican ticket, a large majority of them.

Q. Can you explain why that is?

A. The Republican party in this country corresponds somewhat to what is called the Liberal party in Mexico, which holds a large majority there, and I account for it in that way.

Q. Do they talk those matters over amongst themselves?

A. Yes.

Q. Do you know anybody at this mine of Mexican descent that votes the Democratic ticket?

A. I cannot recollect any one.

Q. Did you ever hear of any rule that a man had to draw boletos or he would get discharged?

A. No; I know several men that do not draw boletos, they wait until they get the money.

TESTIMONY OF ROBERT SCOTT.

By Mr. CROSS:

Q. What is your business?

A. Bricklayer. I am a native of Canada.

Q. How long have you worked here at the mine?

A. I have worked off and on since the winter of 1863 and '64; altogether probably fifteen years.

Q, What wages do you receive at the present time?

A. I get $150 a month.

Q. How long have you been a voter?

A. I think I voted for the first President after Grant. That will be Hayes.

Q. Have you voted the Republican ticket since?

A. Yes; I voted for Garfield and voted for Blaine.

Q. How did you happen to vote for Hayes?

A. I liked the Republican party. That was my free choice.

Q. Did any one here at the mine have anything to do with dictating to you how you should vote at that election, or try to influence your vote at that election?

A. No; nobody has tried to influence me as to how I should vote at any time.

Q. Do you know of any one having ever been interfered with here, or any man having been intimidated, or coerced, or threatened with discharge, or anything of that kind on account of politics?

A. I never have heard or seen anything of that kind.

Q. Did anyone ever bring you word that the management of the mine wished you to vote in any particular way or anything of that kind?

A. No; never.

Q. Has your vote ever been interfered with here in any way?

A. Never.

Q. Have you ever seen anything to cause you to think that the way a man voted here had anything to do with his getting employment or being retained?

A. No; I do not believe that has anything to do with it. I think that it depends on the man.

Q. Did you ever see any attempt to cut people off here from talking about political matters just as freely as they would anywhere?

A. Nothing.

Q. Are you acquainted with Mr. Randol?

A. Yes.

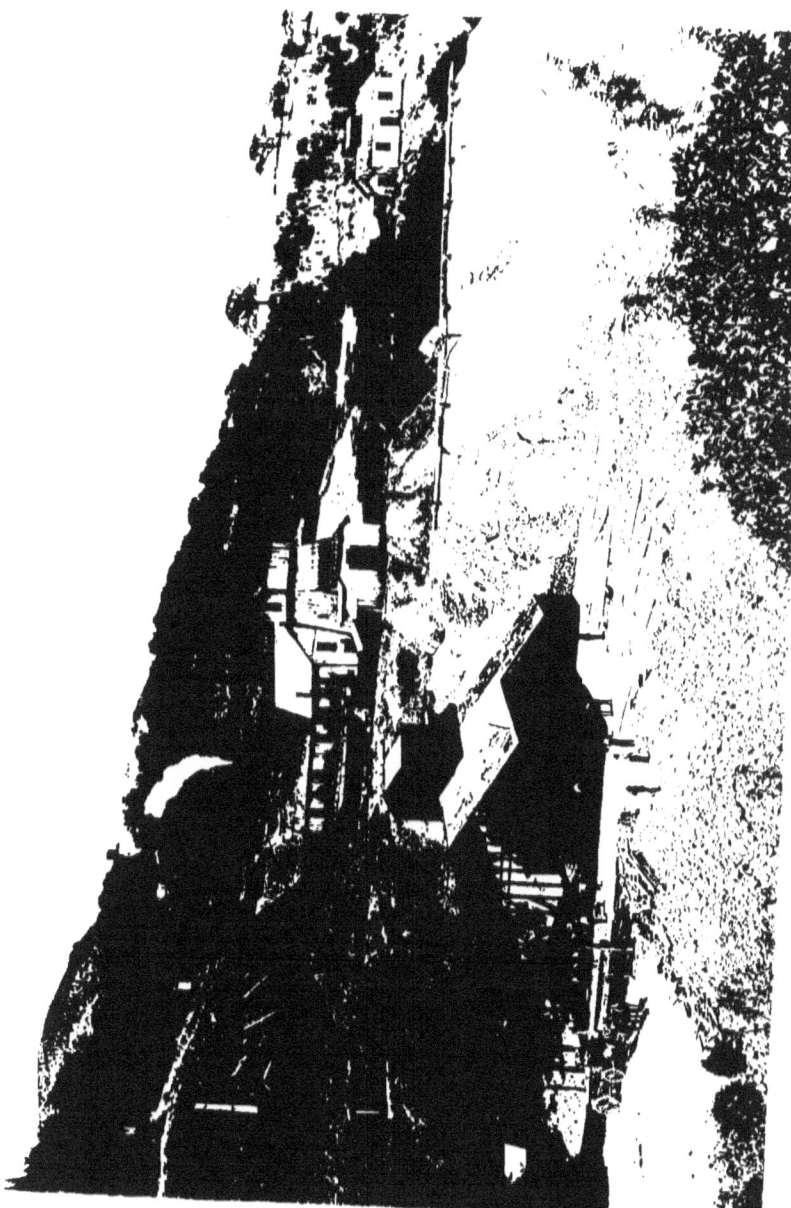

SANTA ISABEL SHAFT.

Q. In this position that you hold, having charge of the mason work, do you sometimes come in contact with him ?

A. Yes; I used to very often, when we were building furnaces, new furnaces.

Q. What is Mr. Randol's manner towards the men that are employed by the company ?

A. Very fair man to deal with; he is very strict, but he is a very straightforward kind of a man to the men that tend to their business.

Q. He wants a man to tend to business strictly ?

A. Yes.

Q. Have you ever seen him act in any manner like tyranny or harshness or unjustness towards the men ?

A. Never.

Q. Tell us about boletos, the way they seem to you and what the course is with regard to the boletos ?

A. I believe that boletos are a very good thing to have. When people draw their pay here they do not generally like to have their money lying around; what money they have over they will send off to a bank or to some place for safe keeping. They do not then have any cash on hand and they go to the store and draw boletos and buy their goods.

Q. Do you think a man is more likely to make a saving than having money by him all the time ?

A. I believe he is; he is apt to be more careful; and then there are a great many that have large families that do not have a great deal of ready cash, and it comes very handy to them to be getting something before pay-day.

Q. You have found it a convenience to you ?

A. Yes. I think the boleto system is a very good thing.

Q. Did you hear of any rule that a man had to take boletos or he was liable to be discharged ?

A. No. I never heard anything about that.

Q. Did you vote the Republican ticket in November, 1886 ?

A. Yes.

Q. State the circumstances.

A. I came down towards the polls and I got a Republican ticket, and a friend of mine wanted me to vote for a friend of his, some county office. I did not know either party; he said that he was a nice man and I could do him a favor; well, I said that I did not know either party. He guaranteed he was a nice man. Well, I said we will put his name down, he wrote it down for me. It was a man here by the name of Richmond I believe, who wrote down the two names for me. I did not have any pencil. I came on further down, and I was inquiring for a pencil, wanted to change another name, and I asked some one there if he had a pencil, and he said he did not, and Mr. Lowe says: "I have got a pencil," I said: "let me have it a minute I want to put down a name here, Mr. Spitzer, I think that he is a pretty good man, I will put his name down," and I handed it to Mr. Lowe and said you put it down—"yes," he says "he is a very good man." That is, Mr. Ralph Lowe, and he wrote it down for me on my ticket.

Q. When you first came here what kind of furnaces were in use at this mine?

A. The old intermittent furnaces were in use when I came here. I was largely employed in the improvement of them.

Witness here explains the various improvements made to the furnaces. These improvements save time, fuel, expense and labor, and are safer for the men.

TESTIMONY OF EDWARD A. WILLIAMS.

By Mr. Cross:

Q. What is your occupation?

A. House carpenter.

Q. When did you first come here to work?

A. In the summer of 1882, and have worked here ever since.

Q. Where were you born?

A. In San Francisco.

Q. Who was the first President you voted for?

A. Grant, at his second election.

Q. What ticket did you vote at that time?

A. Republican ticket.

Q. That was long before you ever were in the employ of this company?

A. Yes.

Q. What ticket have you voted ever since?

A. Republican ticket.

Q. Do you vote pretty straight, or do you scratch some?

A. Very seldom scratch.

Q. Now, you say that you vote the Republican ticket, and have been in the habit of doing so, although you sometimes scratch. What measures, if any, have been taken here at the mine to influence you in your voting?

A. There never have been any at all.

Q. Anybody ever try to dictate to you how you should vote?

A. Never.

Q. Any of the employees or officers of the mine ever try to influence you in that matter?

A. No.

Q. Have you ever had any fear or impression that the manner in which you voted would have any influence upon your employment or the wages you would get?

A. Not at all; not at all.

Q. Have you ever known of anything of that kind amongst the men who did work here?

A. No.

Q. Did you ever see anything to indicate that any man was discharged from the mine here on account of the way he voted?

A. No.

Q. Did Mr. Randol or Mr. Jennings, or any of the bosses or foremen of the mine, ever tell you how you should vote?
A. No.
Q. Or talk to you about the matter?
A. No.

TESTIMONY OF WALLACE J. NALONE.

By Mr. CROSS:

Q. What is your occupation?
A. I am working for Mr. Bohlmann, a teamster.
Q. Where were you born?
A. I was born in Humboldt, California.
Q. Have you ever voted?
A. Twice at general elections.
Q. What ticket do you vote?
A. Democratic.
Q. Did you vote in November, 1886?
A. Yes.
Q. In this precinct?
A. Yes.
Q. What ticket did you vote?
A. Democratic ticket.
Q. Did you do any scratching?
A. Yes; one scratch.
Q. What was it?
A. Frank Branham; I scratched him out and put Sweigert on for Sheriff.
Q. Why did you scratch him?
A. I thought Branham had been there long enough, and better give somebody else a chance.
Q. Anybody ever try to influence your vote?
A. No.
Q. Ever try to dictate to you?
A. No.
Q. Have you ever had any understanding that a man has got to draw boletos or he is likely to get discharged?
A. I never heard of that before.
Q. Did you ever hear of any rule that a man must draw boletos or quit?
A. No.
Q. What wages do you get?
A. $55 a month.
Q. Did you ever see anything here like intimidation of voters or compelling them to vote for certain men?
A. No.
Q. Any electioneering around here?
A. Just about like it is everywhere else.

TESTIMONY OF S. C. NAVARRO.

By Mr. Cross:

Q. Where were you born?
A. Los Angeles.
Q. What ticket did you vote in 1886?
A. Republican ticket.
Q. What nationality are you, or what descent rather?
A. I am of Spanish descent.
Q. What ticket do your people generally vote?
A. Republican ticket so far as I know.
Q. Did anybody in the management of this mine ever try to dictate to you how you should vote?
A. No.
Q. Anybody try to interfere with your right to vote just as you choose?
A. No.
Q. Did you ever have any fear that you would be turned off if you did not vote just as the managers of the mine wanted you to?
A. Never did.

TESTIMONY OF ROBERT COCKBURN.

By Mr. Cross:

Q. How long have you worked for the company?
A. I have worked off and on for the last five years pretty regularly.
Q. Where were you born?
A. New York city.
Q. Who was the first President you voted for?
A. Garfield I believe was the first President I voted for.
Q. What ticket have you generally voted since?
A. Republican ticket; never changed.
Q. Anybody ever try to interfere with your vote at an election?
A. No.
Q. Anybody ever try to compel you to vote in a particular way for any particular man?
A. No. I did never hear of anybody doing so.
Q. Ever had any officers of the company, any of the bosses, or any of the superintendents, or anybody of that kind trying to force you to vote a certain way?
A. No.
Q. Have you voted at any other places besides in New Almaden, ever?
A. Yes, I voted back East.
Q. Did you see any difference in the way they were doing around the polls here than they do at any other places?
A. This is the quietest place I ever saw.
Q. Men are left alone pretty much?
A. Yes, they vote to suit themselves, so far as I could see.

Q. Were there any Democratic tickets around here at the election of November, 1886?

A. Yes.

Q. Men distribute them at the polls?

A. Yes, there were Democratic tickets around. I was offered a Democratic ticket, and I told them I didn't want it.

Q. No trouble about a man getting a Democratic ticket if he wanted it, was there?

A. No.

Q. Is there any rule or custom compelling a man to draw boletos?

A. No, there is not that I know of. I never heard of any.

Q. Did you ever see that it made any difference in what you had to pay for goods, whether you bought for coin or boletos?

A. No, it is all the same.

TESTIMONY OF FRANK BOHLMAN.

By Mr. CROSS:

Q. What is your age?

A. Thirty-three years old.

Q. Where do you reside?

A. Almaden.

Q. What is your occupation?

A. Contractor and livery stable keeper and farmer and stage proprietor.

Q. Where were you born?

A. I was born in Almaden; lived here all my life with the exception of seven years.

Q. What are your business relations with the company?

A. Timber contractor and ore hauling; I do all their freighting, I think.

Q. How long have you had timber contracts with the company?

A. I have been contracting for wood and timber for the last sixteen years with them.

Q. How much timber do you furnish under the contract for the present year?

A. 750,000 feet. I have it cut and hewed.

Q. What other contracts have you with the company?

A. I have a contract to haul the ore from the planillas to the dump, and the coal from the station to the Hill and to the different shafts, that is, coal used in generating steam.

Q. How many horses do you employ in the business with the company?

A. I have about 130 head at the present time.

Q. How many men do you employ on these contracts?

A. I have sometimes thirty-five men employed.

Q. Anybody have a right to employ and discharge them except yourself?

A. No.

Q. Something has been said in the testimony on the part of the contestant about everybody not being allowed to drive teams on the company's private road from the gate up the hill to the different shafts. Explain the reason about that change.

A. Since last September it was thought better not to let them go on the Hill for fear there would be an accident as there were so many teams hauling up and down the hill; for me to keep a livery stable and to take anybody that wanted to go up and show them the shafts and different places, send a man along with them that was

RANDOL SHAFT.

acquainted with the place and the road, one that knew how to look out for teams.

Q. What is there about the road that makes it desirable that only teams and drivers should go on that road who are familiar with the road and the methods of doing business on it?

A. The roads are steep and in some places narrow, and large teams going up there, six-mule teams or horse teams, there are places that if you do not look out they will be liable to run into one another, or if a person has a scarey horse, they are liable to go over the grade.

Q. What is there about the freight teams that is liable to frighten other teams on the grade?

A. There are bells on them—strings of bells.

Q. What is the nature of the road as to it being straight or winding, coming around sharp points?

A. It is a very crooked road. It frequently comes to high points and sharp turns. There are turns that you cannot see until you come right on them.

Q. What would be the effect upon the freighting business done for the company of allowing everybody to drive teams up and down that road?

A. They are liable to meet with an accident of some kind. And they might interfere with the traffic. In the summer time there are a great many teams going up and down there. I should say twenty or more during the summer, loaded teams.

Q. What do you charge for a team and driver to take a load up that hill?

A. I charge $2.50.

Q. Is that a public or a private road?

A. Private road owned by The Quicksilver Mining Company.

Q. They claim the privilege of establishing such rules on their own premises as they see fit?

A. Yes; for their own convenience.

Q. On the part of the contestant there has been some testimony about the men, who work for you, boarding at your sister's house?

A. Yes.

Q. Tell us all about it?

A. I hire these men by the month and I pay them $35 a month and board them, and I have them boarded at that place because I get them boarded cheaper; for that reason I have them boarded there. I think that is my privilege if I hire a man for so much and his board, to board him where it is most to my interest. I think that he has to board where I want him to board; I hire him in that way.

Q. You claim as you pay for his board that you have a right to select the place where he shall board?

A. Yes.

Q. What political party do you belong to.

A. The Republican party. Never anything else. Sometimes I think that there is a good man on the other ticket and I put him on mine.

Q. You know a man by the name of David Bryant who run for Recorder on the Democratic ticket, the last election?

6

A. Yes; I do.

Q. How did you account for him getting more votes here than most of the Democrats did?

A. I suppose on my account; I worked a good deal for him and I have men working for me that I asked to vote for him if they would, and a good many consented to do it. Electioneering as men do at elections sometimes for friends.

Q. You claim that you had a right to do that as an American citizen?

A. Yes; I think I have; it is done everywhere.

Q. Do you know of any reason why they should have a right to send a man out here from San Jose or from San Francisco to work at these polls to get votes for certain men and not give you or any one else that has lived here a right to electioneer for their friends.

A. I do not.

Q. Some claim is made here that they could not get accommodation for their teams here. Do you know anything about that matter?

A. Yes. Mr. Sullivan drove up here the first day, I think, the investigation was going on, and tied his horses under the shed. I asked him why he did not put up at the stable and give me a chance to make a dollar out of him, and he said he did not because he was afraid I would not take him in. I told him to try me the next time he came up and see; so the next day he drove up and came in, and his horses were properly taken care of, and I got the dollar. He did it again the second time. That was the last time he came.

Q. Do you know anything about boletos?

A. Yes, the men who work for me have the privilege of boletos.

Q. Any man who works for you, is he compelled to vote in any particular way?

A. No, he exercises his option the same as other voters.

Q. Has anybody been discharged from your employment on account of political reasons?

A. No.

Q. Was Reedy in your employment at one time?

A. Yes.

Q. When did he quit your employment, and what were the circumstances?

A. He is a man that talks a great deal, and had a great deal to say, and one day when he came out to the stage in front of the store, I told him he could go. He was using vulgar language.

Q. Was it anything about politics?

A. No, nothing to do with politics.

Q. Were you under any obligations to keep him, that you know of, any longer than you wanted him?

A. No.

ST. GEORGE SHAFT.

TESTIMONY OF R. R. BULMORE.

By Mr. CROSS:

Q. What is your occupation ?

A. Accountant and Hacienda foreman.

Q. Where were you born ?

A. I was born in London, England.

Q. Where were you educated ?

A. At Wimberly House Academy, Fulham.

Q. What branches did you give your particular attention to ?

A. General assaying cf the precious metals.

Q. Who were your instructors ?

A. Doctors Boycott and Leibig.

Q. Where were they employed ?

A. In the mint in Calcutta, East Indies.

Q. Did you ever have any service under the Government of Great Britain ?

A. I did; I received a commission and served in a cavalry regiment throughout the Indian mutiny as an officer during the years 1856 to 1859.

Q. What certificate did you have as to your qualification as an assayer ?

A. I hold a certificate from the Bank of England qualifying me to be an assay-master for any of Her Majesty's mints abroad.

Q. When did you come to California ?

A. In 1866; I came out here as an accountant for the Commercial Bank of India; afterwards I was interested in the North Point Dock Warehouse in San Francisco, with E. B. Gothen, until it was destroyed by a fire; I was then engaged as an accountant and Hacienda foreman for The Quicksilver Mining Company by Mr. Randol on the 8th of September, 1878; I have held that position ever since.

Q, When did you become a voter in this country ?

A. I think I first voted in November, 1882; I voted the Republican ticket.

Q. Have you affiliated with that party ever since ?

A. Yes.

Q. There has been some testimony that the night before election you were scratching some tickets. What tickets were they ?

A. Republican tickets; in favor of Democrats.

Q. What Democrats were you scratching in favor of ?

A. Particularly Mr. Moulder.

Q. What reason had you for favoring Mr. Moulder's candidacy over the candidate on your own party ticket ?

A. I am personally acquainted with him, and he is a relation of a friend of mine; I had social relations with him.

Q. Did you try to use your position in the company to coerce or intimidate or force any one to vote for any particular ticket or any particular candidate ?

A. No.

Q. What are most of the voters of this precinct as to their party relations ?

A. Affiliate with the Republican party.

Q. Since you have been connected with this company do you know of any one having been discharged on account of the way they voted or intended to vote, or for any political reasons ?

A. Never; never have.

Q. Do you know of anything having been done during Mr. Randol's administration to control or force the free exercise of the franchise in this precinct ?

A. None whatever.

Q. There has been some testimony about your having a small book here on election day in which you had notes of the men voting. What did that book contain ?

A. That book simply contained an alphabetical list of voters.

Q. Of this precinct ?

A. Of this precinct, as they appear on the great register.

Q. Now, then, what mark did you put upon the book when a man voted ?

A. Simply a pencil mark that he had voted; simply a check mark.

Q. Was there anything in your book at that election to indicate how men had voted ?

A. Not anything of the kind.

Q. State what use there is for having this alphabetical list of voters of the precinct with their register numbers opposite to their names ?

A. To facilitate the voting; when a dozen or more men come down on the stage they cannot all look at the Great Register at once, and they ask me for their numbers, giving their name, and I give each man his number, and in the event of his being unable to write or read or remember the number, I give it to him upon a piece of paper.

Q. How is it a benefit to the men to have the stages run on that day from the Hill to the polling place ?

A. A benefit to the men this way: They can ride instead of walk. It benefits The Quicksilver Mining Company this way: the men are less time away from their duties than they otherwise would be; and are then in better condition for their labor when they return to it.

Q. There has been some testimony given that some Chinamen were sent away from here because they had some soap given them—Chinamen engaged in the wash-house business here. Do you know anything about the circumstances under which the Chinamen left here ?

A. I was told by Mr. Randol to send the Chinese laundry people away in order to give two or three widows that were here a better chance to make a living by washing for the public.

Q. Have you anything to do with the collecting of the rents of the cottages ?

A. I collect the rents of the houses rented by the company.

Q. What are the rents of the cottages ?

A. They will average $5 a month.

Q. How many rooms do they contain ?

A. From four to seven. The company keeps those cottages in repair.

Q. What is your relation to the Miners' Fund ?

MINERS' COTTAGES, HILL.

A. I am Secretary of the Miners' Fund.

Q. As such Secretary do you have custody of the books and accounts of the Miners' Fund?

A. Yes; I keep the accounts and make all collections and disbursements under the direction of Mr. Randol, the trustee. I receive a small salary, the trustee serves without compensation.

Q. Mr. Randol gets no compensation?

A. No.

Q. Have you made up a tabulated statement of the expenses of that fund?

A. I have.

A. What has been the total amount of the receipts of the Miners' Fund for the last sixteen years, from the time that Mr. Randol became Trustee of it up to the present time.

A. $108,954.00.

Q. How much of that amount has come from this collection of a dollar a month from each person who contributes to the fund?

A. $98,909.80; and for other receipts I refer to Exhibit A.

Q. Now you may state what the disbursements have been; what they are for, and the several amounts?

A. The disbursements are: salary of physicians, $60,911; medical stores, $15,820.39, that is the medicine that has been purchased and distributed at the dispensary here, for which was realized $4,558; contributions to the sick and disabled, $4,812.85, that means a person who has been a contributor until he was taken sick or unable to work and could not contribute, then he would be helped along by contribution or donation to him or his family out of this fund; salary paid to the secretary, $4,562.34; hospital nurses, $3,613.07; consultation fees, $1,858. In the event of a serious accident or in a complicated case, the resident physician having some doubt as to the right course of procedure, would telegraph to town for consultation, that would be paid for out of this fund. For livery prior to 1878, $1,425.78, funeral expenses, $1,076.84; board for patients, $1,733.20; furniture, $583.94; office furniture, hospital furniture, beds, chairs, furniture for the dispensary, shelves, scales and weights, and all the general details that constitute a general drug store. Surgical instruments, $501.42; office boy prior to 1878, $418.75; incidental expenses, $638.40; small loans unpaid, $65 at the present time.

Q. Also some cases in which patients made small loans from the Fund?

A. Yes; that is done in many cases; it has been all repaid except $65; subscriptions to medical journals and works—periodicals, $369.80; disinfectants, $330.19; small pox hospital, $117.25; taxes, $18; fuel, prior to 1878, $15.22; apothecary salary, $708; Helping Hand Club, $726.78; care of graves, $20; that makes the total expenditures of the Fund, $100,443.22.

Q. What does that leave on hand in the Fund?

A. It leaves on hand in the Fund $8,510.78 to its credit.

Q. Where is this balance of $8,510.78?

A. Deposited in three banks.

Q. What banks are they?

A. The Security Savings Bank, the San Francisco Savings Union and the Hibernia Savings and Loan Society.

Q. Have you the bank books here ?

A. Yes; they are here, showing the balance on the 31st of December 1886, in each bank.

Q. How is this money deposited; in whose name ?

A. It is deposited in the name of "J. B. Randol, Agent Miners' Fund."

Q. You may state the amount on deposit in each bank on the 31st day of December last ?

A. The Security Savings Bank, $4,141.82: the San Francisco Savings Union, $2,951.07; Hibernia Savings and Loan Society, $2,-379.29, making a total of $9,472.18. You will observe that is in excess of the amount that the balance calls for.

Q. Will you explain how that is ?

A. Yes; in December, 1885, we made a deposit of $1000; in 1886 we had several accidents and our expenses in consequence became greater that year. Greater than the receipts and greater than usual. 1886 was, so far as the Miners' Fund was concerned, unfortunate; we had several accidents and by the end of 1886 we had spent $961.40 more than we had on hand. Deducting the $961.40 from the balance the total amount in the banks you get the exact balance of $8,510.78, the difference between the receipts and disbursements for the 16 years.

Q. Was that $961.40 paid originally out of the Miners' Fund?

A. No, that was advanced by the trustee, Mr. Randol.

Q. What reason was there for that ?

A. He advanced it in the course of the year in order not to draw from the funds in the banks belonging to the fund, so as to be able to receive the full amount of interest on the deposits at the end of the year.

Q. If that money had been drawn it would have prevented the drawing of interest on the deposit, would it ?

A. Yes.

Q. And by advancing that, that amount of interest was saved to the fund?

A. Exactly.

Q. In your judgment is this deposit or this surplus that you now have a large surplus for such a fund ?

A. We have over $8,500 in the banks, but I do not think it is large for the institution.

Q. What amount would be desirable to have, do you think, as a safety fund?

A. As a safety fund, I should think that they ought to have at least $10,000 on hand.

Q. What reason is there for having as large a fund as that on hand?

A. In the event of a serious accident where many are hurt, it would require such a sum to fall back upon and properly care for them, so as not to increase the monthly assessment of one dollar, as it is at present.

Q. You think $10,000 would not be an unreasonable sum to have on hand, considering the extent of the mine where it is possible to have a serious accident which would make a heavy drain on the fund?

A. I do.

Q. Did the amount collected for the Miners' Fund in 1886 meet the expenses of the fund?

A. The amount collected did not.

B. From your connection with the fund, what do you say as to the feeling of the contributors towards the fund?

A. I think it is accepted by everybody as being beneficial.

Q. Does anybody besides the miners and laboring men contribute to that fund?

A. Everybody. Mr. Randol and every officer in the company's service contributes to that fund one dollar a month, and the resident physician attends them and their families. I am of the opinion that it is beneficial to everybody; it is without discrimination; the resident physician responds to a call at any hour, day or night, often having dangerous rides on a dark stormy night in winter to visit a laborer's cottage.

Q. What salary does the resident physician receive?

A. $400 a month.

Q. Has he had occasion to doctor in your family?

A. Yes.

Q. What do you think of his competency to fill such a place?

A. He has been very successful in treating me for neuralgia and general debility.

Q. Have there ever been any complaints made to your knowledge of the management of the Miners' Fund?

A. No; never heard of any, nor of a desire for a change.

Q. How are the drugs supplied which are distributed by the dispensary?

A. The drugs are all purchased from a wholesale house and are of the best quality obtainable.

Q. When those drugs are sold what is done with the money received?

A. It is handed over to me at the end of every month and goes into the Miners' Fund.

Q. What does the company do towards the support and maintenance of the regular physician, if anything?

A. The Quicksilver Mining Company assists the fund by providing gratuitously the house for the physician and the physician's office and the dispensary on the Hill, and the office and dispensary at the Hacienda, livery for his horse and fuel at the dispensaries during the winter, both at the Hill and the Hacienda. Those things are furnished without expense to the Miners' Fund.

TESTIMONY OF THOMAS DERBY.

By Mr. MOORE:

Q. Where were you born?

A. New York.

Q. What is your age, please?

A. Forty-three years.

Q. You are the Derby of the firm of Derby & Lowe, are you not, lessees of the stores at New Almaden?

A. Yes.

Q. State, if you please, your connection with this business; how you first came to be associated with the place, and the history of your connection with the stores?

A. I came to this State in 1864 with Mr. S. F. Butterworth, who was President and Manager of The Quicksilver Mining Company at that time. I remained with him in San Francisco, as a clerk, for several months; about this time The Quicksilver Mining Company erected two store buildings at New Almaden, and leased them to C. J. Brenham; I then left the employ of Mr. Butterworth to take charge of the store business for Mr. Brenham, residing in San Francisco, and purchasing all the goods. I continued in that position until Mr. Brenham died in 1875. Shortly before Mr. Brenham died, Mr. Butterworth purchased the stores from him. I continued in charge of the stores for Mr. Butterworth until he died, on May 5th, 1875. Mr. Butterworth bequeathed the stores to his nephew, Mr. Randol, who was then, and is now General Manager of The Quicksilver Mining Company at this place. About this time I was contemplating a trip abroad, and Mr. Randol came to me and said that he knew nothing about store business, had no use for the stores, and made a proposition to dispose of them to me. I accepted the proposition and became the owner of the business. That severed Mr. Randol's connection with the stores. I then engaged Mr. Lowe, my present partner, to take charge of the stores for me, and in November, 1876, I formed a co-partnership with Mr. Lowe in the business, which has continued ever since.

Q. How do you obtain these stores?

A. We rent the stores under a lease direct from the main office of the company in New York City.

Q. In that lease are there any conditions attached as to what character of stores you are to keep?

A. We agree with the company to keep in the stores a well selected stock of provisions and other merchandise for the use of the employees of the company, not to retail any liquors, and to maintain good order in and around the premises.

Q. Do you reside at Almaden?

A. No; I reside in San Francisco and attend to purchasing goods for the stores. Mr. Lowe resides at New Almaden, and is in personal charge of the stores.

Q. Have you any employees in this business?

A. Yes; we employ six clerks at both stores.

Q. What kind of goods are sold in these stores?

A. We keep a full and well assorted supply of all kinds of merchandise, such as is usually kept in any first-class, well regulated country store, especially goods adapted for miners.

Q. What class of goods is it necessary for you to keep, for instance, in the line of provisions?

A. Our customers demand the best quality of provisions, and are willing to pay the prices of a good article in preference to purchasing inferior grades at lower prices. It is also necessary for us to keep only the best grades of such articles of clothing and other articles of wearing apparel as are suited to the wants of our customers as miners, and they also are fully as particular in regard to goods for dress, demanding the best for themselves and their families.

Q. How do prices charged at your store compare with prices in any other place; for instance, San Jose and San Francisco?

A. I consider our prices compare favorably with the prices obtained in San Jose or San Francisco for the same class and quality of goods; until very recently we were obliged to add extra for freight from San Jose to the Hacienda store, and from the Hacienda to the Hill store.

Q. Is the freight any more from San Jose to the Hill store than it is from San Jose to the Hacienda?

A. It costs as much to haul from the Hacienda to the Hill, a distance of less than three miles, as it does from San Jose to the Hacienda, a distance of twelve miles; this is owing to the steep grade of the road to the Hill.

Q. You say until very recently you were obliged to add for this extra freight. Do you still add that?

A. No; the railroad has recently been completed to a point within two miles of the Hacienda which reduces freight charges to this place.

Q. In regard to purchasing at the stores, it was testified by one of the witnesses for the contestant that he was surprised at an absence of anything like bargaining among purchasers who were buying at the stores; he said that persons would come in and ask for an article, they would never ask the price, but would simply lay down the money or boletos and walk off; he accounted for this, I believe, on the supposition that the store charged just exactly what it pleased for any articles that it sold. How about this bargaining at the stores, can you explain it, or the lack of bargaining, that generally takes place between customers and keepers of stores?

A. We charge but one price to all our customers alike; most of these people have been trading with us for a long time and the cost of goods is well known to them; this fact will probably account for the absence of bargaining and questions as to how much an article costs, that so surprised the gentleman who noted the absence of questions about the cost of the different articles by those buying at the stores.

Q. Now as to the manner in which you conduct your business and the profits arising therefrom, will you state?

A. Our aim in conducting our business is to make a fair and reasonable profit only on the goods we handle; we do not as a rule, sell some goods below cost as is generally done elsewhere for advertising purposes, and for this reason it is not necessary for us to charge exorbitant prices for any article to make up the loss on goods sold below cost.

Q. It was stated by some of the contestant's witnesses that you charge exorbitantly for boots,—"coin" boots I believe they are called. What are those boots?

A. The boot referred to is a particular make of mining boot, especially adapted to the conditions of work here, and is of the best quality and make, which is evidenced by the fact that orders are received by us from miners who have worked here and gone away; they send for it from points as distant as Idaho and other mining camps. These boots are not kept in San Jose or in agricultural communities, there being no sale for them in such places. They are boots especially adapted for miners' use, where the ground is rocky and wet. They are made very strong, full nailed and of the best quality of material, and are imported for our trade here, as I was never able to find a boot good enough in the general stock of the wholesale houses in San Francisco.

Q. Now is the company in any way interested in these stores?

A. The Quicksilver Mining Company, no.

Q. Are they purchasers from you at all?

A. They purchase to a very limited extent, amounting to an average of about $50 a month, and they pay the same prices as any one else.

Q. A great deal has been said about the boleto system. Do you know how that system came into use, and why it came into use?

A. The boleto system was originated by me for the purpose of simplifying the credit system, which is to a certain extent a necessity in any line of trade, and to enable us to issue these boletos without danger of loss to ourselves, I requested privilege of access to the time-book of the company, and the Manager, thinking that this system would be directly beneficial to the employees granted the request.

Q. Is any employee of the company compelled to take boletos or any amount of them?

A. No, the use of boletos are entirely optional with the employees.

Q. Were you ever present at an election in this precinct, Mr. Derby?

A. Yes, I was here at the election in 1886, and was around the polls occasionally during the day.

Q. While you were there did you see anything that indicated coercion or undue influence and compulsion in the voting of any employees of the company?

A. No, I did not see anything indicating bulldozing, coercion or intimidation of the voters by any one, and I know as a fact that such was not the case.

Q. How was the election conducted, that is among outsiders. Of course I do not refer now to what happened in the room, but on the outside, around the polls?

A. Such electioneering was carried on as is in vogue at all places; some worked for party and some for friends. I myself am a Democrat, and upon my party ticket at the last election were three gentlemen whom I considered possessed of superior qualifications, two of them being personal friends, and in the success of these gentlemen I was particularly interested.

Q. Did you try to influence any one else?

A. I myself scratched some of the tickets, Mr. Bulmore scratched some, and possibly some were scratched by others.

Q. Did these gentlemen receive any higher vote than the general party ticket received in this precinct at that time, do you know?

A. Yes, they did.

Q. To what do you consider that increased vote due?

A. I attribute it to my efforts and the efforts of other friends in their behalf.

Q. Who are the gentlemen that you have spoken of, you have said, there were three, I believe?

A. A. J. Moulder, Mr. Hendricks and W. W. Foote.

Q. On what ticket were they candidates?

A. They were on the Democratic ticket.

Q. You speak of scratching some tickets; what party tickets were those that were scratched?

A. Republican tickets.

Q. Where and how were those tickets scratched?

A. We obtained some Republican tickets the night before election, upon which we wrote these gentlemen's names, and whenever we could get a Republican to vote this ticket we certainly did so.

Q. When you speak of using your influence for these gentlemen among your friends, do I understand from that, that it was among the people in this precinct especially?

A. Yes; more especially my clerks and employees in the stores.

Q. Employees of your own?

A. Yes.

Q. Are these gentlemen connected with The Quicksilver Mining Company?

A. No; no connection whatever with the company.

Q. What are your personal relations with your employees?

A. Very friendly and pleasant.

Q. Did you have any reason to believe that any request of yours upon such a matter as this would receive consideration at their hands?

A. I think that they would oblige me in that respect if it was not against the dictates of their own conscience to do so.

Q. Were there any other tickets advocated by workers around the polls that you know of?

A. I understand that Mr. Lowe worked for the straight Republican ticket, and Mr. Heath worked for the Democratic ticket. Mr. Heath was an employee of the mine.

Q. Were there others besides Mr. Lowe and Mr. Heath ?

A. There were others; some were working for the straight ticket on either side, and others for particular friends on each side; during the day I met some men working for one man and some for another. It is difficult to tell who was working for any particular person, as I paid very little attention to the matter.

Q. Your efforts for these gentlemen on the Democratic ticket, who were friends of yours, were something independent of The Quicksilver Mining Company or its management, if I understand you.

A. Entirely so. I was working and exercising my privilege as a citizen.

Q. Now, did you yourself, in that work you did for these men, attempt anything like coercion of any voters ?

A. No.

Q. Were any tickets given folded to men and they compelled to vote them without knowing their contents ?

A. No; they were handed to them openly and legally.

Q. Were they compelled to vote these tickets?

A. No; not unless they chose to do so. What votes I got were upon the grounds of friendship.

Q. Is the present place of taking testimony, in your opinion, convenient for the witnesses who have been here examined.

A. Yes; very convenient.

Q. Is it more convenient than another place, such as San Jose, for instance, would be ?

A. Yes; it is much more convenient than San Jose, for the reason that it would be more expensive for them to go to San Jose. They would lose time from their labors, and the expenses of travel would far exceed the fees that are allowed them in such cases.

Q. Is the present place of taking testimony open to the public ?

A. Yes; perfectly open and free.

Q. How is this building situated as to the public road ?

A. It is situated right on the public road leading from San Jose to the Hacienda.

Q. In what condition regarding travel is it ?

A. Very fine traveling condition. It is one of the best roads in the county.

Q. And the distance ?

A. The distance is about twelve miles, and can be driven over with a good team in about one hour.

TESTIMONY OF RALPH LOWE.

I am 48 years of age. I was born in Massachusetts. I came to California in 1852. I came to Almaden June 27th, 1865; was employed as clerk in the company's office till April, 1870, then went to the mine as outside foreman till July, 1870; I was away at White Pine, Nevada, and elsewhere till December, 1870, after that was employed as clerk in the store till about August, 1873, when I left the store and was employed by The Quicksilver Mining Company till August or September, 1874, and then assumed charge of the stores as agent of S. F. Butterworth till May, 1875, and remained in the same capacity for Mr. Derby till the latter part of 1876, when Mr. Derby and myself formed a partnership for the purpose of maintaining and carrying on the business of merchandising in New Almaden and are still so engaged.

By Mr. CROSS:

Q. Who owns the stores and store business?

A. Mr. Derby and myself.

Q. Does Mr. Randol or The Quicksilver Mining Company or anybody connected with it, own any interest in these stores?

A. They do not. They belong solely to Mr. Derby and myself.

Q. Have you any business connection with Mr. Randol or with The Quicksilver Mining Company?

A. I have not; Mr. Derby and myself lease the stores at an annual rental from the Board of Directors of The Quicksilver Mining Company in New York.

Q. Who are your principal customers?

A. Our principal customers are the employees of The Quicksilver Mining Company and the farmers about the mine, but principally the employees of the company.

Q. Do you furnish supplies to the officers of the company as well as to the miners and laborers?

A. Yes, we do; we have one price for everybody.

Q. There has been some testimony on the part of the contestant that they do not hear dickering going on in your stores; how do you account for that?

A. We have one price for everything; they often come and ask the price, but as our customers are continuous customers, they generally know the prices of these things that do not fluctuate.

Q. Of course prices in some articles fluctuate here as they do in other places?

A. Fluctuate here as in other places; the most of the trading in the store on the Hill is done with the wives of the employees; we offer no goods as a bid; we do not pretend to sell any goods at cost except it is to sell out old stock and old prints; we make leaders of nothing; we sell at a reasonable profit.

Q. I wish you would state briefly what the boleto system is, and how it is operated.

A. Boletos, so called, are simply orders given to the employees of the company by the store for the purpose of purchasing goods; they are issued to simplify the accounts and to accommodate the miners, as an advance on their wages, prior to pay-day.

Q. I suppose while these orders are issued for goods at the stores, that people who get them do a little dickering with them, don't they?

A. They do sometimes, but they finally all work around to the stores.

Q. Are all the goods at the stores purchased for boletos?

A. No.

Q. Do you make any difference in prices between goods purchased for boletos and those purchased for cash?

A. No difference.

Q. What means have you of ascertaining whether or not it is safe to issue boletos to any given man and what quantity it is safe to issue to him?

A. We have access to the company's books, and then I know the men so well and I am here so long that I advance these for them whenever they want them. I take the word of a great many and of others I do not. I ascertain from the office of the company how much they have coming to them and advance a portion of that to them.

Q. Like any other credit system, there are men that you know that you can trust? .

A. Yes, that I have confidence in and I can trust.

Q. Now then, how do you get your pay for these boletos?

A. The amount I report to the office of the company and it is deducted from the men's pay, if they have it coming to them on pay-day, and we are paid that money.

Q. How is this boleto system any better than the ordinary system of credit?

A. By simplifying the accounts and preventing disputes; if persons have pass books that they bring and a book account, there are often disputes, they don't bring their books sometimes and sometimes that way there would be disputes. Now as these boletos are issued in even amounts, the persons drawing them can better keep an account of them, and consequently we very seldom, if ever, have any disputes, and it pretty near saves the trouble and expense of bookkeeping. A great many of the men, as soon as they get their pay, their money, they send it off to town to invest it, as they have no safe and there are no safes here or any convenient places to deposit it; they do not like to keep the money in the house, and they send it off to the banks or other places; and then draw these boletos as they want them for the purpose of furnishing the supplies for the family during the month.

Q. Have you had occasion to transact business for a good many of the men that are employed by the company?

A. I transact some business for them and advise them about investments and so on. A great many parties advise with me about investments—men that work for the company and others.

Q. Do you know whether there are a great many of them that own stock and have money on deposit in the bank?

A. A good many of them have money in banks and money invested in different kinds of stocks and bonds. The San Jose water stock was a favorite stock with them for a while. San Francisco water stock has always been a favorite with them.

Q. Do you know anything about politics?

A. I have been somewhat engaged in politics off and on since I was about sixteen years of age.

Q. Where did you vote the first time you ever voted?

A. My first vote was cast in San Jose for Stephen A. Douglas for President, and I have voted for every Republican candidate for President since. I have not always voted a straight ticket. Not voted for all Republican candidates, I suppose.

Q. You went to the Republican party at the time so many Democrats did, at the opening of the war, did you?

A. Yes.

Q. Do you ever take any part in politics at the mine?

A. I generally do.

Q. What do you do; explain that matter pretty fully?

A. I am a Republican and I have no excuse to offer for it.

Q. Go right along now and tell us what you do.

A. Generally if the Republican tickets are not sent to me, I try to get hold of some of them, and I take and distribute them around to all the men that I know to be Republicans, that I can find, and I give them the tickets the day before election—that is when I take an interest in the election—and I generally come down here to the polls and stay here most of the day and distribute tickets to outsiders and others who have not got them. The ticket that I give out is generally a straight Republican ticket.

Q. If you could get a Democrat to take a Republican ticket and vote it, would you try?

A. If I should succeed, I would think that I had done well.

Q. Do you ever try to force men to vote?

A. No, I never try to force them, never try to buy a man; I have tried to persuade them, but here at Almaden they do not require much persuasion to vote the Republican ticket.

Q. What are the politics of most of the men?

A. Most of the men are Republicans.

Q. The general party vote here for a good many years has been pretty uniform, has it not?

A. It has been pretty uniform. It has been Republican generally.

Q. Pretty strong Republican, is it not?

A. Generally. Four years ago the precinct went for Governor Stoneman, and he was a Democratic candidate. That year General Stoneman carried the State by an immense majority, and he carried this county by a large majority, although I consider this county a Republican county.

Q. Had there been anything like it in the history of politics generally in this State, so far as you know?

A. I never knew any Governor to be elected by such a large majority, although Governor Irwin had a larger plurality, yet it was not a majority. Never been as large majorities cast for any ticket as there were that year for the Democratic ticket. So that the vote of this precinct was not very remarkable as compared with the vote of this State and county. That year for some reason, those prominent in the Republican party did not take much interest in achieving the success of the party, and I believe that was the reason.

Q. Are you about the polls a great deal on election day?

A. I was at the polls on election day from about nine o'clock in the morning to about four o'clock in the afternoon in Nov., 1886.

Q. What were you doing that day?

A. I was distributing straight Republican tickets.

Q. There has been some testimony given about two men going into Doctor Winn's office with you, adjoining the polling place, and

that afterwards they came out and voted. Will you please to un-
bosom yourself, and tell us what transpired in that room ?

A. No person that I know of ever went in there with me for the
purpose of fixing their tickets. I have no recollection of anything
of that kind occurring. I do not think it did occur because I would
have remembered it if it did.

Q. It would not have been anything strange if you went to his
office with two gentlemen ?

A. No; I probably was there several times during the day.
Doctor Winn was in his office and I went in there and had a talk
with him about the election and talked with others in there, but I
never went in there for the purpose of fixing a ticket or controlling
a vote.

Q. There was some testimony given that you said something in
Spanish to a man here that day. I think the testimony was that
Peter Denning, who was distributing Democratic tickets, stopped a
man to talk to him, and you came along and said something to the
man in Spanish, and the man went off rather hurriedly and voted.
Can you state what it was ?

A. Since my attention has been called to it there was a man by
the name of Manuel Selaya who had secured a ticket at some place. I
had not given it to him. He came along and there were some men
here, I think the Redmonds, wanted him to change his ticket, and I
made some kind of a jocular remark to him.

Q. What was the amount of it ?

A. I told him to tell them that, he would vote that way in the
spring, and he said that he would and passed on, and I suppose he
voted. I don't know.

Q. Was Selaya working for the company ?

A. He was not working for the company; does not work for the
company at all. He is an acquaintance of mine who lives in the
Uvas, about four miles from here. Farmer or woodman.

Q. Did you see the tickets before election day in November,
1886 ?

A. I saw them in the afternoon before election.

Q. Where were they left, do you remember ?

A. The tickets were left at the store on the Hill. I got a lot and
took them, some over to the company's office, some to the Helping
Hand Club, some to the boarding house, some to the saloon on the
Hill, and either brought or sent some down here to the Hacienda,
and put some in the store and left some with Mr. Bulmore, late in
the afternoon of the day previous to the election. I left them at the
places where they would be most likely to be seen and voted. They
were Republican tickets.

Q. Were there any other tickets distributed about the polls on
election day besides Republican tickets ?

A. There were Democratic, Prohibition and American tickets
distributed.

Q. Any difficulty about getting tickets if a man wanted to vote a
Democratic ticket ?

A. No. A great many of the voters on the Hill received American tickets in envelopes through the mail. There was no difficulty

about getting Democratic tickets at the polls that day. There were plenty of them around here.

Q. A Mr. Singletary has given some testimony about his getting some extra votes here. Did you procure him those votes?

A. The way Mr. Singletary succeeded in getting those votes is that there was a man by the name of John Varcoe, who is an acquaintance of most of the miners here on the Hill, and of the same nationality or descent, who came here the night before the election, and on the morning of the election he told me that it would be greatly to his interests if Mr. Singletary would be elected, anyhow it would be greatly to his interests if he could secure him a number of votes here; and he asked me, I do not know why, if I had any objection, and I told him certainly not, to pitch in, and he pitched in here till all the votes were mostly polled of the boys on the Hill, and he succeeded by pleading with them and telling them that it was greatly to his interests to have Mr. Singletary elected, if he could get him a few votes here, so that the boys, out of friendship for him, a great many of them, voted for him. The vote was given as I understand by the boys here, as they told me, because he pleaded with them so and they wanted to help him, as he was a pretty good fellow and they thought, if they could show that he got some votes for Mr. Singletary that it would be an advantage to him.

Q. Might get him a deputyship or something?

A. In fact I asked him the question if he was to be Mr. Singletary's deputy, and he did not answer; gave me an indirect answer, and I told him that anyhow whatever he would do he would have no show, as he himself was a Republican.

Q. Who was distributing Democratic tickets about the polls that day?

A. There was Peter Denning and Frank Heath and quite a number of others had them around, giving them out.

Q. Were you electioneering for any particular candidates on that day?

A. I was electioneering for the Republican ticket.

Q. Were you watching and taking notes of how men voted or that kind of thing?

A. No.

Q. Since Mr. Randol has been Manager of this mine have you ever seen anything like the management of the mine interfering with or trying to dictate to the men about their voting or politics?

A. They never tried to interfere with them politically; they could vote always as they pleased.

TESTIMONY OF ANDREAS E. LOPEZ.

By Mr. Cross:

Q. How old a man are you?

A. Twenty-five.

Q. Where were you born?

A. California, United States.

Q. How long have you lived at Almaden?

7

A. Eighteen years.

Q. What is your business?

A. I am clerk for Derby & Lowe in the New Almaden store, where I have been employed for ten years.

Q. Did you vote in this precinct at the last election?

A. Yes, the Republican ticket.

Q. Did you ever vote anywhere except at Almaden?

A. No, I only voted at New Almaden, twice.

Q. That is all the voting you have done?

A. Yes.

Q. Anybody interfere with your voting in any way, or trying to dictate to you how you should vote?

A. No, I never was controlled on the subject.

Q. Are you of Spanish descent?

A. I am of Mexican descent.

Q. Have you had occasion to become very thoroughly acquainted with the residents of the mine of Mexican and Spanish descent at this place?

A. Yes, I am very well acquainted with most of them. They come to the store to trade and I speak their language, consequently I come into pretty intimate relations with them. By a long residence in the place I am very well acquainted with all of them.

Q. What political party do most of the people of Mexican birth and descent generally vote with?

A. In this country, with very few exceptions, they vote the Republican ticket. There are very few exceptions to that.

Q. Do you understand the reason for that, or why they vote for that party, mostly?

A. One reason of the emigrants to this State, that they vote the Republican ticket, is on account of that being the same as the Liberal party in Mexico, the party in power at present, whose views are very much like the views of the Republican party.

Q. Do you have any occasion to know anything about what number of daily papers or weekly papers the Mexican residents of the mine take?

A. About 100 copies of the weekly papers come in Spanish, besides many monthly papers and pamphlets, and books and so forth, that is, regular periodical literature. Some of that literature is of a political character. The weekly papers are so, especially partisan papers.

Q. Those people of Mexican birth or descent who read, are they pretty well informed on public matters?

A. They are, so far as they understand the political questions of this country, as far as the papers define them.

Q. I suppose, like other people, they are considerably influenced by the papers they read?

A. Yes.

Q. What is the feeling of the people of that nationality towards Mr. Randol and Mr. Jennings, and the managers of the mine, so far as you are familiar with it?

A. So far as I know they think well of them. They are well satisfied with the administration of the affairs of the mine, and feel as

MEXICAN CAMP, FROM MINE HILL.

though they were properly treated by the management. Like in all communities, there are probably one or two grumblers, as they call them, but then they are hardly ever noticed.

Q. How do those people who reside on this mine live as to comfort, compared with the laboring people in other localities, so far as you are informed about it?

A. So far as comfort is concerned, they live as comfortable as in any other community of the same class of laboring people.

Q. Is there any real want amongst the Mexican people here?

A. Not that I know of. They all work and get good wages, and are comfortable, so far as their homes are concerned. Of course they are not of the saving kind; most of them spend their earnings in pleasure from month to month as they receive them. There are but few who save their earnings. There are a very few who own their homes and have stock.

Q. Are there amongst those people quite a number of men who have become worn out with years and labor?

A. Yes, there are some few that were miners.

Q. How are those men provided for?.

A. The Quicksilver Mining Company see that they are well treated and provided with work, or in many cases they are provided for by the Miners' Fund. Those who are able to do something get an easy job at light wages. Those who have been here many years and worn themselves out in the service of the company, are well treated and furnished with easy work, others draw on the Miners' Fund for their support.

Q. Are there a good many of those people who do not speak the English language very well?

A. Yes, a good many hardly understand it.

Q. Those people are probably not as well informed about American politics as men who can speak the English language?

A. They are not well informed so far as reading the political questions is concerned; but they get their ideas from others who do, coming in contact with others.

Q. Since Mr. Randol has been here have you seen any coercion or intimidation or pressure put upon those people as to how they should vote?

A. Not that I know of. I have never seen anything of the kind.

Q. So far as you know are those people perfectly free to vote whatever ticket or for whatever candidates they choose?

A. They are.

Q. Do you know anything about the Miners' Fund—you understand it, do you?

A. Yes. The people of Mexican birth and descent generally regard that fund here at the mine, so far as I know, as a very good thing for them.

Q. Do most of those people work on contract or day's pay?

A. Most of them on contract.

Q. What department of mining do they generally prefer to work on, what are they the best at, what do they make the best wages at?

A. They prefer contract labor, they make better wages at contract.

Q. Does the store management have one price which they charge to all persons who buy, or do they charge different men different prices?

A. One price for all goods, one marked price, and they adhere to that price. There is no difference in price whether the goods are bought for coin or boletos.

Q. What would you say of the general quality of the goods bought and sold at the stores?

A. They keep the best quality of goods to suit the miners. The miners are very particular as to the quality; they won't buy anything that is inferior. They are more particular about the quality than they are about prices.

Q. Have you ever seen the tickets about the stores on election days?

A. I have.

Q. Are there tickets of different parties at the stores on election days?

A. There are always enough tickets at the stores to supply everybody of both parties; tickets enough for everybody of all kinds.

TESTIMONY OF J. J. MILLER.

I am clerk in the store; my first vote was for Hayes; I first voted for Hayes and Wheeler, and voted the Republican ticket ever since, but sometimes scratch my ticket; think I have as good a right to electioneer as a man sent here by Mr. Sullivan on election day, who never lived here; tickets of all parties were liberally distributed here on election day; I distributed straight Republican tickets; I was at the meeting of the miners when Dennis Kearney tried to have the vote of the Almaden precinct thrown out and the miners were very indignant at the threat of having the vote thrown out; there has been no searching of wagons that come to the mine for many years; Mr. Randol paid one-half the cost of building the Catholic Church; Mr. Murphy got his large vote on account of personal popularity, Mr. Foote for his anti-monopoly record, Mr. Coombe for his nationality, from the Cornish voters.

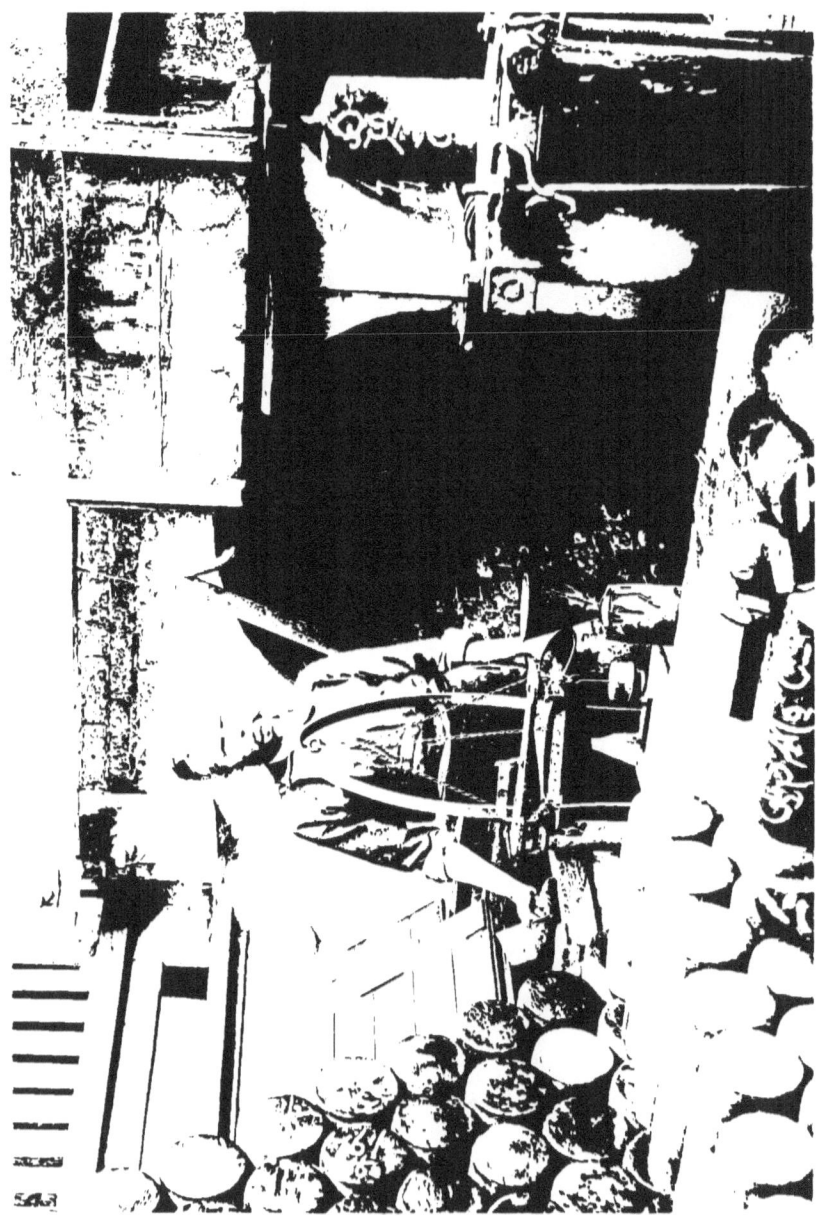

WEIGHING AND FLASKING QUICKSILVER, HACIENDA.

TESTIMONY OF HENRY TREGONING.

By Mr. Cross:

Q. What is your age ?

A. 38.

Q. Where do you reside ?

A. New Almaden.

Q. What is your occupation ?

A. I am watchman and weigher.

Q. Where were you born ?

A. I was born in Wales.

Q. When did you come to the United States ?

A. About 17½ years ago.

Q. How long have you been at the New Almaden ?

A. About 17½ years. I was away a short interval but came right back again in a few months.

Q. Who was the first President that you voted for ?

A. I think Garfield was the first.

Q. What ticket do you generally vote ?

A. The Republican ticket.

Q. Scratch it sometimes ?

A. The national ticket I vote is a straight Republican ticket.

Q. On the local ticket you sometimes do a little scratching ?

A. I always do; yes.

Q. You think that is your privilege ?

A. Yes.

Q. Think that Mr. Sullivan has got any particular right to object to your doing that?

A. No; I do not recognize any such right.

Q. Have you generally voted since you have been at New Almaden from the Garfield election on ?

A. Yes; always.

Q. Anything ever been done here at the mine to intimidate or coerce or unduly influence your vote ?

A. No, no one has ever asked me how I was going to vote.

Q. Have you ever seen anything done here at elections with reference to politics for the purpose of intimidating or coercing, or unduly influencing the vote of any employee of the company ?

A. No, I have not.

Q. What salary do you receive as watchman, Mr. Tregoning ?

A. Eighty-five dollars per month.

Q. What other positions have you filled here besides watchman?

A. I worked about seven years as a miner in the mines underground, under the contract system, and I worked nearly five years as engineer, and kept a hotel here for about three years at the Hacienda, a boarding house, and for a short time I had charge of some men on the Hill, on the surface.

Q. Were you residing here at the time that Mr. Dennis Kearney, the agitator, and others made an effort to have the vote of Almaden precinct thrown out?

A. Yes.

Q. Were you present at a meeting held on the Hill in regard to that matter?

A. I was.

Q. State what transpired at that meeting?

A. I think, as near as I can remember, there was a mass meeting called at short notice, and at that meeting I think Mr. Randol and most of the officials of the mine were present, and the object of the meeting was stated, and the charges that had been preferred against the place, and I remember very distinctly that some not very pleasant things had been said that reflected very much upon the dignity of the citizens here, and the place generally. I remember that I was called by the meeting, not by the officials, but by the men to address the meeting, and I think I did so without let or hindrance, and said all I could upon the subject, and I took the opportunity to throw the indignities back into the face of those who had given them, very freely, and I regarded it as an insult myself, and the community generally regarded it as such, so much so that at the meeting I think they were ready to have shown battle if there was necessity for it—they felt as though they were insulted.

Q. How did the common laboring men then upon the mine, those who were working on contract and for wages, feel about the charges that were made against them?

A. They felt very indignant.

Q. How did they feel about having the vote thrown out?

A. Perhaps they would have to submit to it. I don't think they would like to submit to such a thing.

Q. Felt as though it would be a great wrong?

A. Yes, certainly.

Q. Was there anything said at that meeting as to how men should testify that were going to be taken to San Jose?

A. No.

Q. Any intimation as to how they were expected to testify, or what they were wanted to swear to, or anything of that sort?

A. No, nothing at all. They were only advised by the officials, I do not remember whether it was Mr. Randol or not, but somebody told them: that they were at liberty to go to San Jose, and that they were expected to testify to the truth as they had found it; I know I counseled the men myself in regard to how they ought to conduct themselves there, that the eyes of the State were upon them and it was quite a critical time in the history of Almaden; and they would be brought before the public notice very much, on that day.

Q. You were mining at that time amongst the miners were you?

A. Yes, I think I was working on contracts at that time.

Q. And the men there called you out to express yourself?

A. Yes; at that meeting.

Q. Do you remember who presided at that meeting?

A. No; I do not.

Q. Had there been some serious charges made in some paper?

A. I think there had.

Q. Do you know what paper it was?

A. I do not remember what paper.

Q. Was that charge read at that meeting?

A. I do not remember?

Q. What was the result of that investigation at San Jose; was the precinct thrown out or not?

A. No; the charges were found to be groundless.

Q. Have you been about the polls considerable on election day since you have been here?

A. Yes.

Q. You reside near the polls?

A. Yes; I have been around here, in fact, nearly ever since I have been voting; I have been on the Board of Election.

Q. Do you know a large share of the people that work here on the mine?

A. I know all that have been here in the last sixteen years, with the exception of a few new hands that are here now. I have had the opportunity of being pretty well acquainted with them.

Q. Working right amongst them?

A. Yes.

Q. And at different places on the mine?

A. And in every way, too.

Q. Have you had an opportunity to become informed as to what party most of the men working on the mine belong to?

A. I judge from what I know of them that they affiliate with the Republican party; practically, all of them; especially the Englishmen; 99 per cent of all the Englishmen vote the Republican ticket from choice; that is their natural bent.

Q. How is it among the population of Spanish descent?

A. I think they are inclined to that party.

Q. Have you ever seen anything here, at election, either before or after, or at any other time tending to show that the men employed by the company, do not exercise the elective franchise with the fullest freedom?

A. No; they ought to do it. I have had the same privilege and no more privilege than they have; and I have always done it without any interference at all.

Q. Have you ever seen anything tending to indicate that a man's politics or how he voted had anything to do with, whether he could work at the mine or whether he was retained at the mine?

A. No.

Q. Ever seen anything tending to show that it affected a man's chance of preferment at all?

A. No; in fact, many Democrats I have known here seemed to have preferences that Republicans have not had.

Q. They have held good positions in the company, have they?

A. Yes; almost without exception, perhaps.

Q. They have been a pretty good class of Democrats?

A. I was going to say that nearly all the officials we have had, have been Democrats.

Q. Mr. Jennings was a Democrat when he came here, was he not?

A. Yes.

Q. Do you rent a house from the company?

A. I do; I pay $5 a month; we have four rooms in the house, and a barn, yard and flower garden attached; water is pure and plenty; it is supplied right at the house, flowing water.

Q. What do you pay for that?

A. Nothing; that is included in the rent.

Q. Having been associated with miners all the time, working in different capacities, underground and on the surface, what would you have to say as to how the miners feel toward Mr. Randol?

A. I think they feel very respectful towards him.

Q. Ever seen anything tending to show that they did not feel kindly towards him?

A. No; I think they have had every reason to feel respectful.

Q. You say you kept the boarding house at one time?

A. Yes.

Q. How were the men provided for, the board at the boarding house?

A. They were well provided for; well fed and well housed; they were then, and I am satisfied they are now.

Q. The teachers and others board at these boarding houses as well as the employees of the company?

A. Yes; the public school teachers.

TESTIMONY OF JOHN DUNSTAN.

By Mr. CROSS,

Q. What is your age?

A. Fifty-two years.

Q. Where were you born?

A. I was born in England, in the County of Cornwall.

Q. When did you come to the United States?

A. In 1849.

Q. When did you come to the New Almaden mine?

A. I came to New Almaden in 1869; have been here ever since except four months.

Q. Where did you vote the first time that you ever voted?

A. I voted in Wisconsin for John C. Fremont.

Q. What ticket did you vote?

A. Republican. He was a Republican.

Q. What ticket have you generally voted since that?

A. Republican ticket.

Q. Did you vote here last November?

A. I did; a Republican ticket.

MINERS' COTTAGES.

Q. Since Mr. Randol came here to be manager, has Mr. Randol or the Superintendent, or any of the captains or foremen or bosses ever tried to dictate to you how you should vote ?

A. No.

Q. Since Mr. Randol has been manager have you ever heard any talk amongst the men that they had to vote the way the owners of the mine wanted them to, or they were liable not to get work ?

A. No.

Q. Have you ever known of any officers of the mine interfere in any way with a man's voting just as he chose ?

A. No.

Q. What other places have you voted in besides New Almaden, Mr. Dunstan ?

A. I voted in the States of Michigan and Wisconsin.

Q. Did you ever see anything tending to show that men here at the Almaden, since Mr. Randol has been manager, did not vote just as freely and for their own choice, as they did in other places where you have seen men vote ?

A. I did not.

Q. From what you have seen of men in the United States who were born in Cornwall, how do they generally vote ?

A. They are generally Republicans so far as I have seen them.

TESTIMONY OF CHARLES BERRYMAN.

Q. What is your age, Mr. Berryman ?

A. Forty-five years.

Q. When did you come to the United States ?

A. 1 came here in 1857.

Q. How long have you been here at the New Almaden mine ?

A. Five years. I wish that I were here longer.

Q. Did you ever vote before you came to New Almaden ?

A. Yes; at Lake Superior, in the copper mines country.

Q. Can you remember what the first ticket was you voted ?

A. It was the Democratic ticket.

Q. What ticket have you voted ever since ?

A. Democratic.

Q. Voted the Democratic ever since you have been on this mine ?

A. Yes.

Q. Did anybody ever try to interfere with the way you voted ?

A. No.

Q. Did the Manager or any Superintendent, captain, boss or foreman try to tell you how you should vote ?

A. Never.

Q. Could you ever see that it made any difference in the work you got by being a Democrat ?

A. Not a bit of difference.

Q. Can you see any difference in the freedom of the men here about voting, to the other places where you saw them vote ?

A. Not a bit.

Q. Ever see anything done to show that a man could not vote just as he had a mind to, here?

A. I never did in all my coming down here; I came down here two or three times, and always had my ticket; voted and went home again.

Q. Did you vote last November?

A. I did.

Q. Did you see any of the officers of the company interfering with the men about voting?

A. Neither one.

Q. Where were you born?

A. In England, in Cornwall.

Q. So far as you have been acquainted with men here and in other mines where you have worked how do the men from Cornwall mostly vote in the United States?

A. I believe mostly Republican.

Q. Did you vote for Mr. Sullivan last fall?

A. I did, I'm sorry for it too.

Q. Did you ride down in the stage or walk down?

A. I rode down but I walked up though, they left before I was ready.

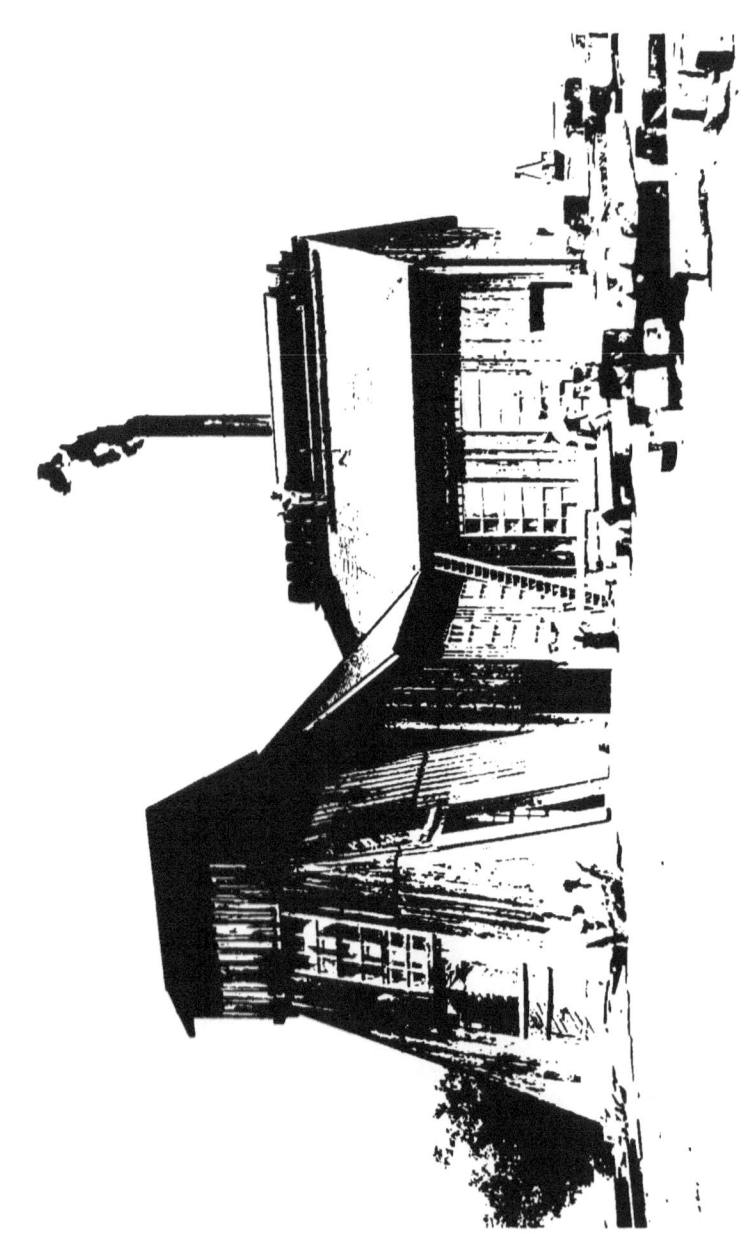

Voters residing in the Almaden precinct were examined as follows:

John Rowe, John Trevarron, Abraham Harris, Thomas Tregoning, James Johns, J. N. Williams, Thomas Prior, Bennett Perry, John Kemp, Thomas Mathews, William Mitchell, William T. Williams, James P. Craze and James Tarcoe, natives of county Cornwall, England, all vote the Republican ticket except one. C. H. James, Nicholas J. Jeffrey, Charles E. Robins and George Stacy, natives of Devonshire, England, and Jacinto Valenzuela, Antonio Vinagu and Juan Hernandez, natives of Mexico, all voted the Republican ticket except two, one of whom did not know what ticket he voted, as he could not read it. Ramon Castro, Emile Victor, Gabriel Norona, Abelino Padillo, Alexander Hernandez, Ricardo Norona, Antonio Sucero, Abraham Martinez, Jesus Barrios, Julio Rios, William Gray, Martin Rios, Miguel Meza, David E. Bohlman, Marcelino Soto and Benito Miramonte, natives of California, and F. A. Dulion, a native of Minnesota, all voted the Republican ticket except two. Two Republicans had voted the Democratic ticket previous to the war. Many of them testified that they scratched their tickets, when they liked the reputation of a man on the other ticket.

Of the above 39 there were 26 who cast their first vote at Almaden, 7 who had cast their first vote at other places in California, and 6 who first voted outside of the State, not one had changed his politics or party alliance since coming to Almaden.

All testified most unequivocally that neither the company nor anyone identified with its management, ever interfered in the politics of the employees or even mentioned them; That the men voted with entire freedom from any influence whatever on the part of the mine management.

Bertrand Tincourt, a native of France, William Ham, Charles E. Pearce and John B. Johns, natives of Cornwall; William James, a native of Devonshire, England, Mathew Dulion, native of Minnesota, Aman Espinoza, Timothy Cooney, Stonewall Jackson Bailey, H. R. Vincent, Manuel Selaya, Benjamin Oswald, Juan Shanave, and C. P. Miramonte, natives of California, D. F. McComas and H. H. Kooser, natives of Pennsylvania, all except two vote the Republican ticket and always have, some vote it straight and some scratch a good deal.

Their testimony was that the management of the mine never interfered or attempted to interfere with their votes in any way. Politics have never been mentioned by any of the officers of the company, and is not considered in the employing or retaining of men.

William Dodge, Charles Harris, William Gilbert, H. H. Reed, William Edward Pierce, James Smith, John Roberts, William Tonkin, Samuel Hocking, William Williams, Joel Wasby, Joseph P. Toy, Peter Barrett, William Drew, William Henry Tonkin, Charles Tonkin, John Reseigh, John Andrews, William Curnow, Thomas Drew, William Eslick, John Job, John Prout, John Hill, Sr., were all born in County of Cornwall, England. John H. Bohlman was born at sea, Amos Poppleworth was born in Yorkshire, England. Antonio Solis, Eufemia Cassus, Theodore Lopez, Francisco Anedondo, Miguel Villegrana, Alisandrio Castro, Antonio Soto, Lazar Castro, Stanislaus Rodriguez, Ramon Herrera, Josia Maria Maltos, Juan L. Hernandez, were all born in Mexico. Samuel Terrill and Domingo Lion were born in South America. Nash Smoot, Lorenza Herrera, Frank Narone, David Villela, Rosario Santobanos, Jacinto Garcia, Eulojia Leal, Thos. Drew and Nicholas Gray were born in California. Of these, all the English born voted the Republican ticket. All the Mexican born voted the Republican ticket, but one, who has worked for the company many years and always voted the Democratic ticket. Forty-five vote the Republican ticket, some with scratches. Three vote the Democratic ticket. One votes sometimes the Republican and sometimes the Democratic ticket. One cannot remember how he votes. One declines to answer how he voted in 1886. Two had voted Democratic once in Nevada when James G. Fair was a candidate for the United States Senate. Thirty-five cast their first vote at New Almaden. Nine cast their first vote outside of Almaden, but in California. Seven cast their vote outside of California. Only one had changed his politics since coming to Almaden.

All testified that since Mr. Randol became manager in 1870, that neither Mr. Randol or any superintendent, captain, foreman, boss or other officer of the company had said anything to them about voting, or how they should vote. That politics or voting had nothing to do with getting work. That there were plenty of tickets of all kinds on election day. That every man votes according to his own free will and choice entirely. Those who had voted in other places testified that the voting here is as free as anywhere and as free as it possibly could be. That there has been no searching of wagons or exclusion of goods for many years. That the boleto system is merely a means by which men can draw a portion of their wages before pay day, and that it is entirely optional with each man whether he draws them or not.

James Williams, Thomas P. Williams and John L. Martin, natives of Cornwall, England; Joseph Henwood, a native of Devonshire, England; Francis Lopez and Adolph Martinez, natives of Mexico; Neil Anderson, a native of Germany; A. D. Malone, a native of Illinois; and Emile Cantua, M. J. Blake, Lucas Patron, Fluencio Cantua, C. J. Costa, James A. Costa, Eugene Baric, Ignacio Cepida, Marcelino Mercado and Estevan Marujo, natives of California. Of these fourteen vote the Republican ticket, three vote the Democratic ticket and one does not know what ticket he votes.

All swear in the strongest language that no manager, superintendent, captain, foreman, boss or other officer of the company has ever had any-

WASHINGTON SHAFT.

thing to say to them about politics since Mr. Randol became Manager of the mine in 1870; that they vote their own free will and choice without any interference whatever by any one connected with the company.

Wilford France, Joseph Bastian, John Bartle, William Floyd, all natives of Cornwall, and Felipe Dorami, Pio Supez, Juan Ortega, Andreas Lopez, natives of Mexico, and Ricardo Tavilo, Luciano Rodriguez, Iguacio Castro and Feliciano Martinez, born in California. All of these voted the Republican ticket at New Almaden in 1886. Six of these cast their first vote at Almaden, and the others had all voted before they came to New Almaden, voting with the same party with which they voted before they came to Almaden.

They all testify that since Mr. Randol took charge, neither Mr. Randol nor any superintendent, captain, foreman, boss or other officer of the company ever mentioned the subject of politics or voting. That all kinds of tickets were plenty on election day last November. That some of the tickets were scratched and some were not, some voted one kind and some another.

John Geach, John Burgess, William Bunney, T. B. Carter, all natives of Cornwall; John H. Bishop, a native of Devonshire, Pedro Carriaga, Ysidro Castro, Jose Ante, Nabor Angulo and Miguel Campos, natives of Mexico, and Alvinza Barraza, Innocencio Campos, Reyes Barazzu, Antonio Bernal and Jose Barros, a native of New Mexico, were examined.

One of these voted the Prohibition ticket. All the rest voted the Republican ticket. Nearly all of them had voted the Republican ticket before they came here, in various places from Lake Superior to San Diego. Two testified that before Mr. Randol took charge of the mine, Dr. Mayo told them they must vote the Democratic ticket or leave the mine.

All testified that since Mr. Randol took charge of the mine that there had been no interference with politics by the company. That the subject of voting or politics or how they ought to vote had never been mentioned to any of them by Mr. Randol, or any superintendent, or captain, or foreman, or boss, or other officer of the company; that they were left perfectly free to vote as they chose. That there were always plenty of tickets of all kinds about on election day and that they voted according to their principles.

John Hill, Jr., John George, natives of Cornwall, England, and Alberto Garcia, a native of California, employees of the company, testified that they had always voted the Republican ticket, *that nothing was ever done by any one connected with The Quicksilver Mining Company to influence their votes.*

The Cornish boys testified that in the mines where they had worked, in Illinois, Wisconsin, Lake Superior, Nevada and California, the Cornish people vote the Republican ticket almost without exception.

The Mexicans mostly testified that they vote the Republican ticket because Mexico is a Republic, but a few said that the Liberal party in Mexico is like the Republican party in the United States, and so they voted with the party representing those principles in both countries.

Every man who voted in the precinct is being called as a witness, and not a single witness has been found, whether in the employ of the mining company or not, but that swears that he has always voted entirely free of any influence whatever on the part of the mine management, for the last seventeen years.

George Carson, *Postmaster* at New Almaden, testified as follows: There are 179 daily papers taken on the mine, being 55 San Francisco *Chronicles*, 33 San Francisco *Calls*, 10 San Francisco *Examiners*, 30 San Jose *News*, 40 San Jose *Mercurys* and 11 San Jose *Times*, besides a very large number of weekly and monthly journals and magazines; that he had compared the poll list of last election with the pay roll of The Quicksilver Mining Company, and that every employee of the company that voted at the election in November, 1886, had been examined as a witness, who is in reach and able to attend; that he was the party who furnished Mr. Kenna (a witness for contestant) the signature of R. R. Bulmore; that he did so openly, and enjoined no secrecy upon Kenna; that he voted and worked openly for Mr. Sullivan's election and for the Democratic ticket; that he had written Mr. Bowden before election that he would do all he could for Mr. Sullivan; that his time was so much occupied that his hands were tied. He wrote Mr. Bowden that Almaden was a very strong Republican precinct, and that he could therefore do very little good for him. He thinks he was the means of securing Mr. Sullivan the extra votes that he received at New Almaden.

Miss Florence Gay gave testimony concerning the Hacienda School.

Nash Smoot and Nels Anderson testified that they, in company with Mr. E. S. Gillan, had scoured the country and served a subpoena, to appear and testify, upon every man they could find who had voted at Almaden in 1886.

HACIENDA SCHOOL.

TESTIMONY OF DAVID E. SKINNER.

I reside about three miles below here, Almaden precinct. I was born in New Jersey; I came to California in 1852; resided in this precinct thirty years; have been in the habit during that time of voting in this precinct; I vote the Republican ticket; I voted in this precinct at the general election in November, 1886; I spent that day in the vicinity of the polls, perhaps half a day; I saw various parties distributing tickets about the polls on that day—Democratic tickets and Republican tickets.

By Mr. Cross:

Q. Did you observe anything on that day indicating that any of the officers or persons in charge of The Quicksilver Mining Company's business were doing anything to coerce, intimidate or unduly influence the votes of the employees of the company?

A. No, not at all.

Q. Have you observed anything indicating that the employees of the company voting in this precinct at the last election, and say for ten years past, were not voting their own free will and choice?

A. No.

Q. What is your businees?

A. I am a farmer, and have 170 acres.

Q. Have you observed anything in the conduct of Mr. Randol or Mr. Jennings since they have been here indicating that they were disposed to coerce the votes of their employees?

A. No, I have not.

Q. As far as you have been able to observe do the voters of this precinct who are in the employ of The Quicksilver Mining Company, vote as freely as they do in any other place where you have observed elections?

A. So far as I know they do.

TESTIMONY OF JOHN H. DUNN.

I am sixty-two years old; I am a farmer; I reside two miles from the polling place in New Almaden precinct; I own 300 acres; I have resided in New Almaden voting precinct since 1864, and during that time I have been in the habit of voting regularly at general elections except three or four years; I voted in the mountains first, in the gold mines; I have no connection with The Quicksilver Mining Company;

I have been in the habit of voting quite regularly at the general elections and voted here in November, 1886; I vote the Democratic ticket; I saw them distribute tickets all over; Democratic tickets and Republican tickets were being distributed; I got my ticket at the store, here in the vicinity of the polls; I got it from Mr. Richmond, one of the employees in the store.

By Mr. Cross:

Q. Did you on election day of November, 1886, observe anything that looked as though the officers or management of The Quicksilver Mining Company were trying to intimidate or coerce or control the vote of its employees?

A. No, I didn't.

Q. Have you, for a number of years past, say ten years, observed anything of that kind at elections here?

A. No.

Q. Have you, during that time, seen anything tending to show that the employees of the company in this precinct did not vote freely and voluntarily of their own choice at elections?

A. They all did, for anything that I know of; they voted freely and voluntarily; and their own choice; I have worked in the mine myself in the summer time and always had my free will and vote; I worked here at the mine about six or seven years during Mr. Randol's administration.

Q. During the time that you say you were in the employ of The Quicksilver Mining Company was anything done to interfere with your vote?

A. I never did see it. I never knew a man to speak of it.

Q. Did you during that time observe that a man getting employment or favors from the company in any way depended upon his politics or how he voted?

A. No, I did not.

Q. Is it your judgment that the voters of this precinct, employed by The Quicksilver Mining Company, vote as freely as other men whom you have seen vote?

A. They vote as freely as they did in the mountains when I voted there, for anything that I know. I was there eleven years.

Q. You were called as a witness for the contestant in San Jose, were you not?

A. Yes.

Q. And testified?

A. Yes.

TESTIMONY OF CHARLES CRANZ.

I am 70 years old; I was born in Germany; I came to the United States in 1834, and came to California in 1882; I reside about three miles and a half from New Almaden; I have been a voter since 1840; I voted in Ohio before coming to California; I generally vote the Republican ticket; I am a farmer; I own my own farm; it contains 103 acres; I voted in this precinct in November, 1886, and before that.

By Mr. Cross:

Q. Do you know whether there were tickets of the different parties being distributed?

A. Yes; I saw one man distributing Democratic and another Republican tickets.

Q. Since you have been a voter in this precinct have you observed anything as though the manager of The Quicksilver Mining Company was bulldozing or coercing or trying to control the votes of its employees?

A. I have not.

Q. So far as you have observed did the employees of the company voting at this precinct vote just as freely as any other place where you have seen elections?

A. Yes; they did so far as I saw.

TESTIMONY OF R. J. BAKER.

I am 52 years old. I was born in Virginia. I came to California in 1859. I have resided in the New Almaden voting precinct ever since 1859. I have been in the habit of voting at general elections; except I have been away about eleven years, when I moved down to Hollister. I generally vote Democratic. I voted in this precinct at the election in 1886.

By Mr. Cross:

Q. Did you on that day see anything tending to indicate that the management of The Quicksilver Mining Company was bulldozing, intimidating or coercing or trying to control the vote of its employees?

A. I did not.

Q. Have you seen anything here since Mr. Randol has been Manager, tending to indicate that the employees of The Quicksilver Mining Company do not vote for such ticket and such men as they individually choose to vote for?

A. No. I am a farmer and reside three miles from the polling place in New Almaden precinct. I farm my own land, about 300 acres. I gave testimony on the other side of this case at San Jose.

TESTIMONY OF GEORGE BOSE.

I am 62 years old; was born in Germany; I have been in the United States since 1844; I have lived in New Almaden precinct a little over 30 years. I have voted in San Jose and Guadalupe; I voted in this precinct last November; I was in the vicinity of the polls that day; all day, that is from 9 till 5 I think; I saw tickets of the different parties being distributed about the place; I did so, myself, a good deal; I seldom ever vote a straight ticket, but generally Republican; I vote the Republican ticket but scratch whenever it suits me.

8

By Mr. Cross:

Q. Did you see anything on election day last November, as though the management of The Quicksilver Mining Company was bulldozing, coercing, intimidating or trying to control the votes of the men who worked for the company?

A. Nothing that I have seen. I saw one of the employees was very prominent here, that is I was informed so. I asked parties here who was the man that was distributing Democratic tickets. He told me he was an employee of the mine on the Hill, he was running an engine there. He was a small man. I did not ask his name; they told me he was engineer on the Hill—a mining engineer there. He seemed to be very officious, distributing Democratic tickets. He had lots of them. I got some from him myself; I ran out once.

Q. Did you see anything else that looked as though the management of the company was trying to force the vote of the precinct?

A. No, I never did—that is something I never have seen in California.

Q. So far as you could observe, what would be your judgment as to the freedom with which men voted in this precinct?

A. I saw that everbody got his ticket and went about his business and voted without any interference as far as I could see; I never saw anyone urging the matter. I generally tend to my own business and I think that other people are allowed the same privilege.

Q. Did you give evidence in San Jose, called as a witness on the other side of this case?

A. I did. I am a farmer; I reside about four miles from the polls on my own farm of 516 acres.

TESTIMONY OF JOHN COONEY.

I am 67 next July. I was born in Ireland. I came to California in 1850; have been living in the New Almaden voting precinct about twenty years, since I commenced voting up here. I am a farmer and own my own farm. I believe I have about 170 acres where I live, and I have 100 acres in another farm. The first vote I cast was in 1844, in Illinois. I will tell you who I voted for then. It was Judge Hoge here in San Francisco—the first man that I voted for—Joe Hoge, in Galena. I voted the Democratic ticket until the time that Blaine ran. I voted the Republican ticket then and since. If there is a man on the Democratic ticket that pleases me and if I like him, I vote for him. I know Mr. Randol ever since he came here.

By Mr. Cross:

Q. Have you observed Mr. Randol's conduct towards the men in the employ of The Quicksilver Mining Company?

A. Yes.

Q. What is his conduct?

A. Very good. I never saw a better man, in fact he cannot be beat. I voted in this precinct in November, 1886. I was in the vicinity of the polls till from about 9 or 10 o'clock until pretty near

BIRD'S-EYE VIEW OF RANDOL PLANILLA AND BUENA VISTA SHAFT.

the time the polls closed. Always different kinds of tickets being distributed in the vicinity of the polls. No difficulty about a man getting any kind of a ticket he wanted.

Q. Did you see anything as though the management of the company was trying to intimidate or coerce or control the vote of the men that worked for the company?

A. They did not; to my knowledge.

Q. You did not see anything of that kind?

A. Never.

Q. During the time that Mr. Randol has been manager of the mine have you seen anything like the mine management trying to control the vote of their employees?

A. Not since Mr. Randol came here. It is better than it ever was before, I never saw a better man, he never interfered.

Q. As far as you could judge from what you knew and saw since Mr. Randol has been here have the voters of this precinct voted for such ticket and such men as they chose freely and voluntarily?

A. Certainly.

Q. Do you know P. C. Moore?

A. I know him well; I know him first-rate; he peddled here for many a long year, and here he made all his money. I think he was a poor man when he came to peddle up here on this mine; he made it all here.

Q. What would you say as to the men that work here for the company as to how they get along and prosper if they attend to their duties, as compared with other men that labor for wages?

A. Get along better here than in any place I ever saw mining, and I have mined in several places. I never saw a mine so well conducted. Every man is pretty well looked after and pretty well off here.

TESTIMONY OF CHARLES PARR.

By Mr. MOORE:

Q. Where do you live?

A. I live about three miles from the Almaden, on what is called the Llagas road.

Q. What is your business?

A. Stock-raiser and farming generally.

Q. How large a farm have you?

A. Between 1,200 and 1,400 acres there where I reside. I own other property outside of it.

Q. How long have you resided and voted in this precinct?

A. Permanently from the last time that I came, about twenty-four years. I have been voting for twenty years at the Hacienda. I do not know of any election that I have not been here, and then I am a frequent visitor outside of the day of election. I do a good deal of my trading, here and I am here two or three times a week, and sometimes every day in the week.

Q. During elections that you have attended since Mr. Randol has been manager of the mine, have you seen anything on the part of

Mr. Randol, Mr. Jennings or of any of the officers of the mine that would indicate an attempt to coerce or unduly influence the voters of this precinct?

A. There never has been a particle to my knowledge.

Q. Have you been around the polls on election days?

A. Certainly I have been there, and if it had been practiced I should certainly have seen it.

Q. What is your opinion then as to the freedom that the employees of this mine have in exercising the elective franchise?

A. I think that a man exercises his own judgment—is free to exercise his own judgment in every respect.

Q. Do you see the miners when they are voting on election days?

A. Of course I see them every election.

Q. Are they free to vote as they please?

A. Free to vote just as they have a mind to.

Q. Have you seen the tickets of the different parties distributed during election day?

A. Yes; I have seen tickets of all the parties, and there has always been more or less people here with tickets electioneering on behalf of each party. Every election all tickets are on the counter in the store, where one could help oneself; they are plentiful; there always have been local electioneers on behalf of the Democracy.

Q. Are those men free, and have they always been so in approaching the electors of the district, whether they were employees or outsiders?

A. They have perfect freedom; there has been coercion practiced here, but not under this administration. I have known every administration since 1846 in Almaden, and with one exception there never was any coercion practiced here; it was practiced under Doctor Mayo.

Q. During his time?

A. Yes; during his time; they practiced it to perfection, too.

Q. Was the coercion of the men at that time observable?

A. Certainly it was.

Q. Has there been any practiced since Mr. Randol came to the mine?

A. Not a particle; he wiped it all out when he came.

Q. What are the nationalities chiefly employed?

A. Principally Spanish and English.

Q. What are the politics of the Cornishmen generally?

A. They are Republicans; a Democrat is almost an exception.

Q. How is it with the Mexicans?

A. The Mexicans are Republicans with a few exceptions.

Q. How is Mr. Randol regarded by the employees of the mine?

A. He is liked very well, very well indeed; they speak very well of him; sometimes they may have some little misunderstanding, for instance, with the Superintendent, or they may not understand things, and they go just to J. B. Randol to rectify such matters: they go to him when it is anything of serious import; if they can get to "J. B." they come away perfectly satisfied.

Q. You trade here to some extent at the store?

A. Yes, I do a good deal of my trading here at the store.

Q. What is the state of the laboring man here compared with what it is in other places ?

A. I think that it is better, it is better in every respect; the Hacienda you would not consider a mining camp; it is much more like an agricultural town; everything is neat and always well kept; they have neat cottages and they wear the best of clothing; vines and flowers clambering over everything, and they have a stream of pure running water; I do not think there is a town within my knowledge that can boast of anything to equal it—running into the houses and running by the doors.

Q. Is the condition of the men employed by the company better or worse under Mr. Randol's administration than it was before?

A. It is better.

Q. Formerly what was the moral condition of the place ?

A. It was very bad.

Q. Has that improved ?

A. That has improved a great deal. There were formerly quite a number of saloons; gambling and prostitution were both practiced, that has been done away with as far as I can see; anything like lawlessness is discouraged by the present manager.

Q. Does this doing away of the gambling houses and drinking saloons have any tendency to cause the employees to save their money to a greater extent than formerly ?

A. That certainly does, it is simply to benefit them that all this has been done away with so far as I can judge; it has worked to their benefit without a doubt.

TESTIMONY OF CHRISTIAN DANNEMANN.

By Mr. MOORE:

Q. Where do you live ?

A. I live on the Llagas creek, in this precinct, Almaden precinct.

Q. How old are you ?

A. I am 58 years old next August.

Q. How long have you been in this precinct ?

A. Since April, 1860.

Q. Have you been a voter here ?

A. Yes, I have voted except when I was off in military service. I was off during the rebellion.

Q. During the time that you have voted at Almaden, since Mr. Randol has been in charge, have you seen anything on the part of the management to indicate that the miners or those employed by the company were forced or coerced to vote any particular way ?

A. No.

Q. You are around the polls when you come to vote ?

A. Always around when the time comes to vote my regular ticket and I vote it.

Q. Have you seen a great deal of voting here ?

A. Oh, yes, I have seen a great deal of voting here.

Q. If there was anything like bulldozing or coercion you would probably have seen it ?

A. I certainly would.

Q. What ticket do you vote?

A. I have voted all my life the straight Democratic ticket.

Q. Have you any difficulty in getting your ticket, your Democratic ballot to vote?

A. I never had any difficulty in getting the Democratic ticket. Anybody that wants to vote one, can get it.

Q. Did you see any one here last election working for the Democratic party?

A. I did. There were some here; some strangers to me, one or two that I did not know.

Q. Were they interfered with, so far as you saw?

A. No, not to my knowledge.

Q. When you come here on election day, are you as free to talk with anybody that you know, whether they are employees in the mine or not, as you are on any other day?

A. Certainly I am.

Q. What is your business?

A. I am a bee-keeper.

Q. Have you any connection with The Quicksilver Mining Company?

A. I have no connection with them. I come over here and trade when I please; if I do not I go somewhere else. I am free and independent; everybody knows me here; I formerly worked for years and years at this mine. I have worked under Captain Young; I worked when the mine was first transferred from the old company to the other, when Mr. Butterworth was here and when Mr. Mayo and Mr. Sherman Day were here. I am what they call one of the old hands, for I am 27 years here.

Q. You have been here a great deal since you left the employ of the company?

A. Certainly.

Q. How do you consider this place for a laboring man?

A. I consider it a very good place for a laboring man if he keeps steady and takes care of himself.

TESTIMONY OF EVELYN P. McCOY.

By Mr. MOORE:

Q. Where do you live?

A. I live on the Llagas; my occupation is a harness maker.

Q. Do you own any property on the Llagas where you live?

A. I bought the place and I have had possession for some thirteen years. It is my permanent residence.

Q. How old are you?

A. I am nearly fifty-two.

Q. Born in the United States?

A. Yes.

Q. Have you been a voter here during that time?

A. Yes; with the exception of two years. I moved to San Jose and then I moved back on the same place again.

Q. During the various elections that you have attended here, have you seen anything during Mr. Randol's administration to indicate that the employees of this mine were being forced or coerced into voting any particular ticket?

A. No; I never did.

Q. Have elections been held as freely as at any other place where you have been.

A. Yes.

Q. If there had been any system of coercion here would you probably have seen it?

A. I should have been very likely to, because I have always been around the polls and up and down the street at the Hacienda, and I have seen people go in and vote.

Q. You have seen the tickets of various parties?

A. Yes.

Q. They are always to be had, are they not?

A. Yes.

Q. During the election days are the employees as free to go where they please, and to talk to whom they please as on any other day?

A. Yes, to the best of my knowledge they are.

Q. Are you in any way connected with the company.

A. No; I never was. No influence has ever been exerted over me in regard to voting or anything else.

Q. Have you seen such electioneering here as you have in other places—as you do in every precinct?

A. Yes, every man working for his friends. I have electioneered myself, and exchanged votes like others do in all precincts.

Q. What ticket do you vote?

A. I voted the Republican ticket last year with exceptions, of course, I scratched it to suit myself. I exchanged votes you know, but it was my own work.

Q. Do you know Mr. Randol?

A. I know him only by sight. I am not personally acquainted with him; never had any dealings with him in any way.

Q. Have you ever seen him attempting in any way to interfere with the liberties of men?

A. No. I have seen him election days here. I don't think that I saw him last election day at all. I have seen him walking up and down the street, or I have heard him arguing some time with some of the outsiders, like Cooney; generally when they meet they would have a little talk. I never noticed Mr. Randol talk to an employee.

TESTIMONY OF JOSEPH CUZARD.

By Mr. Moore;

Q. Where do you live?

A. On the Uvas.

Q. What is your business?

A. Vineyardist.

Q. How many acres have you ?
A. 253 acres.
Q. How long have you been living there ?
A. 16 years.
Q. Where do you vote?
A. Almaden.
Q. How long have you been voting at Almaden ?
A. Since 1877.
Q. Have you ever seen anything here on election day to indicate that the managers of the mine were trying to force the men to vote any particular way?
A. No.
Q. You see the men voting here ?
A. Yes.
Q. Do they vote as they choose?
A. Yes.
Q. Always vote as they please ?
A. Yes.
Q. What ticket do you vote ?
A. Sometimes I vote for Republicans, sometimes for Democrats.
Q. You vote a mixed ticket ?
A. Yes.
Q. You always vote as you choose ?
A. Yes.

TESTIMONY OF GEORGE CROY.

By Mr. MOORE.

Q. Where do you live ?
A. I live up on the Uvas, about twelve miles from here.
Q. What is your business ?
A. I am in the lumber business, and I am farming a little—not much. I own 280 acres.
A. How long have you voted in Almaden ?
A. About sixteen years.
Q. Were you here at the last election ?
A. Yes.
Q. Have you at any election here, either at the last or any previous one, seen anything on the part of the managers of the mine or any persons around, that would indicate that the employees of this mine were being forced, coerced, or influenced in voting in any particular way ?
A. No, I have not.
Q. You have been around the polls, I suppose, more or less ?
A. Been about the polls—yes.
Q. If there had been any coercion practiced here would you have seen it ?
A. I think that I would have seen it; but I did not see anything of the kind.
Q. What is the habit of the men voting here, do they go to the polls themselves or are they taken there by somebody?

A. They go up and vote just as they choose.

Q. Is the voting here such as it is in other places?

A. Just about the same I always thought; it was just about the same as in any other place; there is as much liberty here as elsewhere.

Q. You have seen elections in other places?

A. Yes.

Q. What is your age?

A. 55 years old.

Q. What are your politics?

A. Republican.

Q. Have tickets of all parties been here for distribution on election days?

A. Yes; they can always be had by anybody that wants them.

TESTIMONY OF JOHN R. NORTON.

By Mr. CROSS:

Q. How old a man are you?

A. 47.

Q. Where were you born?

A. Illinois.

Q. When did you come to California?

A. In 1852.

Q. How long have you lived in the Santa Clara Valley?

A. Since 1854.

Q. What is your business?

A. Farmer.

Q. When did you first know The New Almaden Quicksilver Mine?

A. In 1854.

Q. How near have you lived to the mine since that time?

A. Four miles and a half; and had frequent occasion to visit the mine and become acquainted with the people engaged in the operation of the mine here and with the trade.

Q. State what you know about the condition of the people who lived on this mine prior to the time that Mr. Randol came here as Manager. Give a little history of it as you saw it?

A. Under the present management I think there has been improvement in most everything that is connected with this mine.

Q. What was the state of society here just prior to Mr. Randol's coming?

A. There were some very good men here before Mr. Randol came, but there were some very rough characters here in early days.

Q. Those have been gotten rid of?

A. I think so.

Q. Have you had occasion to have business relations with the management of the mine from time to time?

A. Yes; I have traded and dealt with them some considerable, off and on, at different times since 1854.

Q. What changes if any have been made in the methods of trading here at the mine during that time, and methods of doing business that you have noticed.

A. All the business that I have ever done with this company or the stores under Mr. Derby & Lowe's management have been always on a cash basis; I consider them the most liberal buyers, paying the best price in this county for produce that a farmer has to sell, when they want to buy.

Q. There has been some testimony given about searching wagons and the like; have you frequently had occasion to visit this mine of late years and come with a team and go?

A. I have been here with wagons but never had any wagon searched.

Q. Have you known anything of that kind of late years?

A. No.

Q. How many years have you been in the habit of voting in this precinct?

A. I have voted in this precinct since 1860. I would say in connection with that, that the polls were held down in the valley, at the school house, and it being unhandy for the voters to go from here down there, (they had to be hauled down there with teams and wagons) and so the polls were changed to the Hacienda.

Q. Do you think that change as a general thing was satisfactory to the residents of the precinct.

A. I think so; it was a more central location.

Q. Have you been in the habit of being about the polls more or less at elections here at New Almaden since Mr. Randol has ·been Manager?

A. Yes.

Q. What have you seen since Mr. Randol has been Manager, to indicate that the men on the mine, working for the company, had their votes controlled by the management of the company?

A. I have never seen anything of that kind. I have heard exaggerated reports to that effect but consider them groundless and without foundation.

Q. Have you ever seen anything about the polls here indicating any intimidation or coercion or undue influence upon the voters since Mr. Randol has been Superintendent of the mine?

A. I have not.

Q. Could you see any difference between the freedom with which men voted here and other places where you have seen men vote?

A. I do not see any difference. It was generally a very quiet election here, more quiet here than I have seen at any other place.

Q. Very little interference?

A. Very little interference; generally there is good order.

Q. The different parties generally have their tickets here distributed?

A. Yes; I have seen tickets here of all the different parties, men electioneering and so forth, the same as at any other place.

Q. Were you here on election day of November, 1886?

A. I was, and voted here.

Q. Anybody try to interfere with your voting?

A. No.

Q. Some electioneering about, I suppose as usual?

A. Yes, general electioneering; some more active than others.

Q. Did you see anything like any officer or the manager of the company driving the men up to the polls to vote, forcing them to vote this or that way or anything of that kind?

A. I have not; my observation of the officers, of Mr. Randol, and the Superintendent, is that those officers take very little interest in the election. Let it pretty much take care of itself.

Q. How long a personal acquaintance have you had with Mr. Randol?

A. I have known Mr. Randol since 1870; about the time he came here; and have seen him from time to time in his association with the other persons connected with the company.

Q. What, so far as you have observed, has been his manner towards the men in his employ?

A. I think that he is a very able, energetic manager, and has directed and guided this mine for the last seventeen years successfully for the benefit of the stockholders and all classes working here.

Q. At the last election did you notice any stages driving down here with passengers from the Hill?

A. Yes; every election men are hauled down here in stages and wagons and different conveyances to vote, and when they vote they generally return to their work; the majority of them; some few stay around the store here, talking politics and so on; the great majority return to their work after voting.

Q. Did you notice where the stages landed or stopped last election day, such as you saw?

A. They generally stopped at the store or outside of the 100-foot limit, where the register was hanging on the tree, the voters get their number and names off the register.

Q. Did you see Mr. Bulmore have a book on election day about the polls?

A. Yes.

Q. What was he doing with that book?

A. I think he was giving the names and the number to the voters, principally Spaniards that could not read their number in the Great Register; helping them to get their proper register number.

Q. Do you know Mr. Jennings, personally?

A. Yes.

Q. What is his manner towards the employees of the company, so far as you have observed it.

A. So far as I have observed he seems to be a very gentlemanly man in his business; treats everybody with courtesy, I think.

Q. Have you had any occasion to become acquainted with the men who work on the mine here?

A. A good many of them, yes.

Q. What would be your general idea of the men here, as working men?

A. My idea is that those men are paid the highest wages and are well taken care of, and have the best of everything supplied to them here in the stores, better I think than any other corporation of this kind on the coast.

Q. You know something about what wages men receive here, do you not?

A. Yes.

Q. The last month's pay roll on contracts shows the average wages of all the men employed on contract to be $2.87 a day per man. How would that compare with the average wages of the laboring men in other capacities in Santa Clara County, so far as you know it?

A. I think that they are better paid than any other laborers in Santa Clara County.

Q. Do you have occasion to see how these people are fed and clothed and taken care of?

A. Yes; I have noticed that these people are generally well dressed, and always have plenty of big dollars in their pockets, and look as though they had been pretty well fed.

Q. Did you ever see anything about the people employed on this mine, the way that they were living or acting, or the way that they were treated, that looked like slaves or peons, or anything of the kind?

A. No; I think a prudent man here who attends to his own business and lets other people's business alone has a good life situation here.

Q. Did you ever see anything since Mr. Randol was here that looked as though the man who did not vote the way the management wanted him to, was liable not to get work or to be any worse off than others?

A. No; I have not.

Q. What do you think about such talk as that, from your acquaintance with the men, living right here close to it?

A. I think that those reports are, as I said before, entirely groundless.

Q. Do you think of anything else you would like to state in this examination?

A. I would say that I think that this Almaden Mine is a living monument of industry and enterprise, that has been guided and directed by the present able manager, J. B. Randol, and his illustrious predecessor for the last thirty or forty years, and that it is to-day the peerless Quicksilver Mining Company of the American continent.

TESTIMONY OF ERNEST DESACHY.

By Mr. MOORE.

Q. Where do you live?

A. On the Uvas creek. At Mr. Cuzard's vineyard. I am his son-in-law.

Q. How long have you been voting at the Hacienda?

A. Since 1877. I have been up here about every election since.

Q. Have you ever seen anything on the part of the management of this mine that would indicate that they were forcing the employees to vote any particular ticket?

A. No, never. As far as I have seen, the employees of this mine are as free to vote for whom they please as they would be if they were living any other place.

Q. What ticket did you vote?

A. Can you force me to answer that?

Q. No; not without you want to answer it.

A. I voted the Democratic ticket, except just one vote for Mr. Moore.

Q. Did you have any difficulty last election in getting a ticket to vote?

A. No; they were here, plenty of them. Anybody could get them that wanted them.

Q. Have you ever seen anything like bulldozing in this precinct?

A. No.

Q. Anybody being compelled to vote any ticket?

A. I never did.

Q. Are elections conducted here as they are elsewhere?

A. Yes.

Q. Are you employed by the mining company?

A. No. I have nothing to do with the company.

TESTIMONY OF JOHN PFEIFFER.

I am 24 years old, a native of Kansas, I am a stonecutter by trade, and worked for my father at the Goodrich quarries, about three miles from the Almaden voting place. I voted at New Almaden last November and once before. I voted the Democratic ticket, except that I voted for Felton, Rea and Watson. I never saw anything that looked as though the management of The Quicksilver Mine was trying to control or influence the votes of its employees or any one else.

TESTIMONY OF MOSES BRAY.

I am 55 years old; was born in Maine, and have lived and voted in New Almaden precinct 23 years. I voted the Republican ticket here last November. I have never seen anything, since Mr. Randol has been Manager, as though the company was trying to control the votes of its employees. I am a bee raiser.

TESTIMONY OF W. P. JOHNSON.

I am a farmer, 43 years of age. I was born in Missouri; have lived in California 35 years and in Almaden precinct 18 years. I have been voting at Almaden. I vote the Democratic ticket straight through. I voted the Democratic ticket last November. I got my ticket at the store near the polls. I worked for The Quicksilver Mining Company and Frank Bohlmann, off and on for 15 years. I saw nothing at the election in 1886 or at any other time since Mr.

Randol became Manager of the mine, indicating that any one connected with the mine was trying to control the votes of the precinct, or of any one employed by The Quicksilver Mining Company.

By Mr. CROSS:

Q. If anything of that kind had been going on do you think that you would have been likely to know it? ·

A. I think I would.

Q. Since Mr. Randol has been here and while you were employed by the company, was anything done to control or unduly influence your vote?

A. No.

Q. By the management of the company?

A. Not at all.

Q. During the time you worked for the company were you in the habit of voting the Democratic ticket?

A. Yes.

Q. Could you ever see that it made any difference with what employment that you got or what pay you got, the fact of your voting the Democratic ticket?

A. I could not.

Q. Have you any reason to think that the way a man votes has anything to do with his getting employment or obtaining promotion in the employment of The Quicksilver Mining Company?

A. I have not.

TESTIMONY OF JAMES HARRY.

I am 53 years old; was born in England, in the county of Cornwall. I came to the United States in 1869. I have been a miner since I was 17 years of age. I have mined in Cornwall, England, in the State of California, in Nevada county and Santa Clara county. I have lived at Almaden since 1871, and have been in the employ of the company all that time.

By Mr. CROSS:

Q. I would like to have you give a history of the different employments you have had under the company from the beginning up to the present time ?

A. I came here in the year 1871 and started to work on contract at so much per yard in drifts; the contracts in those days were let every two weeks. I have worked some contracts for as low as $6 and my board for two weeks. That would be $3 a week, and I have made as high as $70 and board for two weeks on contracts. I have also worked some on tribute in the ore bodies; we mined the ore at so much per carga of 300 pounds, and I made on tribute from $2.50 to $3.50 per day. I have also worked as timberman; my business was then to go through the mine putting in timbers in the labores and drifts and shafts; my pay then was $3 per day. I have also worked as pumpman at $4 per day; my work then was putting pumps in the different shafts. About this time Mr. Randol thought that there could be some improvement made in the hoisting of the ore from the mine, and he talked the thing over with me and others, and it was thought that it could be done, so I took charge of the work and put in a skip in the Randol shaft; after the skip was in running order I was put on as shift boss. Previous to this the ore had been hoisted in buckets, the bucket was attached to the end of a rope and held from 400 to 500 pounds; that was hauled by steam; the bucket was swinging around free in the shaft in going up. The skip is an iron box with a door in front, and the bottom stands at an angle of 45°, the rock is dumped in the top of the box, and is discharged through the door in front, which runs in guides; each skip car holds a ton and a half of rock; that is a great improvement in the method of raising the ore; we raise a ton and a half where before we hoisted 500 and 600 pounds at a trip, and the skip being landed on a door that is hung on hinges at the same angle as the bottom of the skip, and when you drop the door in front, the skip-load is dumped into the car, which is drawn to the planilla; I made that improvement, that is I gave him the idea and put it in. From that time I went as shift boss; that was in the year 1873, I think. About 1876 I was foreman of the Cora Blanco, one of the mines of the Quicksilver Mining Company at New Almaden, and in 1877, soon after the Santa Isabel shaft was started, I was put in charge of that shaft and remained there till the shaft was down to the 2,000; I had charge of the work; I put in the skip and the pump works in that shaft, and in 1881 I was appointed mining captain and I have held that position ever since; I started the Randol shaft on contract; worked the first contract in the Randol shaft, sinking the shaft; that shaft is 1,800 feet deep.

Q. What are the duties of Captain?

A. The duties of the Captain are to take the orders from the Superintendent, at the present time Mr. Jennings. Previous to Mr. Jennings it was Mr. Randol, and I carry out the work under ground, running drifts, sinking shafts, and raising and sinking winzes and seeing that the mine is kept properly timbered, well ventilated, and to do everything that we know for the safety of the men in regard to the timbering, and to take out the ore in the cheapest way, putting in shoots to conduct the ore from level to level and transport it to the shaft in cars, and to work the mine as economically as we can. I have always had instructions from Mr. Randol to do everything that I thought best for the benefit of the company. Mr. Randol's watchword is economy. I have charge of all the work below the surface. I have worked in all the different departments of underground mining, before I became Captain.

Q. To whom do you give your orders directly?

A. I give my orders to the shift bosses, one by day and the other by night.

Q. How many men work under your direction, Captain?

A. About 350.

Q. Of what nationalities are most of the men under your charge?

A. A few of every nationality; but mostly Mexicans and Cornish and their descendants.

Q. When did you vote the first time?

A. I think that my first vote was for Garfield.

Q. What party do you belong to and what ticket do you vote?

A. I have always voted the Republican ticket.

Q. You always vote the straight ticket, or do you sometimes scratch a ticket?

A. I sometimes scratch.

Q. Under what circumstances do you scratch the ticket?

A. My reasons for it are, that I read the papers and we talk a little, and I have felt as a citizen that I have a right to scratch for any one in preference to another man; but as between parties I favor the Republican party.

Q. What reason can you give why you, and if you know, the Cornish boys generally, feel favorably to the Republican party?

A. I find, but I do not mean to say it is always the case, but a good many of the Democrats are Irish, and they are generally Roman Catholics, the English people are Republicans because they are

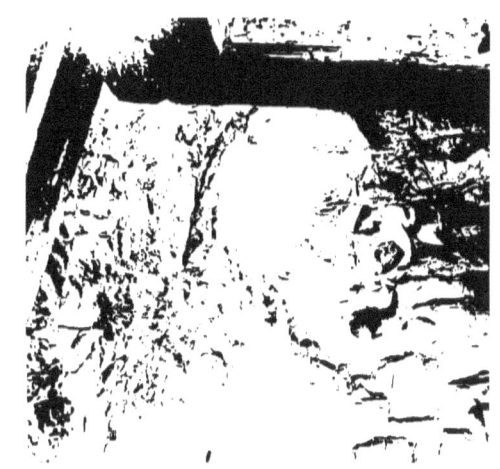

Protestant, and that they do not want to be governed under a Roman Catholic administration; don't want the Catholic influence in politics; that is one reason why the Cornish boys are so strongly Republican. Naturally there is not a great deal of sympathy between the Cornish boys and the Irish boys; that is another great point; they do not harmonize as a general rule.

Q. Since you have been connected with the mine have any orders ever come to you from any one above you about voting or politics?

A. No.

Q. What was the first experience that you had about politics with the management of the mine after you became a voter?

A. I remember on one occasion, I do not remember now what election it was, that I asked Mr. Randol whether there was any man on the Democratic ticket that he was in favor of or not; that I was not personally acquainted with any candidate at that time, and he said no; he did not leave any influence on me that he wanted me to do anything at all for him, and he made so light of it that I never asked him more from that time to the present, and he has never spoken of politics with me since.

Q. The purpose of this question that you put to him was to give him a chance to talk about politics and the ticket if he chose to?

A. Yes.

Q. You say he made so light of it?

A. Yes, he made so light of it that I thought I would not ask him any more unless he spoke first, and he has never spoken to me.

Q. Has Mr. Randol ever said anything to you about getting the men in the mine to vote for this man or that?

A. No, never a word.

Q. Has Mr. Jennings, the Superintendent?

A. No.

Q. Has there ever been any effort on the part of those who were in the management of the mine over you, to control your vote or to get you to control the men's vote, or anything of that kind?

A. No.

Q. Have you ever seen anything of that kind going on at this mine?

A. No, never. I go through the mine the day before election day, and notify the men that to-morrow is election day, and every man who wants to cast his vote can meet at the store early in the morning, and there will be teams there to convey him to the Hacienda to vote; so as not to lose time.

Q. If the men go and come back and get back in reasonable time do they get their pay?

A. They can get back quicker in the stages; men who go and come back in reasonable time get their pay; men who do not come back are checked.

Q. Do you keep the time?

A. I keep the time of all the men; all the mechanics, the machinery men or engineers; and I checked some men last November for not being back in time and going to work; because they came down and lingered about the polls. I could not afford to pay them if they wasted the day.

9

Q. Do you when you are giving notice to the men in the mine, do you say anything about how they are to vote?

A. No.

Q. In giving notice do you make any distinction between those that you know are Democrats and those that you know are Republicans?

A. No.

Q. Do you know of anything to prevent a man who wants to vote the Democratic ticket from having just as much freedom to come as any other man?

A. No.

Q. Have you since you have been on this mine done anything to control the men's votes?

A. Never.

Q. In letting out contracts or hiring men, do you make any difference with men according to what ticket they vote.

A. No.

Q. In giving men promotions and preferring men, do you make any difference on account of politics?

A. No.

Q. Does it have any influence at all?

A. No. Whenever a man is promoted it is because he merits it by his work.

Q. Have you had men working under you all this time that have been voting the Democratic ticket?

A. Yes; and I knew it.

Q. Why do you distribute Republican tickets?

A. Because I think that I have the right to, as an American citizen. I have been a Republican and believe in the Republican party.

Q. Do you know anything about boletos?

A. Yes; I know that there are boletos used.

Q. Do you take boletos?

A. Yes; occasionally.

Q. Are you compelled to?

A. No.

Q. Why do you take them?

A. Sometimes I take them because coin is not very flush.

Q. Do you understand the boleto business, they give out boletos for what a man has earned that is not due him until pay-day?

A. Yes; men who want to get some money or want some provisions in the house before pay-day, can draw boletos.

Q. Are men compelled to take boletos?

A. No.

Q. Does it make any difference as to a man getting work whether he takes boletos or not?

A. No.

Q. You get a pretty good salary; is it necessary for you to take boletos?

A. Sometimes I have an opportunity to send some money to town and use it to advantage, and I send all the money I have on hand, and go to the store and take boletos before the next pay-day.

Q. Do you know whether there are other men working for the

company, who are on the pay-roll, send some of their money away and then take boletos during the coming month ?

A. I know that some of them have a little bank account.

Q. What is your idea as to the proportion, for instance, of the English boys who have got a little stake in the bank ?

A. I think that the majority of them have a little, what they call, laid by for a rainy day—a little accumulation that is saved out of their wages.

Q. Do you know anything about the men having stock in the Water Company in San Jose ? Have you any information about that ?

A. Yes; there are several have ten, and some have fifteen, and some twenty, and some have as high as fifty shares in the San Jose Water Company—the company that supplies the city with water. Those deposits in the bank and in this water stock represent some of their savings while they have been working here for the company.

Q. Has there ever been any trouble about the men getting their pay ?

A. No; it comes regularly at pay-day every month.

Q. How does Mr. Randol treat the men in the employ of the company, so far as you have observed ?

A. He has treated men as perfect gentlemen. If a man is employed by Mr. Randol and performs his part that he is employed for, and is economical and careful of the company's property that is intrusted into his hands, Mr. Randol has been very kind and very generous to him.

Q. He requires men to do their duty ?

A. Yes; and I have known him to reward men for their industry and their carefulness and for their acts of bravery in their work very liberally, and I have also known him when a man fails to do his duty to discharge him. That is, he would not keep a man unless he did his duty.

Q. Does Mr. Randol have much to do with the men directly or is it mostly through the officers that he acts ?

A. Mostly through the officers.

Q. In managing so many men and carrying on so large a work are there little difficulties arising among the men about their work and one thing and another ?

A. Sometimes the men will appeal to the Superintendent, and Mr. Jennings and myself at this time generally settle the difficulties, but previous to Mr. Jennings' coming, it was referred to Mr. Randol.

Q. Since you have been here have there been any serious difficulties in the mine ?

A. No.

Q. Do you know anything about what the men make on an average at contract. For instance, have you looked at what they made last month ?

A. Yes; the average of contract on yardage last month was $2.88 per day per man.

Q. Are there some that made a good deal more ?

A. Some made as high as $5.00 per day—between $4 and $5.

Q. Do men that work here and quit for one reason or another, and go away ever seek to come back to work ?

A. Yes. I have a letter now that I received from men in the early part of this week, who had been away only one month, and they have written me saying they have been unsuccessful in getting work, they have worked some few days somewhere, and they would lose the money that they worked for and they would very gladly come back to Almaden to get employment if they could.

Q. Is it often the case that men who have quit and gone away come back for employment again?

A. Yes. Good miners. I will say in connection with this, if it is necessary, that these same men, as I have said, were in San Francisco in the Wisconsin Hotel, and a party came in and told them that if they would go on the stand and testify against the New Almaden mine that they could get some work from Mr. Sullivan at $3.50 a day for them.

Q. Who are the miners in the main that have something saved up; those who have stayed here all along or those who have stayed here, gone away, and come back again?

A. Those who have stayed here right along have been the men who have made money; they are the men who have saved something.

Q. What do you know about the building of the church here and how it came to be built, and the history of the church?

A. I do not exactly remember the date that the first church was built, but the first church was built one-story, built by subscriptions here at the mine. The first time Mr. Randol gave $250 and the company $250; the first winter the church blew down. Mr. Randol said if we wanted a good church to go on and take up our subscriptions and that whatever we subscribed in the community that he would double it; that he would give as much as all the rest; the whole amount that we had from Mr. Randol and the company that time was $848; afterwards the church was again destroyed by fire: that was, I think, in 1884, and again we had to appeal to Mr. Randol, and again he gave from the company $500, and his own personal subscription was $355, and the balance of the money was raised by subscription from the people working on The Qicksilver Mining Company's grant; that church cost $3,450. That is the present church; Mr. Randol has subscribed towards the Protestant church on the Hill $2,203 since he has been here.

Q. How many people will that church accommodate?

A. About 250 or 300.

Q. How is it generally filled at religious services?

A. Filled to the fullest capacity. In fact our pastor is talking about enlarging; the Sunday school is held there Sunday afternoon. We have a fine Sunday school with an average attendance of 165 to 170; those are the children of the people who work for the company; the Good Templars' Lodge meets in the basement story, and the Miners' Benevolent Society.

Q. What have you to say as to there being any want in this community in the families of the men working for the company?

A. There is no such thing as want; I do not know of any; I have known the old, worn out Mexicans to come to me and tell me that they wanted some assistance.

Q. What would happen under such circumstances?

BUENA VISTA SHAFT.

A. I would report it to the store or the Miners' Fund, and they would have support from the Miners' Fund.

Q. What can you say as to the men and their families living here at the mine—as to how they dress and feed ?

A. I should think that they live and dress, to all appearances, as well as at any mining camp that I was ever in.

Q. What can you say as to the quality of the supplies that they get at the stores and as to their eating meats freely, and the like of that, as to showing generous living ?

A. I think that they keep the best of supplies at the stores—that is the kind that the men buy.

Q. Now you have been giving some statement of the church here and its strength and organization and support, have you any official relation to the church ?

A. Yes; I am one of the Board of Trustees, and a member of the Board of Stewards; I also hold a position as class leader in the church.

Q. How long has it been since you have had a fatal accident in this mine ?

A. Three years July coming; that is very remarkable in the history of a large mine.

Q. You have been paying some attention to the evidence; reading the evidence about this contest between Mr. Sullivan and Mr. Felton, have you not ?

A. Yes.

Q. What do you think of the matter as you consider it ?

A. I think that Mr. Sullivan has been mislead by some party or parties. I think he has accused The Quicksilver Mining Company and this precinct in an unjust way, and without cause.

Q. Do you know of any particular reason why Mr. Sullivan was not likely to get a large vote amongst the English boys in this precinct ?

A. Mr. Sullivan circulated a pamphlet some time ago that did not take very well among the English boys; finding fault with their mother country and with the English people; a good many of the boys feel a good deal attached to the mother country; although they are American citizens, they feel attached to home; they do not like to have the country abused, although they now belong to America. I have got a copy of that pamphlet. [Here Captain Harry read an extract from the Sullivan pamphlet.] Such language as that would have the tendency to make the English boys feel less favorable to him than to a man of Irish descent generally. I know that it has. I have heard them talking about it. It made them feel somewhat hard.

Q. What do you think about this attempt to prove that the men here on the mine are treated like slaves and peons, and bulldozed and compelled to vote, and all that kind of talk ?

A. I think that it is nothing but humbug; it is all false.

Q. Have you ever seen a place where the employees have more freedom of action and to vote than you have here ?

A. No; I never have. You speak of the men being treated as slaves. I would just say in reference to that, that whenever there is a place such as a hot-drift to run or a wet shaft to sink, or where men cannot work to the best advantage, they are paid extra wages on account of its being a hard place; that is not done at other mines.

Q. There have been some claims made that the men here on the mine do not have any chance to read the papers, or to be informed about public matters, or what is going on. Do you know whether or not there are a good many papers taken on the Hill?

A. I do not think there is a family on the Hill but what takes one, two or more papers; I take three dailies and a weekly, and I believe that most every family takes one or two or more papers; I suppose that more than a hundred papers come on the Hill daily; all the party papers come up on the Hill and are distributed. The *Chronicle*, the *Call*, the *Alta*, the *Mercury*, the *Times*, the *Christian Advocate* and the San Francisco *Examiner*. Yes, a good many of the boys take the old country papers; the *West Britain* comes there regularly; the London *Times* comes there regularly.

Q. Do the men working for the company show a great deal of disposition to read the newspapers and to keep posted and to talk about what is going on in the world?

A. Yes, as a general rule, they do. Some of them are posted very well, and others do not take as much interest as some do.

Q. How long is a day's work in the mine?

A. Ten hours, where the men are working by day's pay. If they are working on contract and want to work a little more nobody can prevent them. Some of these contracts they work only an eight-hour shift.

Q. Is there anything else you wish to state?

A. I may say that for myself I have found that Mr. Randol and Mr. Jennings and all the officers of the mine have treated me as a gentleman, and as long as I am able to work I want no better place than New Almaden. I think that there is man enough in me to know it if I was a slave, or if I was driven, or if I was compelled. I know since I am an American citizen that, if I do not like, it I can go where I like. I think that as an American citizen I have a right to stand my own ground, and no man can bulldoze me or ill-treat me. I have been here for sixteen years, and if all be well I see no reason why I may not remain here. Men are not confined in Almaden to the Benevolent Association; there are parties that belong to the Odd Fellows; quite a number of Odd Fellows on the Hill and Masons and Workmen and Knights of Pythias. They are connected with all these associations just the same as people of other communities.

Q. What can you say as to the class of men generally in the employ of the company, as to what kind of men they are?

A. I should say they are up to the run of politics and societies and everything; they are pretty well informed men. I have a remembrance now of the great change that has taken place in this mine from what it was when I came here. I remember before I came here I have heard that the Almaden was a den of cutthroats and thieves and robbers and murderers. Almost the first thing I saw when I came to New Almaden, was a man shot on the Hill. I went on the Hill and saw the man lying in his blood, and I remember the remark that was made to me then, that that was a woman's third husband who had been shot. But of latter years there has nothing hap-

pened more than in any of the camps; of course quarrels happen anywhere and we have quarrels here; we have got human nature to contend with.

Q. What could you say of the men working here, so far as you can say, about them as to being independent spirited men ?

A. I think they are as independent spirited men as there are anywhere I ever saw. There is no way here to compel a man or to bind him here; if he does not like it, he feels he can get up and quit, and he does.

TESTIMONY OF S. B. CHRISTY.

I am thirty-three years of age, and reside at Berkeley, California; I am Professor of Mining and Metallurgy at the University of California—the State University.

By Mr. Cross:

Q. What attention have you given to the study of mining, first, in the study of mining as a theory?

A. I have devoted my entire time for the last fourteen or fifteen years to the study of mining and metallurgy; that includes both the theory and the art of mining; I was educated at the University of California.

Q. What qualifications have you as an expert upon mining subjects generally?

A. I have devoted my entire time for the last fifteen years to these studies and have in connection with that work made it my business to visit and study most of the different types of gold, silver, lead, quicksilver and coal mining in California, Nevada, Colorado and some other States, principally in Nevada, California and Colorado. I have paid particular attention to quicksilver mining and reduction. I have made it my business to familiarize myself with the literature in English, French and German. I have made numerous translations from works in these languages with particular reference to quicksilver, and particularly with the methods used at Almaden in Spain, for mining and working these ores, and also at Idria in Austria.

Q. What quicksilver mines in the State of California and Nevada have you visited, inspected and studied personally?

A. I have visited nearly all of the principal quicksilver mines in California, among others the New Almaden, the Sulphur Banks, the Great Western, the Great Eastern, the Oat Hill, the Guadalupe and the Redington.

Q. State whether or not you have spent considerable time at these mines, investigating the methods of extraction and reduction of ores?

A. I have made myself personally familiar with the methods in use for mining and reducing ores at all these places.

Q. What facilities have you had and used for the purpose of investigating mining and reduction, and the condition of the mines at New Almaden?

A. My first visit to New Almaden was made in the year 1875, on which occasion I spent about a month at the mine and reduction works; since then I have visited the mines very frequently at inter-

REDUCTION WORKS, HACIENDA.

vals during the last twelve years, for the purpose of very careful and minute study of the work done at this place. I have probably spent as much as six months, total time, at the mine and the reduction works in this study.

Q. That time has been devoted to the investigation of the problems involved in quicksilver mining at this mine, has it?

A. Yes; it has been entirely devoted to a careful professional study of the subject, and I have been afforded every possible facility at all times by the officers of the company for making that study a careful and complete one, and have been allowed the privilege of examining the books and papers of the company, as well as the works themselves.

Q. Have you examined the reports made at different times to the company and stockholders by the officers of the company?

A. I have read most all of these reports through carefully.

Q. Have you read the literature produced at the mine with reference to the affairs of the mine?

A. I have kept myself informed, I think, very completely of everything that has been published here of any technical interest.

Q. State whether or not you have visited the underground workings of the New Almaden Quicksilver Mine?

A. I have always made it my habit at each visit to the mine to go underground and see all that has been done, and nearly all of the principal workings that were going on at the time, and have also explored all of the old workings of the mine that were operated in former times which were accessible.

Q. State generally and briefly the character, extent and quality of the ore deposits as you have observed them in this mine?

A. Quicksilver deposits as a general rule are very different from those of the ores of other metals. Many other metals occur in well defined fissure veins, so that there is no difficulty in following the ore, and in many cases of calculating beforehand the amount of ore in sight, but with the exception of the deposit at the old Almaden in Spain, and to some extent the deposit at the Idria in Austria, the quicksilver deposits, particularly those of California, are characterized by a great and persistent irregularity, so that it makes the mining of these ores much more difficult than that of other metals. New Almaden is a striking example of this irregularity. It has often occurred in the history of the mine that there was no ore or scarcely any in sight, and it has often looked as though the mine must of necessity be shut down, and it has only been by the most careful and painstaking prospecting or dead work that it has been possible to keep up the production of the mine. Very frequently large bodies of ore will almost completely run out, and there will be visible in the face of the works only a slight coloration in the vein matter, which indicates that there is any ore left in that particular place, and by following out this little string of ore very carefully it may lead into a large deposit. As a result of this the workings of the mine are necessarily very irregular, and it requires the greatest skill on the part of the engineer in charge of the works to keep up a regular and steady output of ore. Many times in the past history of the mine the prospecting work has not been carried on on a sufficient scale, and this largely accounts for some of the irregularities of the production of the mine in former times. I have noticed a steady improvement in the carrying out of this prospecting work, which of itself is necessarily very expensive and requires the greatest judgment on the part of the person in charge of the work.

Q. Is it cinnabar ore?

A. The mineral that characterizes the ore is cinnabar mainly, although native quicksilver is occasionally found.

Q. What statement, if any, can you make with regard to the means and methods of reductions employed in connection with the New Almaden Quicksilver Mine?

A. When I first visited the mine in 1875, there were two iron-clad monitors in existence, one was already running, the other was just being built; the rest of the furnaces in use at that time were the old-fashioned, so-called "Almaden Furnaces" that had been in existence here for many years. These furnaces were intermittent furnaces, and when the ore had been roasted the workmen had to enter the furnace while it was still in a partly heated state, and withdraw the hot ore by hand from the furnace, and then they had to charge the furnace, going into it for that purpose; this, together with the irregular nature of the operation, caused considerable expense to the mine and considerable exposure and suffering to the men who were compelled to endure the heat, and danger of poisoning from quicksilver fumes. The great success that the continuous acting monitor furnaces met with, in treating the coarse ore, occasioned Mr. Randol to institute a persistent endeavor to find some approved furnace for continuously treating the fine ores, which furnished a great bulk of the ore from the mine; that is, ore in the shape of pieces from an inch and a half in diameter down to the size of dust. Probably two-thirds or more of the ore produced at the mine was of this nature. And beginning with that time, and since then the experiments that were induced for the purpose have been eminently successful, and at the present time there exists at New Almaden probably the best equipped plant for roasting fine quicksilver ores, that there is in the world. It is certainly much more efficient than the means used at old Almaden in Spain, or at Idria, in Austria, for this purpose.

Q. What is the proper name for the kind of furnaces now in use at the New Almaden mine?

A. They are perhaps best described as shelf furnaces, and are continuous in their mode of operation.

Q. What is meant by the term continuous as used in connection with the furnaces?

A. The meaning of the term is, that the ore is continuously fed in at the top of the furnaces and drawn out at the bottom, that is, that there is no intermittence in the nature of the operation, that it goes on continuously. Metallurgists are well aware of the advantage, economically and otherwise, of furnaces of this type.

Q. What is the advantage, economically, of using the continuous furnace now used as compared with the intermittent furnaces formerly used, and very generally used in other places?

A. There are many advantages. In the first place they require

QUICKSILVER FURNACES, Nos. 1 & 2

less fuel for the roasting of ores, because they are continuously kept the proper temperature and not allowed to cool down, thus avoiding the necessity of needless waste in reheating them to the proper temperature; in the next place being maintained at a constant temperature, they are not subject to alternate cooling and contraction, which causes a rupture of the enclosing walls sooner or later, thus giving rise to a loss of quicksilver in the form of drops and also in the form of vapor. They involve much less labor on the part of the workmen; they are more easily controlled, and they give a higher efficiency, moreover the workmen are no longer subjected to the poisonous action of the fumes.

Q. Thus very much decreasing the dangers attendant upon the men who are engaged in the operation of the furnaces, as I take it?

A. Certainly; the men need never be exposed to the action of the fumes in working a furnace as now constructed, unless through their own carelessness or neglect of proper precaution.

Q. What can you state as to what was necessary under the former methods of treatment of fine ores or tierras, as compared with the methods which are used now for the treatment of the same class of ores?

A. Formerly it was impossible to roast the fine ores in the old furnaces at all, except in very small quantities at a time, unless they were previously mixed up with clay and made into adobe or large sun-dried bricks; these had then to be fed into the furnace, and carefully piled in by hand before they could be roasted at all, and even then they were liable to break into dust in handling and heating, thus interrupting the draft of the furnace and exposing the men to the fumes, and, of course, involving considerable additional expense.

Q. Is all of that avoided by the present methods of reducing that class of ores?

A. All of these difficulties are entirely overcome.

Q. In speaking of the methods of mining, what facilities are in use by this mine for the purpose of pumping and hoisting from the underground works?

A. Originally, at the time of my first visit, the appliances in use were of a rather primitive nature, they were those that had been in use for many years, and were not well adapted to the economical handling of large quantities of ore or of water. Improvements have been constantly going on during the last twelve years, and at the present time the mechanical arrangements for pumping, and hoisting the ore to the surface, and of handling the ore both underground and at the surface, compare favorably with those of any other mine on the coast.

Q. When you speak of pumping, you mean the pumping of water from the mine?

A. Yes.

Q. Under whose administration of the New Almaden Quicksilver Mining property have all of these changes and improvements, that you speak of, been made?

A. They have been made under the administration of the present manager—Mr. Randol.

Q. Have you during your visits at this mine had occasion to observe, and have you observed the condition of the employees of this company, speaking of the manner in which they are housed and clothed, and also the manner in which they are cared for and looked after by the management of the mine, as to their comfort, safety and protection, and their social condition on the mine ?

A. I have become personally acquainted with many of the miners in the course of my visits to the mine. Have visited them in their houses, as well as conversed with them underground, and have attended some of their public exercises, both in their church and on public occasions, such as public wrestling matches and games, and I think their condition will compare very favorably indeed with that of any set of miners that I ever came in contact with. In fact, I think that, taken as a whole, their condition is considerably superior.

Q. What would you say as to the condition of the miners here, as you have observed it, as compared with the condition of laboring people in other classes of industry, as you have had occasion to observe them on this coast ?

A. I think their condition would compare favorably with that of workmen in any other industry.

Q. What would you say as to how the men employed here compare in skill and efficiency with the miners that you have observed in other places, where you have had occasion to study the subject of mining ?

A. My judgment of that is, that the English and American and other miners, Anglo-Saxon miners, are very skillful miners; that they understand their business and are very content; regarding Mexican miners, they seem to have a great deal of skill in finding new deposits of ore; the English miners, Cornishmen, are extremely valuable in doing hard work, such as driving drifts and sinking shafts and other work of that class.

Q. In your judgment, Professor, what conditions as to compensation and surroundings would be necessary in order to attract and hold the character and quality of miners that you have observed here; what would be your judgment as to the management of a mine in this locality being able to attract and hold such a class of miners as you find here, if the conditions of living were unfavorable or the compensation inadequate, compared with other mines.

A. As I understand it, miners, as a rule, go to the place where they are best paid and best treated; they naturally gravitate towards those centers. The mining population, as a rule, is an extremely intelligent class of workingmen; they keep themselves well informed as to the conditions that are maintained in the different mining centers, and they always gravitate towards the places where they reckon their compensation and their treatment is the best.

Q. So that a good quality of workmen would tend to indicate that the compensation and surroundings were favorable, would it ?

A. Certainly; miners, of all men, go where they are best treated; as a class of laborers they are somewhat wandering in their habits.

Q. So that they have, as laborers, opportunity to be well informed as to where are the most desirable places for good miners ?

A. Yes.

Q. Have you given to the subject of Miners' Funds, so-called, or Miners' Aid Funds, particularly with reference to the providing medical skill and treatment for those employed in mining—have you given to that class of subjects considerable investigation?

A. I have always taken a great deal of interest in that subject.

Q. Why have you taken particular interest in that subject?

A. I have always considered it was the duty of both the employers and those in the engineering profession to see that the workmen who might be under their charge were properly looked after and provided for, so far as it was possible that the matter could be done. I always believed that the men should be well treated, and should be made as comfortable as the nature of the circumstances permitted.

Q. What is there in the nature of the business of mining, as compared with other industries, that makes it especially desirable that that particular matter should receive especial attention?

A. The work of the miner is in some respects difficult, and above all it necessarily involves the men in the constant exposure to danger from causes that can hardly be foreseen in the best regulated mines; the men are often subjected to danger from their own carelessness, and it is a very curious fact that any class of men who are constantly in the presence of danger soon get used to it. So that they become reckless of their own means of safety, and the miners are, particularly as a class, examples of this state of things; and more than that, they very often are indifferent as to the future; they do not look ahead far enough. As a class they are less provident, I think, than farmers and people of other industrial occupations.

Q. How is mining classed as to hazard as compared with other industries?

A. It is naturally regarded as more hazardous than farming or many other of the ordinary industrial pursuits of life.

Q. Does the business of mining necessarily result, in your judgment, in frequent accidents and injuries to the men employed in underground work?

A. In Europe, where the government has taken the most stringent measures to prevent accidents in mines, they occur in spite of all that, and it is only by the constant exercise of the greatest care on the part of the managers of the mine and of the miners themselves that they are not more frequent.

Q. What recent accident do you recall which is an example of the hazards and serious accidents that transpire in mines?

A. An explosion occurred only the other day in British Columbia, and a very large number of men—something over a hundred—lost their lives at one catastrophe.

Q. What particular class of dangers would you think would be especially common in the business of quicksilver mining?

A. In quicksilver mining, particularly at New Almaden, the accidents that might happen would be from the carelessness on the part of the men in charge of the hoisting engines, or on the part of those engaged in watching the cables, the ropes that lift the cages; from accidents owing to the premature explosion of blasts, or from caves that would come down upon the men; this latter is one that is necessarily a constant source of danger in some of the ore bodies, because the ground is rather of a treacherous nature and is liable to come down without any previous warning, when it appears to be sound. All these conditions tend towards the necessity of being provided at hand with the best of medical and surgical skill.

Q. Do you know whether or not funds of this character have been common in other mining localities and mines besides at New Almaden?

A. It is very common in industrial enterprises of a large size, such as the management of a railway or of a large mine, to make some provision to protect the men against unforseen accidents or the results of their own carelessness. In the Eastern states, particularly in the coal and iron mines of Pennsylvania, these are quite commonly connected with large and well-managed mines. On this coast they have not been very common; numerous attempts have been made in some of our larger mines to introduce funds of this character, but they have mainly met with indifferent success, and I know of no other that has been anywhere near as successful as the one at New Almaden.

Q. What classes have there been of organizing or furnishing the fund for such a purpose that you have known or learned of from your reading?

A. In some places attempts have been made to establish funds of this nature by subscription, and immediately after some great catastrophe a subscription is a very great help to alleviate distress, but it is as a general rule found impracticable to maintain a fund of that character by voluntary contributions only.

Q. What has been the general result, so far as you know, as to a fund of that kind becoming permanent when it was depending entirely upon subscription or the voluntary action of the miners?

A. As a general rule, I think that such attempts have never been followed by permanent success. Miners, as a rule, live from day to day, and are not, as a general rule, fully alive to the importance of laying by something for a rainy day, as the saying goes.

Q. What, in your judgment, is necessary with regard to contributions in order that such funds should be permanently successful and beneficial?

A. I am of the opinion that it must necessarily be compulsory in order to be successful. I believe it is the result of experience here as well as elsewhere.

Q. Did you ever have occasion to give the Miners' Fund of New Almaden a critical examination by inquiry and examination of the books of the fund and its workings.

A. I have taken pains to satisfy myself as to the practical workings of the fund. I prepared tables with reference to that matter, the data for which were taken from the records of the company.

Q. Will you state by reference to any such table you have prepared at any time in the past, what you ascertain to be the average cost of medical attendance for those belonging to the Miners' Fund at New Almaden?

A. The record of the total number of cases treated by the physician during ten years from 1874 to 1883 inclusive, amounted to over 84,000; the total amount disbursed during the thirteen years ending

with the year of 1883 amounted to over $79,000; the records previous
to 1875 as to the number of patients treated were not kept, but taking the rate to be the same during the first three years that it was
during the last ten, it would make the total cost to the members of
the fund something less than forty-four cents a visit.

Q. Would that include nurses and hospital expenses?

A. Including all other expenses incurred in the interest of the
Miners' Fund, such as medicine, nurses, loans, and so forth, the total
cost would be seventy-two and one-half cents a visit.

Q. How would that compare, so far as you are advised, with the
ordinary cost per visit for medical attendance in the cities of California where you are at all acquainted with the matter?

A. It is very much less than the citizens of any city or town have
to pay, that I know of.

Q. And these visits would include surgical as well as ordinary cases
of the administration of medicine?

A. Certainly, that includes all cases and funeral expenses, too,
in cases of indigence.

Q. Have you given any attention to the subject of contract work
in the mines?

A. Yes.

Q. Do you know whether that system is pursued to any considerable extent at the New Almaden mine?

A. It is largely in use here.

Q. State what you think of the contract system as a method of
underground mines, what are its merits and what its demerits, so far as
you are familiar with them?

A. The contract system, as applied to mining, really had its rise
in Cornwall, England, and has been in use there for many years, and
it is well recognized among mining engineers that this is one of the
chief causes to which the skill of the Cornish miners is due, that it
has given them an interest in the success of their work, and has consequently made them feel that the success of their work was their
success, and naturally developed the greatest possible amount of
skill upon the part of the Cornish miners, for which they are famous.

Q. Do you know whether or not that system has been practiced
to any considerable extent in the mines of California, Nevada and
Colorado?

A. The practice varies; in some places it is not in use, and in
others it is.

Q. What, in your judgment, are the benefits to the employee
growing out of the practice of the contract system?

A. It gives him the advantage of his skill and industry.

Q. What are the advantages to the employer in the practice of
this system of mining?

A. It secures to him the best return for the investment of his
money. I would state in this connection, to explain that matter a
little more fully, that mining is in many respects different from that
of the employment of men in other industries; the men are necessarily divided up into small gangs, and they are working alone,
largely at points necessarily more or less scattered underground,
and it is very difficult to properly supervise them, and if men are

paid by the day some of them frequently take advantage of the opportunities to do very little work, and they are all paid alike, the skilled with the unskilled, but if they work together in gangs who have a common interest, each man sees that the other man does his fair amount of the work, and each man feels that in doing the work he is going to get the reward of his exertion.

Q. What system of mining, in your judgment, is most likely to attract the best class of miners, employment by the day or the contract system?

A. I certainly think that experience shows that the contract system is the one that skilled miners prefer.

Q. There has been offered in evidence here an exhibit found in volume thirteen of the transactions of the American Institute of Mining Engineers, an article commencing at page 647 of the book entitled "Quicksilver Reduction at New Almaden." Was that exhibit compiled and written by you?

A. That is my work.

Q. What facilities had you for obtaining the information contained in that article?

A. I had every facility extended to me for getting the information there presented that I could wish; I had access to the original records at the office of the company, to their drawings and maps and to the furnaces themselves.

Q. And also to their reports?

A. And also to their reports, and I would state that I took great pains for my own satisfaction to get the exact facts that are there presented, and to convince myself that they were correct, and when the material had been put in shape, Mr. Jennings not only assisted me in gathering the material, as did also Mr. Randol, but both took the pains to go over the work very carefully and to check off any errors or omissions.

Q. That was after you had prepared the work?

A. That was after I had prepared the work, so that I have every reason to believe that it is essentially correct in all particulars.

Q. These productions have become well-known parts of the quicksilver mining literature of this coast?

A. Certainly. They are part of the transactions of the Institute of Mining Engineers.

Q. I believe that is all, unless you think of some other matter that you think would be pertinent to state in this connection.

A. I think you have covered almost everything, except that I would like to add that, in my judgment, but for the improvements introduced at New Almaden by Mr. Randol, and his exceptionally good management, the New Almaden would, like so many other quicksilver mines, have been long ago shut down. But for the sustaining of this mine, it is hard to tell what prices the gold miners would have to pay for foreign quicksilver produced at Almaden, Spain, or Idria in Austria.

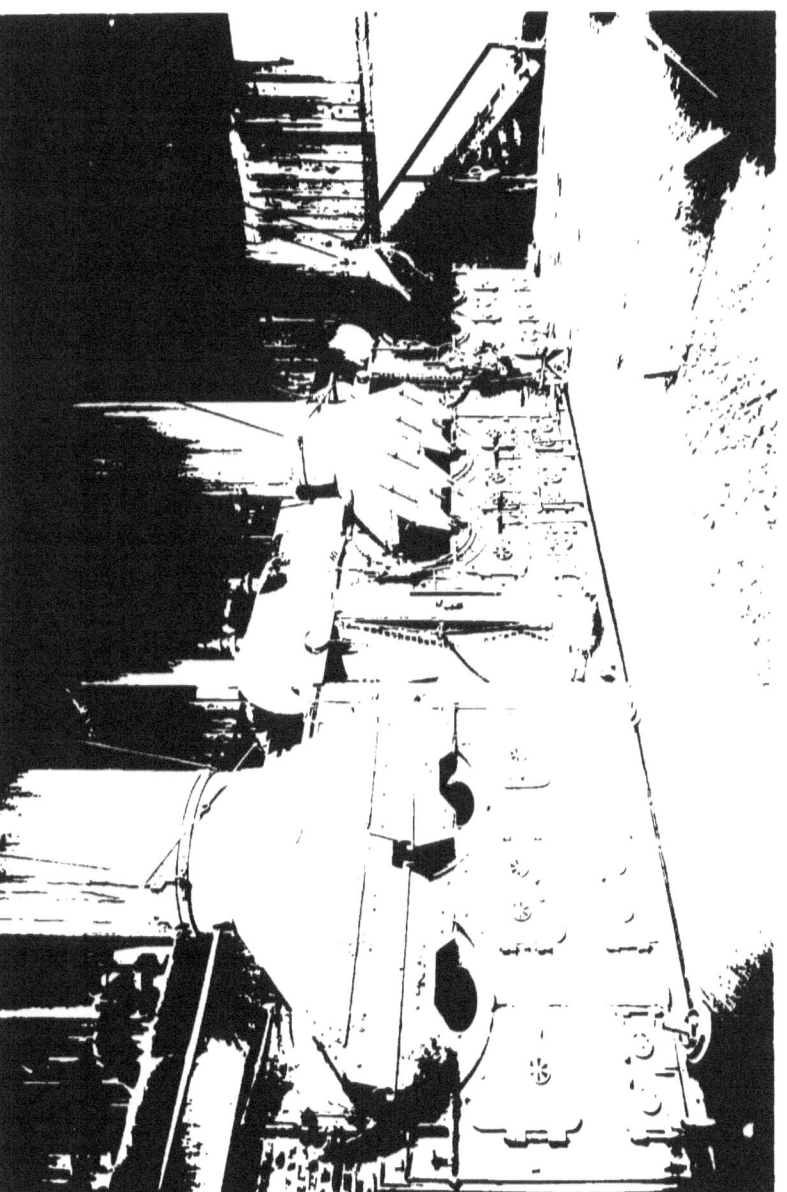

BOILER ROOM, BUENA VISTA SHAFT.

EXHIBITS.

10

RULES AND REGULATIONS

— OF —

THE QUICKSILVER MINING COMPANY,

NEW ALMADEN, CALIFORNIA.

1st. The Company, its agents and employees, will not be bound to indemnify any employee for losses suffered by the latter in consequence of the ordinary risks of the business in which he is employed, nor in consequence of the negligence of another of its employees, unless the Company be proved to have neglected ordinary care in the selection of the culpable employee.

2d. Each employee is required to perform his service in conformity with the usages of the mine and the works, unless otherwise directed by his superior officer.

3d. Every employee is desired to use such skill as he possesses, so far as the same is required for the service in which he is engaged, and also to use material and time in the most economical manner.

4th. No material nor tools will be allowed to any employee unless by permission from the office, and employees leaving must bring a receipt from their foreman in full for all tools used, or pay for them.

5th. Every employee will be held liable for all damage caused to the Company's property by his blunders, mistakes or carelessness, and will be paid for the value of such services only as are properly rendered.

6th. The Company reserves the right to discharge an employee at any time in case of willful breach of duty, or in case of his habitual neglect of the rules, regulations and usages established for the welfare of all employees.

7th. Employees by the month must perform all the requirements of their respective service without charge for extra time, and such employees, in case of absence, must first obtain leave from their superior officer, if they wish to retain their positions. If they desire to quit the Company's service, they must give one month's notice, or forfeit one month's pay.

8th. Regular pay-day will be on the last day, or the last Saturday of each month, as may be most convenient, when payment will be made for the preceding month. Payments will not be made at any other time, except it shall suit the Company to do so. All payments are due at the Company's office in New Almaden, and at no other place.

9th. It is required of every foreman to call the attention of each and every employee to the foregoing rules before he begins work for the Company, and it is understood that in consideration of their employment each and every employee agrees to recognize the foregoing rules as a specific contract between employer and employee, and to faithfully abide thereby.

February, 1883.   THE QUICKSILVER MINING COMPANY,

J. B. RANDOL, Manager.

EXTRACTS FROM CIVIL CODE OF CALIFORNIA.

Division III, Part IV, Title VI, Chapter I.

ARTICLE II.

Sec. 1970. An employer is not bound to indemnify his employee for losses suffered by the latter in consequence of the ordinary risks of the business in which he is employed, nor in consequence of the negligence of another person employed by the same employer in the same general business, unless he has neglected to use ordinary care in the selection of the culpable employee.

ARTICLE III.

Sec. 1981. An employee must substantially comply with all the directions of his employer concerning the service on which he is engaged, except where such obedience is impossible or unlawful, or would impose new and unreasonable burdens upon the employee.

Sec. 1982. An employee must perform his services in conf rmity to the usage of the place of performance, unless otherwise directed by his employer, or unless it is impracticable, or manifestly injurious to his employer to do so.

Sec. 1984. An employee is always bound to use such skill as he possesses, so far as the same is required for the service specified.

Sec. 1988. An employee who has any business to transact on his own account similar to that intrusted to him by his employer must always give the latter the preference.

Sec. 1990. An employee who is guilty of a culpable degree of negligence is liable to his employer for the damage thereby caused to the latter; and the employer is liable to him, if the service is not gratuitous, for the value of such services only as are properly rendered.

ARTICLE IV.

Sec. 2000. An employment, even for a specified term, may be terminated at any time by the employer, in case of any willful breach of duty by the employee in the course of his employment, or in case of his habitual neglect of his duty or continued incapacity to perform it.

Sec. 2002. An employee dismissed by his employer for good cause, is not entitled to any compensation for services rendered since the last day upon which a payment became due to him under the contract.

RULES OF THE MINERS' FUND.

This fund, instituted for the benefit of the residents of New Almaden, is established upon the following basis:

I.

Employees of The Quicksilver Mining Company, heads of families, and all other adults residing at New Almaden, each pay, monthly, into said Fund, the sum of One Dollar. The money so contributed is held by J. B. Randol, Trustee, to be paid out for the following purposes:

1. The salaries of a resident Physician, and of a Druggist, and for the purchase of medical supplies.

2. For relief of contributors, whom circumstances may entitle to the same, and for other contingent expenses.

II.

Contributors are entitled, without further payment, to the attendance of the resident Physician for themselves and their immediate families (except that cases of confinement will be charged five dollars), and will be furnished with medicines prescribed by him, on payment of cost.

III.

When the Fund is subject to any expense for relief of persons indigent, or otherwise—say, for medicines, nurses or supplies—it will be regarded in the nature of a gift, or as an advance, to be repaid, as the Trustee may decide to be just, considering the circumstances of each case.

IV.

It is expressly agreed that when the resident Physician is called to attend any person not a contributor to the Fund, that there shall be a charge of not less than Five Dollars for each visit to be paid into the Fund, and to be charged against and collected from the head of the house where such non-contributor may be living.

V.

The Trustee serves without pay, and, in consideration thereof, it is understood that the foregoing rules and regulations will be observed by all persons interested therein; and it is expressly agreed that all sums due, or to become due, to the Fund by the contributors, or any of them, shall be a lien upon any property of the contributors at New Almaden, and upon any money due, or to become due them, for wages from The Quicksilver Mining Company, which money said Company is authorized to pay over to said Fund, without further notice.

J. B. RANDOL, Trustee.

NEW ALMADEN, February, 1883.

MINERS' FUND.

Receipts and Disbursements for Sixteen Years, ending December 31st, 1886.

RECEIPTS.

Collections..	$98,909 80	
Medical stores, sales	4,549 59	
Obstetric cases..................................	1,705 00	
Outside practice................................	154 00	
Donations.......................................	29 75	
Sale of horse...................................	126 50	
Interest on deposits in bank....................	3,479 36	
		$108,954 00

DISBURSEMENTS.

Salary of physicians............................	$60,911 00	
Medical stores, purchases.......................	15,817 39	
Contributions to sick and disabled..............	4,512 85	
Salary to Secretary.............................	4,562 34	
Hospital nurses.................................	3,613 07	
Consultation fees...............................	1,958 00	
Livery—prior to 1878............................	1,425 78	
Funeral expenses................................	1,076 84	
Board for patients	1,733 20	
Furniture.......................................	583 94	
Surgical instruments............................	501 42	
Office boy—prior to 1878........................	418 75	
Incidental expenses.............................	638 40	
Small loans unpaid..............................	65 00	
Subscriptions to medical journals and works.....	389 80	
Disinfectants...................................	330 19	
Small-pox hospital..............................	117 25	
Taxes...	18 00	
Fuel—prior to 1878..............................	15 22	
Apothecary's salary.............................	708 00	
Helping Hand Club...............................	726 78	
Care of graves..................................	20 00	
		$100,443 22

Balance credit Fund, 31st December, 1886........	$8,510 78

MINERS' FUND.

Amounts Collected during the Year 1886 and part of Year 1887.

1886.	Mine Pay Roll.	Hacienda Pay Roll.	Totals.
January...............	$432 75	$62 50	$495 25
February.............	443 00	62 00	505 00
March.........................	417 00	65 00	482 00
April..........................	406 50	59 00	465 50
May...........................	401 50	60 00	461 50
June..........................	404 00	58 50	462 50
July..........................	411 00	60 00	471 00
August........	407 00	61 50	468 50
September...............	381 00	57 00	438 00
October........................	380 50	57 50	438 00
November.................	395 50	58 00	453 50
December....................	396 50	56 00	452 50
Totals................... ...	$4876 25	$717 00	$5,593 25
1887.			
January........................	$385 00	$57 25	$442 25
February.......................	378 75	55 50	434 25
March..........	400 00	56 00	456 00
Totals....................	$1,163 75	$168 75	$1,332 50

Average per month for year 1886........... .... $466 08
    "   "   " three months 1887............................. .... 444 16

NEW ALMADEN.

Analysis of the Employees in Accordance to Occupation.

November 1st, 1886.

Total number of men employed on Hill............................	416
Contractors 248	
Day's pay......................................109	
Month's pay............ 59	
	416

Total number employed at Hacienda................................	61
Contractors... 1	
Day's pay.. 46	
Month's pay.. 14	
	61

Analysis of the Voters of the New Almaden Precinct at the General Election Held November 2, 1886.

Total number of votes polled..................................		256
Voters not in employ of The Quicksilver Mining Company.......	100	
Voters in the employ of The Quicksilver Mining Company.......	156	
		256

NATIONALITIES OF VOTERS.

American...114		
English....... 81		
Mexican 28		
Irish... 11		
Other nationalities.. 22		256

Of the 156 in the employ of The Quicksilver Mining Company, there were:

Americans...52
English...71
Mexicans..25
Irish.. 2
Other nationalties...................................... 6

Of the above 156 voters there are still employed by The Quicksilver Mining

Company........................... 149
Dead... 2
In jail... 1
Gone to Mexico 1, Hollister 1, San Jose 1, (All left of own accord)........ 3
Discharged for Drunkenness 1

NEW ALMADEN.

Earnings of the Yardage Contractors for the Year 1886, and the First Three Months of 1887.

1886.	No. Days Worked.	Highest Earnings Per Day.	Average Earnings Per Day.
January.............................	2207	$4 38	$2 19
February...............	1853	4 18	2 86
March....	2042	3 75	2 25
April.............................	1627	4 15	2 52
May.......	1880	5 96	3 26
June.............................	2678	3 95	2 42
July	1327	4 80	2 50
August...........................	1322	3 86	2 13
September........................	1620	3 46	2 57
October....	1112	3 12	1 93
November...'......................	1123	4 25	2 47
December........................	1673	4 92	2 98
1887.			
January	1518	4 54	2 53
February......................	1659	4 93	2 38
March...........................	2153	5 41	3 02

Total number of days worked... 25,794

Total Earnings.. $63,934.81

General average per day......................... .... $ 2.48

Statement of Houses on the Company's Land.

April, 1887.

Number of Persons who rent Company's Houses........ ....　122

   "   "   " have   "   " free. 7

Number of Houses owned by 91 men on Company's land. 119

Number of Americans owning houses.................. 2

   "   French   "   "   3

   "   Mexicans   "   "   38

   "   English   "   "   48

     Total.......................... 91

Total number of Company's employees, -　-　-　-　-　***477***

   "   ***"***   ***"***   ***"***   ***"***   ***voting,*** -　-　-　-　***156***

     11.

EARNINGS AND EXPENSES.

FOR SIXTEEN YEARS, ENDING DECEMBER 31, 1886.

Earnings.

Quicksilver produced, 317,822 Flasks.

Average value... $35.11^{34}	$11,159,822	55
Miscellaneous...............................	629,727	65
	$11,789,550	20

Operating Expenses.

Mine and Hacienda Pay Rolls........	$5,132,519	53		
Miscellaneous and Taxes.......	705,337	44		
Materials consumed in operation of Mines and Furnaces.............	1,656,512	95		
			7,494,369	92
Profit balance..............			$4,295,180	28

Which is accounted for as follows:

There have been expended for Improvements and Repairs, as below:...........................			$855,354	25
Furnaces and Condensers.............	$299,499	96		
Hoisting Works, Machinery, Pumps and Shafts........	442,681	37		
Houses and Shops	74,162	31		
Flumes, Ore-cleaning Floors, Waterworks, Roads, and other surface Improvements................ }	69,010	61		

ADD:

Real Estate purchased......	$14,500	00		
Legal Expenses and Patents.$42,219 62				
Less collected account Patent 2,250 00				
	39,969	62		
"Black debt" of 1870................	9,342	68		
			63,812	30
Forward.......			$949,166	55

Profits expended in California brought forward.. $949,166 55

Accounted for by increase in Personal Property accounts in California, and by consignments abroad,
as below: 136,288 37

On December 31, 1870, the property accounts showed
balances of—

Cash.............. ...	$47,201 20	
Quicksilver..........	9,207 00	
Supplies..............	59,844 52	
Ore.................	35,675 95	
		$151,928 67

And on December 31, 1886—

Cash................$	17,994 95	
Quicksilver....	165,787 50	
Supplies.............	63,743 57	
Ore.................	40,691 02	
		288,217 04

Total profits accounted for in California............ $1,085,454 92

Profits remitted to New York office................   3,209,725 36

Total profits accounted for..... $4,295,180 28

Remittances to New York office $3,209,725 36

Funded debt and dividends paid in
New York, as below.............$2,552,453 55

Interest on funded debt, taxes, legal expenses, etc., and assets in New York   657,271 81

  $3,209,725 36

The Company is entirely free from debt.

Payments for Funded Debt and Dividends.

First Mortgage Gold Bonds, paid June
1st, 1873............ .... $500,000 00

Second Mortgage Gold Bonds, paid July
1st, 1879..... ....   1,000,000 00

Forward. $1,500,000 00

Brought forward. $1,500,000 00

Dividends.

$9.25 on 42,913 shs. Preferred Stock.		
$2.25 on 57,087 shs. Common Stock..	525,391 00	
August 4th, 1881.		
$6.00 on Preferred Stock.		
$0.40 on Common Stock.	280,312 80	
May 3d, 1882.		
$3.00 on Preferred Stock, February 26, 1884.	128,739 00	
$1.50 on Preferred Stock, February 15, 1886.	64,369 50	
$1.25 on Preferred Stock, August 16, 1886.	53,641 25	

$1,052,453 55

$2,552,453 55

Dividend $1.50 on Preferred Stock declared January 12th,
payable February 15th, 1887, $64,369.50.

EARNINGS FOR SIXTEEN YEARS.

Year.	Production, Flasks.	Quicksilver Value.	Average Value per Flask.	Miscellaneous Earnings and Ore Account Increased.	Total Earnings.	Total Profits.	Profits per Flask.
1871	18,568	$575,608 00	$31 00	$63,931 57	$639,639 57	$238,742 07	$12 86
1872	18,574	876,406 00	47 18	32,964 72	909,370 72	451,759 17	24 32
1873	11,042	746,457 05	67 60	80,712 23	827,169 28	428,502 27	38 80
1874	9,084	897,561 12	98 80	95,121 93	992,683 05	499,243 85	54 95
1875	13,648	678,917 37	49 74	45,502 00	724,419 37	218,704 81	16 02
1876	20,549	782,120 16	38 06	33,569 95	815,690 11	381,007 96	18 54
1877	23,996	782,633 42	32 61	30,914 78	813,548 20	376,668 89	15 69
1878	15,852	489,186 40	30 86	40,382 00	529,568 49	132,969 32	8 39
1879	20,514	563,436 10	27 47	17,839 30	581,275 40	112,094 74	5 46
1880	23,465	677,442 85	28 87	16,982 30	694,425 15	242,118 88	10 32
1881	26,060	727,249 90	27 91	59,031 52	786,281 42	415,103 88	15 93
1882	28,070	765,645 77	27 27	17,839 86	783,535 63	264,139 27	9 40
1883	29,000	755,601 24	26 05	20,050 04	775,651 28	287,687 04	9 92
1884	20,000	587,419 53	29 37	23,202 28	610,621 81	103,578 99	5 18
1885	21,400	624,116 79	29 16	21,476 63	645,593 42	37,413 70	1 75
1886	18.000	629,970 85	35 00	30,206 45	660,117 30	105,444 64	5 86
Totals and Averages.	317,822	$11,159,822 55	$35 11	$629,727 65	$11,789,550 20	$4,295,180 28	$13 51

EXPENSES FOR SIXTEEN YEARS.

Years.	Mine and Hacienda Pay Rolls.	Miscellaneous, Taxes and Ore Account Reduced.	Supplies Consumed.	Totals.	Total Cost per Flask.	Net Cost per Flask. *
1871	$321,565 51	$ 26,538 13	$ 52,693 86	$400,797 50	$21 58	$18 14
1872	343,748 17	55,942 95	57,920 43	457,611 55	24 64	22 86
1873	317,573 69	24,848 03	56,244 29	398,666 01	36 10	28 79
1874	389,190 69	31,505 33	72,743 18	493,439 20	54 32	43 85
1875	381,758 44	31,240 49	92,715 63	505,714 56	37 05	33 72
1876	310,266 61	30,334 49	94,081 05	434,682 15	21 15	19 52
1877	291,801 06	41,909 81	103,168 64	436,879 51	18 21	16 92
1878	283,839 60	30,346 57	82,413 00	396,599 17	25 01	22 47
1879	263,229 92	107,600 23	98,350 49	469,180 66	22 86	22 00
1880	240,157 76	100,748 63	111,399 88	452,306 27	19 27	18 55
1881	238,580 76	29,098 52	103,498 26	571,177 54	14 24	11 98
1882	330,806 33	54,822 59	133,767 44	519,396 36	18 50	17 87
1883	314,684 73	35,953 23	137,326 28	487,964 24	10 80	16 13
1884	333,084 98	34,296 91	139,661 03	507,042 82	25 16	24 19
1885	387,644 52	43,501 45	177,033 75	608,179 72	27 76	27 42
1886	384,686 86	26,650 06	143,495 74	554,732 66	30 81	29 14
Total and Averages.	$5,132,519 53	$705,337 44	$1,656,512 95	$7,494,369 92	$23 58	$21 60

* Ascertained by deducting amounts to credit Miscellaneous and Ore Account increased.

STATEMENT OF MINE AND FURNACE WORKS FOR SIXTEEN YEARS.

YEAR.	TOTAL ORES PRODUCED.		TOTAL ORES ROASTED.		PERCENTAGE YIELD OF QUICKSILVER.	FLASKS QUICKSILVER PRODUCED.
	Tons.	Pounds.	Tons.	Pounds.		
1871	11,134	1,600	11,017	700	6.44	18,568
1872	10,716	1,875	10,707	1,800	6.63	18,574
1873	13,602	225	8,665	850	4.87	11,942
1874	18,560	125	11,727		2.96	9,084
1875	17,407	400	15,553	200	3.35	13,648
1876	16,883	1,725	16,658	950	4.09	20,549
1877	18,539	1,600	18,615	1,300	4.93	23,996
1878	18,328	780	18,472	1,808	3.28	15,852
1879	21,048	380	27,532	1,135	2.85	20,514
1880	23,798	964	30,677	850	2.92	23,465
1881	33,815	1,900	32,070	1,135	3.11	26,060
1882	34,216	480	36,073	1,200	2.98	28,070
1883	41,087	1,520	38,581	500	2.87	29,000
1884	39,267	440	39,625	1,090	1.93	20,000
1885	37,616	1,280	39,534	1,300	2.07	21,400
1886	37,985	1,980	40,699	690	1.69	18,000
TOTALS	394,009	1,274	396,212	1,418	Av'ge 3.07%	317,822

Statement of the Number of Tons of Ore of all Qualities REDUCED, and Flasks of Quicksilver PRODUCED, at the New Almaden Mines in 1886.

MONTHS.	GRANZA.		TERRERO.		GRANZITA AND TERRERO.		TOTAL.		Average Per Cent.	Flasks Quicksilver.
	Tons.	Pounds.	Tons.	Pounds.	Tons.	Pounds.	Tons.	Pounds.		
January	528	......	89	390	2,698	......	3,315	390	1.65[1]	1,431
February	324	200			2,743	......	3,067	200	1.37[2]	1,100
March	703	200			3,503	......	4,206	200	1.38[4]	1,522
April	568	1,200			2,051	1,000	2,620	200	1.83[4]	1,256
May	752	800			2,374	......	3,126	800	1.95[7]	1,600
June	837	100			2,824	1,000	3,661	1,100	1.88[6]	1,806
July	646	700			2,929	1,000	3,575	1,700	1.68[1]	1,572
August	333	1,800			2,943	......	3,276	1,800	1.44[7]	1,240
September	336	800			2,836	1,000	3,172	800	1.45[8]	1,210
October	347	1,300			2,930	......	3,278	300	1.49[3]	1,280
November	780	1,800			2,845	......	3,625	1,800	2.00	1,900
December	822	1,400			2,951	......	3,773	1,400	2.11[1]	2,083
Totals and Averages.	6,981	300	89	390	33,629	......	40,699	690	1.69%.	18,000

Ores Roasted..................81,398,690 pounds, or 40,699 690/2000 tons.

Quicksilver Produced............... 1,377,000 " " 688 1000/2000 "

Total Product of the Mines on the Company's property from July, 1850, to 31st December, 1886, 853,359 flasks or 65,281,963½ pounds Quicksilver, estimated value, $32,640,000.

Table Showing Tons of Rock and Ore Extracted from the Mine for 10 Years.

Year.	Rock from Drifts, Shafts, and Crosscuts.	Rock from Vein.	Ore.		Total.
			Granza.	Tierras.*	
1877	30,348	27,282	5,980	11,034	74,644
1878	29,926	26,537	6,322	9,359	72,144
1879	30,223	30,009	6,655	8,549	75,536
1880	24,529	35,340	7,401	12,125	79,395
1881	18,063	38,417	8,021	14,097	78,598
1882	40,909	45,095	9,237	14,706	109,949
1883	32,345	44,147	9,584	20,289	106,365
1884	42,077	44,795	7,625	20,038	114,534
1885	56,096	44,927	8,485	25,334	134,842
1886	48,289	34,124	7,183	24,718	114,314

*Terrero and Tierras from Dumps not included.

Drifting, Sinking, and Prospecting, "Dead Work," for 10 Years.

1877 . . . . .Total Feet 8,390.^{55}

1878 . . . .   "   "   6,941.^{70}

1879 . . . .   "   "   6,404.^{38}

1880 . . . .   "   "   5,144.^{79}

1881 . . . .   "   "   4,574.^{25}

1882 . . . .   "   "   9,133.^{00}

1883 . . . .   "   "   6,699.^{50}

1884 . . . .   "   "   6,814.^{50}

1885 . . . .   "   "   11,370.^{50}

1886 . . . .   "   "   11,926.^{00}

PRODUCTION OF QUICKSILVER IN CALIFORNIA.

MINES.	1877.	1878.	1879.	1880.	1881.	1882.	1883.	1884.	1885.	1886.
New Almaden	23,996	15,852	20,514	23,465	26,060	28,070	29,000	20,000	21,400	18,000
Aetna and	2,229	3,049	3,605	4,416	5,552	6,842	5,890	2,931	1,309	3,478
Napa Consolidated								1,376	2,197	1,769
Great Western	5,856	4,963	6,333	6,442	6,241	5,179	3,869	3,292	3,469	1,949
Sulphur Bank	10,993	9,465	9,249	10,706	11,152	5,014	2,612	890	1,296	1,449
New Idria	6,316	5,138	4,425	3,209	2,775	1,953	1,606	1,025	1,144	1,406
Great Eastern	505	1,366	1,455	1,279	1,065	2,124	1,669	332	446	735
Redington	9,309	6,636	4,516	2,139	2,194	2,171	1,894	881	385	409
Guadalupe	6,241	9,072	16,540	6,670	5,228	1,138	84	1,179	35	....
Various	13,861	8,289	8,047	1,600	584	241	101	7	392	786
TOTAL......Flasks,	79,396	63,880	73,684	59,926	60,851	52,732	46,725	31,913	32,073	29,981
Lowest Price, per flask	$30 60	$29 85	$25 25	$27 55	$27 90	$27 35	$26 00	$26 00	$28 50	$32 00
Highest " "	44 00	35 95	34 45	34 45	31 75	29 10	28 50	35 00	32 00	39 00
Average " "	37 30	32 90	29 85	31 00	29 80	28 25	27 25	30 50	30 25	35 50
Total Value, at Average Price	$2,960,000	$2,100,000	$2,200,000	$1,860,000	$1,810,000	$1,500,000	$1,275,000	$975,000	$970,000	$1,060,000